Gravity Hill

Gravity Hill

Susanne Davis

Lake Dallas, Texas

FIRST EDITION

Requests for permission to reprint material from this work should be sent to:

Permissions
Madville Publishing
P.O. Box 358
Lake Dallas, TX 75065

Author Photograph: Tara Doyle
Cover Design: Jacqueline Davis

ISBN: 978-1-956440-06-5 paperback
ISBN: 978-1-956440-07-2 ebook
Library of Congress Control Number: 2022932006

For my mother, Margaurite Hogan (1940-2021), who always believed

Chapter 1

Jordan Hawkins sat on a metal stool inspecting amber beer bottles as they spun by her lamp. Built out of sky blue sheets of metal and plopped in the middle of a paved lot, Glass and Company offered the highest paying factory jobs in Connecticut's eastern corner. Twenty-four hours a day, florescent light shone over the lines and the furnace blasted dry heat over the workers, finding moisture and sucking it back up into the air.

Jordan was looking for split necks and cherry stones, the two most common defects in the bottles. Split necks were easily detected because light shone through the crack in the lip of the glass, whereas the stubborn pebbles that resisted melting could only be found by scanning for shadows in the body of each bottle. Jordan twisted her ponytail around her hand and tugged. The pain felt good. Down the line a pair of cherry stones danced. The inspection lamp caught the imperfections each time the bottles turned, so that they looked like bugs encased in amber. She kept her eyes on the pair. Beer bottles spun by very fast, a combination of their size and shape, about sixty a minute, but Jordan liked that—she liked to feel that nothing on the line was too much for her to handle, and when they reached her, she knocked them off the conveyor belt down into a hole in the floor. Another belt would carry them back to be fired over again. "Better luck next time, losers," she whispered.

Jordan had barely taken off her high school graduation gown when she filed into Glass and Company's orientation with the other new recruits weeks earlier. Mr. Tilchek, one of the shift supervisors, filled a beer bottle with water and rapped it lightly against a counter. The bottle popped wide open, revealing a pebble and he joked, "Resistance is futile." Jordan got the joke, but grief had a way of flattening everything, especially humor. Tilchek explained that every bit of sand had to be melted to make perfect glass. "Defects weaken the bottle," he said, pointing to the flashing light of the furnace where the bottle would be fired again, and the best Jordan could do was nod in acknowledgment. She saw not the furnace but an ambulance and lights splitting open the darkness.

That was only a month ago, but it felt like somebody else's lifetime. Tonight, at eight p.m. just as he did every night, Mr. Tilchek tapped Jordan on the shoulder for her break. He was a short, stout man with straight brown hair that hung over his ears and hid the top of his gold-rimmed glasses. His smile hitched up on one side, apologetic and hesitant. Jordan removed her Styrofoam earplugs, and the roar of the plant filled her head.

"You want to work a double?" Tilchek shouted.

A double shift meant overtime and the third shift made the most money. She would make $25 an hour, $200 extra for the night. Her bank account had $7,000 before starting at the factory, the total accumulation of her lifetime wages. In just a month, she had added another $2,000.

She plucked a split neck from the line.

Tilchek smiled. "I was going to tell you this at the end of your shift, but I might as well tell you now. I'm giving you a 3% raise, starting next week."

"Gee, thanks," she said without taking her eyes off the line. She knew that by taking the double she wouldn't get home until after eight in the morning and that meant her father would have to do most of the morning milking alone.

"You have a 97%, Grade A inspection rate," Tilchek added, pushing his glasses up on his nose. Jordan saw not her green eyes, pale skin, and blonde hair pulled back in a ponytail, but rather her frown lines reflecting back to her.

She'd been taught to deflect compliments and she knew

Tilchek's admiration wasn't just for her bottle inspecting. She kept her head down, glad for the baggy shirt that hid her compact form.

Tilchek touched her arm lightly. "Hey," he said. "I know you've had some bumps in the road. But you're gonna make it."

Jordan jerked her arm away and punched three split necks into the gutter.

Tilchek seemed to get the message. He stepped back. "Why don't you go take your break? And then go to Line 3 and start packing."

Jordan slid off the stool. "Thanks again for the raise," she said, but Tilchek had already put his earplugs in, which was a good thing because her thanks sounded ambivalent.

Workers milled about the break room, but even in the crowd, Jordan picked out Tom Hesip, Regional High's sexy football star: doe-eyed, streaked blond hair and fat, juicy kissing lips. He sat in the corner at one of the square Formica tables, his lunch box open in front of him. Since graduation he worked full time at the glass factory and lived in a reno-vated mill apartment in Putnam with the high school French teacher. Jordan had flirted with Hesip once at a football game, and he'd responded by asking her to go with him to a party after the game, but she'd left the party early to get home for chores.

The vending machine was in that corner and she was hungry, having already eaten her sandwich on the way to work. She pretended to study the bills in her wallet as she stood in front of the machine and selected a bag of peanuts. She got as far as stuffing the peanuts in her back pocket, when Hesip called out.

"I'd know that ass anywhere," he grinned. "What are you doing here?"

"Same as you. Working," she said flatly. She looked into his lunch box, which held two sandwiches with lettuce and tomato, a package of baby carrots and an apple. In the high school cafeteria, he'd filled his plastic tray with bags of chips and starchy entrées and carried it to Room 107 to eat lunch with Mrs. Logee, a cute pixie of a woman in her late twenties. Jordan hadn't believed the rumors of the affair, but two weeks before the end of school Mrs. Logee was fired, and a substitute took over the French classes.

"When did you start working here?"

"Last month." Jordan started to move away when Hesip slapped his head and said, "What a jerk I am. Sorry. Are you still going to college in the fall?"

Jordan shook her head. "I'm taking a year off."

"It's too bad," Hesip said. "About your brother." His gaze slid away. "I know how much school means to you."

Some of the men sitting at the table with Hesip stopped talking and looked at her. Hesip picked up one of his sandwiches and unwrapped it. Were they waiting for her to say that she wished she were the one who had died? Because she wasn't going to say it.

"And I'm sorry Mrs. Logee lost her job. I know how much it meant to her."

Hesip dropped the sandwich. His face reddened. "You are such a bitch."

Jordan whipped her gloves out of her back pocket and moved out of the break room. She didn't want to admit how good it felt to hurt Tom Hesip. When she reached Line #3, Norma Helfin didn't look up to see her there, although she certainly must have, but instead heaved a box onto the conveyor belt and poked Jordan in the side. Norma scowled as she adjusted the box but made no apology. Jordan didn't expect any. Norma was a lifer and even though Jordan worked at the factory, she wasn't a lifer, and everyone knew it. The lifers hated the college kids because they came in, made good money to pay their tuition, and then they were gone. So, the lifers did what they could during that time to make factory life miserable for them. If they could leave a line backed up with bottles, they did. If they could put the college kids working on the lines nearest the furnace, where they fainted like flies, they did. Then they belittled them for being so weak. If lifers found defects that the college kids hadn't caught, they'd save them all until the end of the shift and then take them to the shift supervisor. But the lifers hadn't been able to get anything on Jordan and a few showed their grudging admiration for her. She had the best eyes of the teens on her shift and her life of farm work made her tough enough so that the heat of the plant, long hours, and heavy boxes didn't faze her. But those attributes seemed to make Norma even madder.

"Hey, Norma? You want to work third shift? Well, you can't, because Mr. Tilchek asked me," Jordan called out as she started flipping bottles into boxes.

Norma glared at her and veered over to where Tilchek watched the lines.

Jordan heard Norma shouting at him. Although she couldn't hear what Norma said, she knew the general content. The rule was that the person with seniority always got the offer to work overtime first.

Tilchek hefted his pants over his belly. He wore navy blue work pants with a crease ironed down the front of the legs. He kept his thumbs inside the waistband as if he feared Norma might tear him to pieces. He spoke in a low tone to counter hers. Norma frowned over at Jordan, and then spun away toward the break room. Jordan looked at the bottles spinning down the line toward her. They were backing up so that the person at the inspection lamp, someone she didn't know, didn't care to know, shouted. "Hey, get packin'!" The empty boxes began falling off the overhead line.

Tilchek hustled over and started throwing the bottles into boxes. His practiced motions jump started her own. He was pissed. A man from the next line over, someone Jordan had never seen before, tall and wiry, wearing a ponytail of long hair and a Harley T-shirt came to help. The line started running smoothly.

"You got this?" Tilchek snapped.

Jordan nodded and the two men went off.

The plant's smells—damp sand, wet cement, dry fire, and the sweat of hundreds of people—filled her lungs. She packed bottles into boxes and heaved them onto the conveyor belt to be carried into the warehouse. The muscles of her forearms roped over bone and her small hands swelled. She thought about her mother and father at home in bed and she thought about the way her house looked in the moonlight, the white paint taking on a blue hue of the night, so that the house itself looked peaceful. Ever since she'd been a little girl, she had a recurring dream that a giant came along and lifted off the roof of the house, to see each of them, her mother, father, brother, herself, huddled in sleep and then the cows in the barn, lying in their stalls, and the calves in their sheds. The giant never scared her, he was just a curious giant and after he'd checked on them, he always went away. She thought of God and the giant as one and the same.

Across the factory floor someone yelled, "Watch out!"

The girl on the line next to Jordan had fainted and her line jammed solid. A box tumbled and crashed near Jordan, sending shards of glass everywhere. Jordan stepped over the broken pieces and continued from the other side flipping bottles into boxes and heaving them onto the belt. She didn't want the lifers pointing at her, saying she was weak. She saw the girl being helped up by another supervisor, a short woman with broad shoulders and leather wristbands. The supervisor got an extra to fill in and she led the pale girl to the staff lounge. Jordan could see why they hated the college kids.

As she turned back to her line and reached for the next bottle, her hand touched something soft and furry. There on the line lay a rat, bloated stomach, eyes congealed with death, scrawny claws clenched. She stifled the scream in her throat and whipped around in time to see Hesip and two other guys peering out of the warehouse. They laughed, slapping each other on the back. Jordan grabbed the rat by its tail and marched to the door of the warehouse, where the guys were too busy enjoying their joke to look up and see her.

"You're so funny, Hesip," she said, whipping the rat down at his feet. "This place is just the right speed for you. I can see that."

"Look at Miss High and Mighty. She fell down to Earth. Boo. Hoo."

"At least I'm not a lifer." Jordan saw the hurt cross his face for a second time. She glanced at the line, backed up all the way to the flashing fire of the furnace. The supervisor was looking for her. Jordan could get docked for leaving the line unattended. She ran back to it. Hesip's words, her own words, everything hurt. She pounded bottles into cartons, trying to pack it all away.

"You got a problem in the warehouse?" The supervisor stood next to her, tightening her wristbands. Muscles bulged in her forearms, the byproduct of years of lifting bottles and boxes.

"No." A hypotenuse was the longest side of a right-angled triangle. The theme of Plato's Cave was about shadows and reality and helping others out of the shadows.

"Then don't leave the line. Or next time I'll write you up."

Willa Cather wrote *My Antonia*, *The Song of the Lark*.

"Do you hear me?" The supervisor put her hand over the box so that Jordan had to stop and acknowledge her.

"Yeah. I hear you." Jordan tried to give the woman the kind of look she'd seen Clay and his friends give to the people who hassled them: the *you can't hurt me* look. Jordan had never been able to perfect that look before, but it came easy now. The woman turned away and for the next hour Jordan packed, waiving her five-minute break to the girl who'd fainted.

The girl came off her line. She still looked pale. "How do you do this?" she asked.

"What?"

"You're like a machine. Doesn't this place get to you?"

Jordan breathed in the vapors coming off the bottles. The smell burned her lungs. "There are worse things," she said.

"I don't think I can take this," the girl said. "I thought I could, but I don't think I can." Her voice trailed off as she walked away.

At her last break of the double shift, Jordan avoided the break room and stood outside with the smokers, the group of older workers in their late fifties and sixties, those who had already raised their children, some of those children working in the factory now. Most lived within thirty miles of the plant and conducted their lives within that radius. The July night sky was a solid lapis blue, lit by the lights around the plant except for the one chute of foggy steam from the smokestack. The parking lot was filled with American cars and trucks, a few motorcycles. Someone drove a Mustang. That had always been Clay's favorite car. He'd been saving money to buy one. Someone mentioned the rumor that the plant might close soon.

"We make more bottles than the country needs."

"Automation," someone muttered.

"They speed us up and put us out of work."

One of the guys changed the topic. "How 'bout a bike ride this weekend? We could go over to the Bean and get lunch." Jordan knew he rode a motorcycle to work. His name was Merle, stitched on a jacket with a red embroidered patch. He took a silver pocket watch out of his pocket. The plant management forbade workers to wear jewelry on the line because of the danger of it getting caught in the machinery. Many of the older workers carried pocket watches instead of cellphones.

The other man looked like a gnome to Jordan. He was small and stooped and his skin had an unhealthy pallor; even in the dead of night she could see that.

"Nice watch," he said to Merle. "Is it new?"

"My kids gave it to me last weekend for my birthday."

"That a train etched on there?"

"A barn," Merle said, rubbing his thumb over the cover before he offered the watch for his friend to see. "My daughter takes jewelry classes, and she did it for me after we had to sell the farm."

Merle's daughter was a year ahead of Jordan in high school.

She'd gone away to college and Jordan never saw her anymore. Jordan wondered if Merle had pressured her to stay and work at the factory or if he'd encouraged her to leave.

The gnome shook his head and handed the watch back. "How many acres?"

"We kept twenty-five." Merle stuffed the watch back in his pocket. "And the barn. The rest is gone."

"That seems to be the way of it," said the gnome as he stroked his beard and took another puff off his cigarette. Jordan watched the two men pull the nicotine in and hold it in their lungs as if the smoke was a solid word of comfort.

Chapter 2

The twenty-minute ride home wound through the quiet corner of eastern Connecticut, more like Appalachia than the Connecticut people associated with the wealthy west of the river. Jordan passed the donut shop, the decrepit Our Lady of Sorrows Catholic Church, and Fill 'R Up gas station in Moosup, and the lonely grinder shop in the center of Ashville itself. She took the long way around to the farm, avoiding Gravity Hill. When she pulled her truck into the driveway, she saw that the rose bush had wept a blanket of petals overnight, but what she saw—really saw—was the white farmhouse on a knoll. Small and empty. To her the house looked sad no matter how many bushes bloomed around it. An enormous gray cloud stretched over the house and the fields, and the smell of cow shit seeped into everything, even her skin. The calves bleated out their hunger and while they might have looked cute to visitors, to Jordan they were a reminder of constant work and everything she didn't want to do with her life but was doing anyway.

A Toyota Tercel zipped into the barnyard behind her, kicking up gravel. A young man in wire-rimmed glasses climbed from the car. Tall with a narrow build like a runner, he glided toward her. She noticed his dark curls, like Clay's. He wore a blue button-down shirt with a plastic identification badge fastened to the front pocket on his upper chest. He tucked a clipboard under his arm and offered his hand.

"Eugene Martin," he said. "Department of Environmental Protection."

Cyclists sometimes peddled by the farm, but cars rarely stopped unless they took a wrong turn trying to find Gravity

Hill. This guy looked out of place even before he shook Jordan's hand so gently. Just then, her father, Sam Hawkins, opened the barn door and Martin headed toward him.

The African geese started squawking. There'd been a whole gaggle of geese, before the day the milk truck driver driving too fast into the yard, and unable to stop, had flattened those sunning themselves in a mud puddle. And an eagle had gotten one. Jordan secretly wished the eagle would take these last two. They were loud and obnoxious. Since the eagle attack, however, the geese rarely left each other; even an airplane overhead started them honking out warnings.

"Mr. Hawkins?" Martin wasn't watching the gander as he introduced himself to Jordan's father and didn't see the gander lurch forward. The goose latched on to his leg and Martin swatted at him, dropping the clipboard in the process. He shook his leg, trying to detach the goose, but the gander wouldn't let go.

Jordan started laughing. She couldn't help it. How this would have amused Clay.

"Jordan, stop," her father commanded, but she couldn't. Tears leaked from her eyes and her stomach hurt, but still, she couldn't stop. Where was Clay?

Finally, after a couple of failed attempts, Sam was able to grab the goose. He threw him in the barn. "Jordan, get some ice," he snapped.

The young man rubbed his leg and regarded her with a hostile stare.

"Sorry." She wiped her eyes before she turned to the house. This was the first time in a month that she'd laughed. No wonder it hurt. She cracked the contents of an ice tray into a dishcloth and brought it outside.

Martin rolled up his pant leg to show an ugly mass where blood pooled beneath the surface.

"Looks painful," Jordan said.

"Thanks for the concern." He dumped some ice into his sock, pulled his sock up over the bruise and handed her the dish towel.

Jordan and Sam helped him retrieve his papers and when he'd organized them all in a neat sheaf, he held out a black-and-white photo and botanist's illustration of what looked to Jordan like some kind of vine.

"This is the Hartford Fern," Martin said. "It's registered as a species of special concern." He turned to Jordan. "That means it's a native plant that has a restricted range of habitat and a high demand by man so that it needs to have its population protected. Our records show it's growing down by the Quanduck River, on your property."

"Someone was here years ago. Probably before you were born," Sam said, but when Martin didn't laugh, he went on. "Melvin Kind. Sent me a certificate for agreeing to keep a buffer between the field and where it's growing next to the river down there."

Jordan bent over the paper. This was the first she was hearing of the fern. "Really? That thing? Dad. You never told us—"

"Best not to advertise it," Martin said to her before turning back to her father. "Melvin retired recently, and I was hired to take his place and I was going through some files. We're supposed to do field visits every five years to check on the plant life. From the file it didn't look like he'd been here in ten years. Have you checked on the Hartford Fern lately, Mr. Hawkins?" Martin asked.

"No. We've been kind of busy lately." Sam's long arms hung loose at his sides and his eyes radiated sadness. The gray around his temples spread through his hair and even into his eyebrows, springing wildly about, as if surprised by the direction in which grief took them. His broad shoulders sagged, shoulders that had heaved a thousand bales of hay without sloping under the weight. Jordan saw the signs of him losing patience, but she didn't think this young environmentalist did.

"The fern's not looking too healthy, and I wondered if you'd come down and take a look at it with me."

Sam looked back at the barn. "We've got animals to feed."

"Dad, we can take a few minutes," Jordan protested.

Sam frowned at her, but he relented. "We gotta make it quick."

Jordan and her father got into her truck and Martin followed behind in his car. Jordan turned off Main Street and bumped along the back edge of the field, following the tire marks left by the manure spreader.

"We don't have all day to spend on this guy," Sam warned. "We're already behind. You worked a double last night?"

Jordan nodded.

"When we get back to the barn, you'll have to clean up from milking. I've gotta spread manure."

Jordan slid out of the truck, thinking what a nice distraction this Martin provided. She tried to give the young man a friendlier smile, but he looked away and she could tell he was still sore at her laughter. She didn't try to explain, she barely understood herself.

"This is pretty country out here," Martin commented.

"That's why they call it the quiet corner," Sam said as he led the way through the thick undergrowth and towering pines to the soft, mossy bank of the Quanduck River.

Martin walked beside Jordan. "The Hartford Fern was the first plant species named to the federal government's endangered species list, way back in the 1890s."

"What made it endangered?" she asked.

"Back then, people picked the greens and used them as Christmas decorations." His excitement over seeing the fern seemed to temporarily override his annoyance at her.

He pointed to where the water surged over the rocks, sucked itself into crevasses and spewed white froth. A curtain of vines clung to a backdrop of pine trees. Little hand-shaped leaves waved in the breeze. It didn't look at all like a fern.

Martin took his pencil from his clipboard and pointed to the top of a frond. "These are the fertile leaflets," he said. "See how they're dry and brown?"

"I guess I do see that," Sam nodded.

"New growth comes from here and I can guarantee you

we won't have any new growth next year if they continue like this. I'm wondering if cow manure or some pesticide product is washing down here to the banks and burning the plant. Have you changed your product usage or cleared more land along the edge of the field there?"

Sam shook his head.

The younger man looked skeptical. "Well, what do you think is killing this plant?"

"I don't know," Sam said. "I appreciate what you're trying to do here, but I'm telling you we haven't changed a thing."

Martin's glance slid from him to Jordan, then back again. He seemed puzzled about the fern, but satisfied that Sam was speaking honestly. He pinched off three of the dried leaves and a healthy section of the vine and placed them in a plastic bag he removed from his back pocket.

"Well, I'll take these leaves back for testing. We'll see what the test results say. We may want to talk about implementing some agricultural best management practices as a safeguard measure."

"Just what I want to talk about," Sam said, "adding more work to my day."

Sam started up the path and Martin followed him.

"But I don't need to tell you, if we lose the Hartford Fern in Connecticut, we lose part of what makes Connecticut—"

"... changes the ecosystem and you never know—"

The water, with its swollen belly of rain, carried his voice away. Jordan stopped to pick up two bottles, one Smirnoff, one beer, almost embedded in old tire tracks—and thought, here's something about the river that hasn't changed.

"Come on, Jordan," Sam yelled back. "We've got work to do."

When she reached the top of the path, she waved at the receding taillights of Martin's car. She felt sad to see him go.

That night the town held a memorial service at the Living Bible Church for the three boys. While the accident had

14

happened a month earlier, the families had been slow to coordinate the difficult service.

The Hawkins pulled into the parking lot of the church, a small white building with cement steps, a black door, and a wooden cross on top, located in the town's industrial park, above the river. The industrial park had been created on land polluted by the Riverside Textile Mill. The mill had mysteriously burned down and left barrels of dye and solvents leaching into the ground. The illegally buried barrels had been discovered and removed. Now, the town's only industry was the tire-burning plant, which replaced the mill. From the Hawkins' car, one could see white smoke, but not the plant itself.

The parking lot was almost full, and Pastor James stood at the door, waiting. The Hawkins were members of the church, or at least attended at holidays, which was more than the other two families. As Pastor James escorted them through the foyer into the room where he'd set up folding chairs, Jordan noticed two clumps of people standing in the back, looking uncomfortable and ill at ease. Only a few sat in chairs, including Mr. Z, a beloved elementary school teacher, who was going above the call of duty, Jordan thought, since he'd already attended the private funeral for Clay. He'd always liked Clay and his crumpled features told her just how terrible he felt about the whole thing.

Mary Coty and Ruth Green reached out their arms as she approached.

"How you doing?" Mary whispered. She tried to hug Jordan, but when Jordan stepped aside, Ruth pulled Mary back to give Jordan space to pass.

Jordan shrugged. In truth, the hug felt good… hugs were scarce at home these days; although she would never admit she missed them. She just didn't trust herself not to fall apart in an embrace. "I'm okay." Her voice on autopilot sounded like someone else's.

"*We'd* be better if you returned our phone calls." Mary

batted her green eyes so that the matching eye shadow blinked in and out of focus. Jordan remembered her in seventh grade, putting on that color. It was part of her signature style now.

"Do you want to come out with us tonight?" Ruth asked.

"I can't. We've got to go home and milk after this." Jordan moved away to where Pastor James had seated her parents in the front row, wishing she'd been able to explain to Ruth and Mary that it felt too exhausting to talk, but that she appreciated them trying.

Each day since the funeral, Jordan had wanted and yet dreaded the attention of her peers. She wanted the world to stop and acknowledge her older brother's death; instead, her high school classmates had shunned her. That entire month of May, as she walked numb through her days at school, it seemed as if they feared death might be contagious. They made her invisible and so she made herself so small that no one saw her. She avoided eye contact and conversation, waiting for the bell to ring at the end of the day. It was more a relief, not a celebration, to graduate. At home, she worked side by side with her father and they plowed and planted all the fields, while on the ridge above them, Clay lay in his grave. It felt strange to plant seeds when all she felt was death all around her. One of Sam's farmer friends sent his three sons to help with the planting. They were good looking, but she barely acknowledged them. They got the corn in the ground in six days and then they were gone. Now, Sam and Jordan mended fences, fixed the hinges on the barn door, repaired a section of the stonewall, working each day until they collapsed, exhausted.

Sitting in the midst of all these people Jordan wished she could escape back to the fields. When would Pastor James get started? It was quarter past the hour. He stood in the center of the room, adjusting the ceiling fan.

Jordan got up and went over to him. Glancing back, she saw a ring of empty seats surrounding her parents. Some of those standing at the door now filled the chairs, but no one came to sit next to the Hawkinses.

"Pastor? I was just wondering. Could we get a copy of the comments you made at the funeral?"

"Of course," Pastor James said, seeming satisfied with the fan adjustment. "How are you doing, Jordan?"

"Okay." She tried to step away, but he called after her.

"You going to say a few words?"

"I don't know." She fingered the paper in her pocket. Her hands trembled. "I don't know if I can."

"Sometimes we get a little extra strength, just when we need it," he said.

"I'll try," Jordan said as she moved back to her seat.

Pastor James lit the candle and the wick sputtered to flame. He set his Bible next to the candle on the pulpit and the room fell silent.

"Thank you all for coming." His voice was simple and warm. People leaned toward him.

"We come together tonight to remember Clay and Tim and Tony, all of whom died together in April. We come to pray for them and their families." At this point he smiled at the Hawkinses first, and then at Tony Barbo's mother and father. Mr. Barbo wore a flannel shirt pulled tight around a swollen stomach, although the rest of him was skin and bone. Jordan remembered hearing that he was wasting away from cancer or drinking, and Mrs. Barbo leaned away from him toward the pastor. Tony's sister, Tina, stood beside her father, rubbing his shoulder with one hand and holding her toddler in her other arm.

Pastor James gestured toward the Hawkinses. "Sam and Diane helped me organize this memorial so we could come together as one family." He held up the big black Bible and opened it as if he were greeting a friend. "I want to start with this reading, from 1 Corinthians 13." His voice sang out, "If I speak without love…"

Jordan caught just snatches of what he said as she looked at the people crying, hanging their heads and hiding their tears as if they'd done this too many times and were worn out by their grief. Mr. Z was the only one besides Sam and Pastor James wearing a tie and Diane was the only woman wearing a dress and high heels. Jordan wouldn't wear black, but she'd exchanged the heavy wool skirt she wore to the funeral for a jean skirt, blue cable-knit top and sandals. Tony's mother wore sweatpants and an athletic jacket with a big M on it for the high school where Tony had played football. She looked up and Jordan, catching her gaze, smiled at her, but Tony's mother shot back a look so full of anger, Jordan felt she'd been punched in the chest.

"... a gong booming or cymbal clashing. If I give up my body... if without love, will do me no good whatever."

The stark candle bathed Pastor James' face in light. He finished reading and nodded at the Hawkinses.

Sam cleared his throat, but Jordan jumped to her feet before her father could stand. She knew if she didn't do this now, she never would. Her father squeezed her hand, and she squeezed back, then she reached into her pocket for the poem she'd found on the Internet. It contained someone else's grief, and when she first read it online, she'd recognized that grief; now, looking at her community knit together, reading the poem seemed wrong. She wanted to use her own words. She took a deep breath, and her voice shook but she managed to say: "Everything makes me think of you, Clay." And it was true. She felt as if he was right there in the room, and he was the one she was talking to. "I can't do anything without thinking of you." She looked at the people. "My brother had the best heart of anyone I know. He was always doing things for people. He never judged anyone. He was always there for me. Until now."

"Bullshit!"

Jordan's hands started to tremble. She crumpled the paper and put it in her pocket. Who had said that?

"Don't forget it was your brother driving. He's to blame."

"He wasn't as drunk as the others," she snapped. It was true that Clay had been driving but all the boys had been drinking and while blood alcohol for each of them was above the legal limit, Clay's was just barely so. This was the only explanation for Clay driving Tim's car and for Tony leaving his truck and also getting in the truck. Still, no one could understand the speed at which the truck had crashed down the hill. Why had Clay been driving at such a speed? Why hadn't he hit the brakes before they flew into the tree and burst into flames?

Sam stood up and walked over to her and put his arm around her. "We're sorry for all the loss." He spoke evenly. Clay and his best friend, Tim Hatch, both sitting in the front seat, had been killed instantly, but Tony Barbo had been thrown from the truck He suffered extensive injuries and third degree burns over sixty percent of his body and had died three days later. "We grieve every day, knowing Clay was driving. But we *all* lost them. And I'm sure we *all* wish we had them back. But all we got is each other." He sat down and pulled Jordan down next to him.

Pastor James stepped into the center of the circle. "We want to lay blame because we are in such pain, but we're here as a community, trying to help each other."

Chairs squeaked. People shifted. Then Mr. Z stood up. "I taught all three of these boys. I say 'boys' because they still had their whole lives ahead of them and they all had some growing up to do." He ran his hands up and down his tie, looked over at the Hawkinses and said, "Clay Hawkins was a good boy. From a good family. That this could happen to him, to any of these boys, is just plain tragic all around."

"We love you, Tony," his sister shouted. Her father leaned over and smoothed her hair. Tony's mother pressed a handkerchief over her mouth and shook her head. Tony's sister, Tina, was wearing a low-slung jean skirt with a rope tattoo around her ankle and her toddler wrapped around her leg. Tony's father clamped his hands on his knees and stared at the floor. He chewed the inside of his cheek.

Jordan remembered Tina pregnant in high school. She'd been sixteen and in a remedial reading class, just like Clay.

Tina finished her junior year, delivered the baby in the summer, and never came back to school. Now she worked behind the grinder counter of the general store. Jordan never heard who the father was. People didn't question it, not in Asheville. The town had one of the highest teen pregnancy rates in a state that didn't seem to see them.

Pastor James looked to the back corner. "There are some others who want to speak. Let's see—Win?"

A man stepped out from the back of the church.

He wore his long hair pulled back in a ponytail. He was much older than a teenager; it was clear by the way he held himself, as if he shouldered some of the world's weight. Even at a quick glance, Jordan could see by the clean lines of his profile, the high cheekbones and straight nose, he was handsome, but there was something else, an energy that caught her attention. He cleared his throat. He seemed to be having trouble, then the words tumbled out: "Pastor said it would be okay if I sang a song. A song to Tim."

Pastor James nodded, relieved. "Now would be a good time for it."

"It's hard to see history repeat itself here," the man said. "Both Tim's parents died before him. I'm sure you know they were hard drinkers and Tim followed right along behind." The man talked intimately, as if Tim Hatch was right there beside him and Jordan felt close to him then because that's how it seemed to her sometimes, as if Clay was right there beside her. Everybody strained to see Tim's cousin, but even though he'd stepped out of the corner, he still stood in shadow. "They took me in for a while when my own folks couldn't handle me. And they couldn't save me, really, but they tried. Now, I'm the only Hatch left and so this song, 'Remember Me' by Jimmie Lee Robinson, is the one I want to sing. He was kind of a lonely traveler and so was Tim." He cleared his throat, and the notes came out powerful and clear, full of grief and longing. The man leaned into the rhythms he created and the people in their seats melted into each other, and the hard edges of grief softened. Tony Barbo's mother looked at Diane Hawkins and the two mothers recognized each other's longing.

Diane reached across and took Jordan's hands. Jordan took her attention off the man for a moment to see the room and the people, to see them as she had never seen them before and hoped she would never have to see them again. It was as close to crying as she had come since Clay died and that seed of bitterness nearly choked her.

The man went on to sing the refrain, and his voice hit a bump, so Jordan started to sing along, not well, but still she did it through her tears and when the song was done, Tim's cousin hurried out the back door, and Jordan was both glad and disappointed to see him go, leaving them weeping and Pastor James rushing through the closing prayer.

As the Hawkinses left the church, they passed the familiar and eerie figures of Brother Michael and Sister Rachael, dressed in their white robes, Brother Michael with staff in hand. He believed he was the second coming of Christ and had long ago convinced Sister Rachael of it. She belonged to a large family with two dairy farms and a grocery store and a long local history. He and Sister Rachael traversed the five-mile corridor between Asheville and Moosup, preaching their Second Coming gospel and accepting public assistance. But now they stood in their robes, watching people file from the church. When Sister Rachael saw Jordan, she waved and beckoned to her.

Jordan turned away. "Please," Sister Rachael said. "I have something to tell you. Don't be afraid."

But Jordan was afraid of Sister Rachael. She didn't know how Sister Rachael had let herself come under the power of a man like Brother Michael. She skirted around her parents and got into the car, locking the door even though Sister Rachael hadn't followed.

The Hawkinses didn't speak on the way home or even much through milking, but Jordan knew her parents were thinking about the recrimination hurled across the room. Her own anger frothed up inside her and she tried to keep it contained there.

Chapter 3

Jordan found the accident site between the bridge and the bottom of Gravity Hill, the place where Clay had died. She was on her way home from work and having avoided it since Clay's death, she wanted to sit for a while by the river and hear the water. Almost every first date in town started or ended at Gravity Hill. The hill wasn't really a hill at all if you believed the scientists, rather, an optical illusion of a hill created by a false horizon; a slight downhill slope that appeared to be an uphill slope. But it didn't feel like an illusion to Jordan. Three white crosses glowed in the dark and bunches of dead flowers lay in a heap. In one hand Jordan carried a warm beer and in the other a pack of peanuts.

The moon made a silver path across the Quanduck's surface. The peanut shells made no sound as they fell away from her hand and floated like tiny boats. She and Clay loved the river, all the kids did.

From downriver a light plunged out and showed on the water. Then there was a splash and a bobber surfaced and floated. Often there were fishermen at night shining trout, the beam of flashlight illuminating the fish. She wanted to be alone and at the same time it wasn't helping her find the comfort and strength she was seeking. She broke more peanuts and flung the shells in the bushes out of courtesy to the fisherman.

"You stupid ass, Clay." She removed the long-sleeved flannel shirt that she wore at the glass factory to protect her arms from the hot bottles and tossed it aside. The night was warm, and the air felt good against her skin. Underneath, she wore a plain white T-shirt, which had come untucked from her jeans. The jeans were stiff and uncomfortable, one of the several pairs she'd bought for the factory. She took off her steel-toed work boots and socks, tossed them near the flannel shirt and sunk her toes in the water.

The light of the fisherman moved closer upstream, but Jordan heard no sound until a fish broke the surface with a splash. Then she saw the line play like silver thread being pulled through the water and a moment later a trout arced in the air, gleaming in the light as the fisherman pulled it to shore.

The burn mark from the accident started high up on the trunk of the oak tree, which towered over all the others. There was no undergrowth there; it would have burned away in the fire. There was a rustling in the brush; Jordan thought it was probably a deer, who smelling her, would now skirt around the clearing. She watched the spot, hoping to catch a glimpse of it, when the fisherman emerged into the clearing.

"Hey, how you doing? Catchin' anything?" Jordan stood and brushed off her pants. She felt nervous and kept her distance so she could run if she needed to, but she'd always felt safe by the river, and she didn't think she would need to.

"Yeah," the guy said. "It's okay."

He had a loose build, broad shoulders, and strong legs. A bunch of trout hung on a line looped through his belt, strung through the gills, their dead eyes staring at nothing. He wore a wide-brimmed hat so she couldn't see his eyes. But she recognized he was the guy who sang at the memorial service.

"Want some peanuts?" Jordan held out the few that were left.

The guy took the peanuts. "Figured someone was up here. Saw your peanuts going by."

"Sorry 'bout that. Once I saw your light, I tossed 'em over there." She pointed to the bushes. The empty beer bottle shone in the moonlight, along with the scattered shells.

"You want a cold one?" he asked. "I sank a six pack near the bridge."

Jordan picked up her shirt, socks, and shoes and they started toward the bridge.

The man asked, "What brings you out this time of night?"

What brought her out was none of his business. "That your piece of shit truck up the hill?" Jordan asked. "I saw it coming in."

The guy laughed. "Okay. You got any more lines like that?"

"Maybe."

He shined his light into the water until it caught a silver gleam, then he pulled the six-pack from the water and handed one to her. "You hungry? I'm gonna cook these trout. Only way to eat 'em. Straight from the water."

Jordan nodded. Drinking beers on Gravity Hill was what Clay and his friends had done every weekend. She hadn't eaten anything but the peanuts since her sandwich that afternoon. Drinking wasn't a good idea, but she took a long drink, and then followed the guy onto the bridge. He leaned his pole against the cross beam and opened his tackle box. A knife lay on the top tray. He took it and cut a fish from the line, laid it on his tackle box, and whop! The head splashed into the water below.

"You want me take the bones out?" he asked.

"Yeah," she said.

He sliced down the body, holding it gently between his fingers. His hands weren't clean, but they were thick and strong like the rest of him. He took the point of the knife and lifted the skeleton, peeled it right away from the fish then went down to the river and rinsed his hands and the fish, once, twice, three times. While he did that, Jordan rifled around for some twigs to build a fire. He helped her get the fire going and then he cooked the fish until it turned the color of a toasted nut, lifting it off to put a piece on each of the two tin plates he took from the bottom of his tackle box.

"This is good," Jordan said.

"You eat much trout?" the man asked.

"My brother and I used to fish," Jordan said, taking a

mouthful of beer. The man waited. "This is where he died in the crash. Stupid fuck." The man watched her stab a piece of trout and stuff it in her mouth. "There are so many better ways to die," Jordan said. She drained the can of beer and reached for another.

"My cousin was with him," the man said.

Jordan looked at the man more closely. "What's your name again?"

"Win Hatch." He was handsome with a long nose and blue eyes as pale as water. She was a sucker for blue eyes. Fine lines curved around his mouth. The beer was giving her a buzz.

"You sang that song." He nodded. "I wanted to talk to you, but you left."

"Didn't feel much like talking. It wasn't a talking crowd," he said, looking down at the fish on his plate.

"You blame Clay?" Jordan asked.

"No more than the others," Win said.

"Well, you're in the minority there," Jordan said.

"Give them time. They'll settle down."

"You made everyone cry. You live here?" she asked. Asheville had a population of 2000. There weren't many people she didn't know.

His fork glinted as he put a piece of fish in his mouth. "Not anymore. Like I said at the service, I lived with Tim's parents for a year when I was in high school."

"When was that?" The skin around his eyes was thin like onion skin.

"A long time. Ten, twelve years ago."

"Which is it? Ten or twelve."

"Twelve."

"Why are you still here?"

"I'm sorting through Tim's stuff, getting the house ready for sale."

Jordan remembered then he'd said he was the last one left. She thought it must be hard to be the only one. "Tim was Clay's best friend. I liked him."

"He was a good boy. He had a good heart," the man said.

"I was supposed to leave for college. I had a scholarship. But I gave it up to stay home this year and help my dad."

"It's just a year," he said. "You worried about him?"

"Yeah, both him and my mother. But mostly him," she said, raising the can to her lips.

They drank without speaking, until a faint drum of thunder started in the distance. A jagged line of lightning parted the clouds, and another arced up from the ground to meet it.

"Did you see that?" Jordan asked.

The man dipped a shoulder. He looked darker now. A crack of thunder split the silence and another thread of lightening lit the clouds.

"Is Win short for something?" Jordan asked.

"Winthrop." His eyes traveled down her body. "What's your name?"

"Jordan." She pulled her jacket tight. Something had changed in the exchange between them, and she couldn't say why she was still there.

"Jordan. That's not too common. We're gonna get a storm, Jordan," he said. "I'm headed for that shelter, just across the bridge."

"Whatever," she said. The dilapidated shack had been a tool shed for loggers in earlier decades when they ran logs down the river to the sawmill, now defunct. Clay and his friends had partied there, but since the accident, the resident state trooper patrolled the bridge area and the parties had moved elsewhere. Jordan was surprised the trooper hadn't been by yet this evening, but perhaps he'd assumed the impending storm would keep people away.

Win kicked some dirt on the fire and collected his gear. They'd finished the six-pack.

Jordan stood and brushed herself off. "I'll take this with me," she said. "They're trying to clean this place up and keep the kids out of here." But she didn't move, just held her boots and shirt and socks in one hand and the empty six pack in the other.

When the rain hit, Win offered her his hand, and she took it.

They reached the shack, and Win let Jordan go in first. She stumbled and fell, dropping the beer carton and her clothes on the packed dirt. The smell of mold rose up as she felt around for the scattered items. One window let in some light. Win took off his hat and his hair tumbled down, all the way to his shoulders. It was thick, beautiful brown hair. He looked a little wild, his eyes darting over Jordan in a way that made her look at her own body. Her legs were spread; her T-shirt clung to her breasts.

She shivered.

"You're chilled from the rain." His voice sounded husky. He knelt between her legs and put his coat over her shoulders. She tried to push herself away, but her back met the wall.

"You don't have to be afraid," he said. "Tell me, what does your name mean?"

She wrapped the coat tight around herself. Her mother had picked the name for the baby girl she dreamed of having long before meeting her father. "It means descending, flowing down."

Even with the coat, her teeth chattered.

"Well, that's real pretty."

"Fuck, it's cold," she said and wondered how she came to be there when she knew better. But knowing better was never a guarantee.

Win started unbuttoning his shirt. He put that over her shoulders too. "If you lay back, I can hold you and warm you up. You can tell me about Clay."

She was scared, but his voice was soft, and she wanted to hear more of it, just not her brother's name. "I don't want you to say his name."

"Okay." His hand brushed over her face. "Were you crying earlier? I think maybe you like people to think you're tough."

"I don't care what people think. Sing to me," she said. "Sing me that song."

Win pushed his hair back from his face. The T-shirt he wore exposed his stomach, a stomach defined by muscle and a thin line of hair diving below the waist of his pants. He leaned back, watching her. Outside the rain pounded the tin roof and a flash of lightning lit the space between them. His face shifted and softened. He cleared his throat and opened his mouth, and his sad, sweet voice filled the air again, just as she remembered it.

"Remember me. I'm the one who loves you."

It sounded even sweeter than in the church.

Jordan thought of Clay and Tim and Tony. The rest of their lives gone. With each word Win sang the dark empty space inside her grew smaller. She reached for him and kissed him, and he kissed her back with such force that she gasped and when she opened her mouth, his tongue darted in, seeking her out and then it was just her and this Win. Tim and Tony and Clay went somewhere else while Win's warm tongue spread like liquid, finding all her hollow spaces. He wasn't singing anymore but she could still hear his voice. Something came blowing up from a deep part of her and her tongue slid into his mouth too, although not as sure as his. He curled his tongue around her ear, and she said, "Is that all you've got?"

Win raised himself up. "I don't have a condom."

"I'm on the pill." It was a lie, but now that she'd come this far, she wasn't going to turn back. Win moved with an appetite that made no apologies. She knew that without the beer she wouldn't be in this situation but now she was, and she felt her own appetite for the first time since Clay had died. The ceiling was spinning when Win flowed inside her like cold silver. She shuddered around him.

The roof leaked and water dripped, dripped, dripped onto her leg. Jordan didn't move.

Win rolled off her. "Was that enough?"

"No," she said, not knowing if he meant sex or singing or which she meant, either. The aching emptiness had disappeared for a short time but now it was back.

He stroked her face. "You're all out of lines?" He kissed her cheek. "I got my own demons," he said. "Sometimes they lay still, and I think they're dead. But then they kick me in the teeth." The shack was so tiny he had to remain lying down to be next to her. Finally, he stood and adjusted his clothes.

She sat up, but when she did, the shack and everything in it slid to the side.

Win pulled his hair around one hand, wrapped it and tucked it up under his hat. His face disappeared again, until he opened the door and light caught his eyes. Whatever he saw in Jordan made him come back to her. He pulled her shirt over her breasts, pants up to her hips, looped behind her ears the wisps of hair that had fallen from her ponytail. Then he took his shirt and jacket back. He held her chin and looked into her eyes.

Jordan shook her head. She felt closer to tears now than any time since Clay's death and she promised herself she wasn't going to cry. She couldn't, not now, not here.

"Can I walk you back to your truck?" he asked.

"No," Jordan said. "I can find it just fine."

He looked down at her as if he was waiting for her to ask him to stay, but she didn't, so he stepped out into the night.

She knelt before she stood, holding the wall for support. The keys. She found them in her pocket and the next thing she knew she was in her truck, jamming the key in the ignition, flying down Gravity Hill. She knew she shouldn't be driving, but she didn't care anymore as she sped into the fog, thinking, *I—am tough–I am,* but still she held her breath until the tires touched pavement.

Chapter 4

The Rhode Island Red rooster strutted around the barnyard with ratty tail feathers high in the air, faded from the beautiful red of autumn leaves to the color of rust. In his old age, he'd become senile and crowed day and night. Jordan went to her window, slid open the screen, grabbed a small stone from the pile on the sill and winged one at him. The first missed, but the second one hit him in his bald butt, sending him squawking and fluttering back to the barn.

The haze above the horizon told Jordan it was going to be a hot one. She stood in front of her mirror, pulling on a pair of shorts and a T-shirt, removing the bits of leaves tangled in her hair, reminders of the previous night, just in case the burn marks running down the front of each thigh, where Win's open zipper had chaffed her legs, weren't enough. Her thin legs fit into narrow hips and tapered up from years of milking and carrying hay to the cows. "Who's stupid now?" she asked the stranger in the mirror. She got no answer. She didn't need one. Losing Clay was no reason to act like Clay.

Jordan went into the bathroom and ran the water as hot as she could stand it, undressed and stepped into the shower. She lathered up, rubbing soap into the chafed area and over her vagina, which also hurt, then turned and let the hot water run down her back and legs. When her whole body had been scalded pink, she got out and dressed in jeans, T-shirt and a flannel shirt. She tied her hair back in a ponytail and went down to the kitchen. Chestnut was lying on a mat by the door, and he wagged his tail as if to say, don't expect anything from me. It's too hot. But Jordan felt chilled to the bone.

The coffee on the warmer meant that her father was already outside. He hadn't been sleeping well, except for little catnaps where he curled up on a bale of hay in a fetal position. Most of the time he moved through his work with a stone face.

Jordan drank a cup of coffee and forced herself to eat a piece of toast with peanut butter. She'd lost ten pounds since the funeral and her mother had threatened to take her to the doctor if she didn't gain some weight back soon. Her mother's cookbooks were spread over the counter—*Cooking with Whole Grains, Cooking for a Small Planet,* a book about something called community supported agriculture. Diane had always enjoyed growing a garden and the previous summer she'd started selling vegetables and over the winter wrote a newsletter announcing plans to sell more produce, but Clay's death had changed things. She'd planted the garden this spring but weeds now threatened it and Jordan never knew where her mother was because she no longer posted her work schedule. She'd been working a lot of doubles. This morning, like many mornings, she wasn't home.

Sam stood in the milk room, studying the wall calendar that tracked the cows' heat cycles. Despite Clay's death, the farm had had a good spring, twenty heifers born and only seven bulls. More cows needed to be bred and Sam was making note of their tag numbers.

"You want me to call Dave?" Jordan asked when she entered the milk room.

Instead of answering, her father threw the switch to disinfect the pipeline, a task that preceded every milking.

"Dad?" Anger flickered in her at his nonresponse. All she was doing to help, and it was as if he didn't see her or hear her. She felt invisible.

He jiggled the milking machines on their stand, making sure the suction was tight so they would get a clean wash. "It's not too late to sign up for some classes, Jordan."

"We've already been through this. I made my decision."

"But why, Jordan? I want you to go. Mom and I both do."

31

"Next year. We're just not ready for me to leave."

Sam shook his head and before he could speak, she stomped out into the milk parlor, phone in hand. It was five a.m. The call went through to an answering service, which would forward the message to Dave the breeder, who would come that day with his vials of bull semen. The sun streamed through the high windows cut into the cement walls of the parlor and light gleamed on the stainless steel pipes that would suck milk from the machines attached to the cows, to the 500-gallon bulk tank in the milk room. The cows lined up at the gate, mooing from the pressure on their udders and their hunger for grain.

Jordan slid open the gate and let in the first cow. "Sassie, you slow poke." Jordan hoisted the long pole, meant to tap the cows on the rump if they dawdled, and nudged the cow on the spine. Sassie grunted and shied away.

"Hey," Sam said, coming into the room. "Careful."

He was a cowman, through and through. Everyone in town said it. There wasn't a farmer who took better care of his herd. He loved the milking parlor as much as Clay had hated it.

"Morning, girls." Sam called them all girls, no matter how old. Greeted them every morning the same way. Even now. He reached up to the radio fastened to one of the metal posts and turned it on.

Jordan reached up and turned the radio off. Her jeans chafed against the raw skin on her thighs as an image of Win appeared before her, his hair flowing over her as he thrust himself inside her. She shivered.

"You cold?" her father asked.

"No." Shame spread across her face. She didn't know what or who she was anymore, drinking and having sex on Gravity Hill right where Clay and the others died.

The room filled with noise—the automatic pipe cleaner and the roar of the vacuum and disinfectant swishing through the stainless steel pipes to cleanse them before they would then be rinsed for milking. Without speaking, they each took a bucket and filled them at the grain chute at the front of the parlor. Sam took the left side, Jordan the right. They poured grain into the hollowed cement dish and the cows' steamy breath, sweet from corn belches, rose up to mix with the grain dust. At the end of the line, six on each side, they stepped off the ledge at the same time, making it look like a syncopated dance as they descended the three cement steps, into the milking pit, to the bucket of steamy water that stood on a crate in the middle of the pit. They dipped their hands in; each took a wash rag and starting at the head of the line, Sam still left and Jordan right, wiped it over each cow's bag and teats, brushing away dried sand and shit from where they had lain in the stalls. Some let down their milk immediately, streams of white painting the cement floor and grates beneath their feet. Jordan worked quickly, keeping pace with her father even though she hated the farm work. When all the machines were on, their soothing pulse filling the room, Jordan felt not good, but better.

"What time did you get up?" she asked.

"A little after you got home," Sam said, shooting her a glance.

"I went to the river." Jordan bent under one of the cows, pretending to adjust a machine for better suction.

"At that hour?"

"What hour should I go, Dad? I work the whole light of day between the barn and the factory." Jordan couldn't help it. Anger bubbled up and it had nowhere to go but out.

Tires crunched over gravel in the drive. Jordan looked out the window to see her mother behind the wheel of her little blue car, arms draped over the steering wheel, staring at the house. Her friends who'd planned the farmer's market often stopped by to keep her updated, but at moments like this, when she thought she was alone, grief immobilized her. The steps leading up to the porch sagged; off to one side stood a rusting, broken grill, but her mother's gaze was fixed on the second-floor window... Clay's room.

33

"Mom's home," Jordan said, stepping back down to the milk pit.

A moment later, the door swung open. Diane wore green scrubs with a patterned smock and platform shoes that made her look taller. She had the same build as Jordan, only softened by age. She tipped her head to the side and with the back of her hand, nudged a wisp of silver hair away from her face. She wore no jewelry other than her wedding band. She didn't need dressing up to be beautiful, Jordan thought, although the blue gray of her eyes, once fluid like an ocean, had been compressed by her suffering to the steel gray of cable.

Sam's depression made it hard for him to offer much of anything, even a greeting, but he looked up and nodded. Jordan had heard her mother encouraging him to see someone, but so far, he'd refused.

"Hi, Mom." Jordan said. "How was work?"

"Busy. Three hard labors and a C-section. But they're all healthy. No real trouble with any of them." Diane worked third shift as an OB nurse at County General.

"Well, that's good."

"I heard something today at work," Diane said, descending the steps. She went and stood beside Sam.

Even though sound filled the room, the gush of milk through the line, the cows belching, the vacuum seemed to suck it all away, clearing the air for her. "I heard Mrs. Barbo plans to sue us."

Sam dropped the milking machine. He scowled at her before he picked it up and disconnected the hose to rinse it in the bucket of water. "You sure?"

"Bobbie Thompson told me. She says Barbo's telling everyone that she's filing a claim against us since Clay was driving and against Tim Hatch's estate, since it was Tim's truck."

Jordan wondered if Win had heard this.

"She could take the farm," Sam said.

Diane touched his shoulder. "Don't say that, Sam. She's just hurting. She'll settle down. Maybe I should try to talk

34

to her. Mother to mother." She looked at Jordan. "Can you keep your ear to the ground at the fair? You might hear something there."

"I don't know, Mom. I was thinking I might not show the calf." Jordan wished she'd never agreed to show Clay's calf at the fair. How stupid to take her dead brother's animal and parade it around the fair grounds. What did it matter, anyway? Clay had never wanted to show the stupid thing, not really. And now, she was going to go parade it around when people were angry with them for Clay's accident. How did her mother think this would help things? "I don't want to show the calf, Mom."

"Jordan, don't be selfish. Showing Clay's calf is a way to remind people of Clay's good qualities," Diane urged. "He had a lot of them, and we need to help people remember that."

Jordan knew better than to pick a fight with her mother. Clay was dead and still her mother defended him. Diane walked past Jordan, keeping her gaze locked in a glare as she passed. The parlor door slammed shut after her.

Sam struggled to get the machine back on. He was trying and not really succeeding in being more flexible since Clay's death. "You don't want to show the calf, then don't," he muttered. "I never expected you to fill his shoes."

"The cement shoes you put on his feet, Dad? Nobody could fill those."

"Asking someone to take a little responsibility isn't putting cement shoes on their feet," Sam said. "And you talk to me with respect." He straightened and looked at her. "I knew my son. He would have come around."

But Jordan believed otherwise.

Chapter 5

All year, people looked forward to the Woodstock Fair. Kids planned on showing their animals, farmers dreamed of simpler times, of owning draft horses and plowing their fields with those horses. Teenagers started romances on the fairway that often ended in marriage and kids and years of going back to the fair and trying to rekindle the fire and romance of those early encounters.

They waited weeks to hear more about the rumor of Mrs. Barbo filing a claim against them, but when no letter arrived in the mail and no more information filtered in through town gossip, Diane went blueberry picking. She'd begun selling muffins at the Saturday farmer's market. Jordan could always tell when her mother had trouble sleeping because the smell of muffins baking wafted up the stairs in the wee hours. This morning, she'd brought home a pail full of plump berries, made a pot of coffee, spread out her mixing bowls, five-pound bags of flour and sugar, eggs and milk on the kitchen table, and started mixing wet ingredients with dry ones, flicking away the bad berries before she added the good ones to the batter. Jordan watched her for a few minutes before she headed out to work with Clay's calf.

When her mother had the first batch of muffins cooling on the windowsill, she called to her.

"I should be able to pack up these muffins in a few minutes. Will you come with me to see Mrs. Barbo?"

"This stupid calf. I'm so frustrated!" Jordan yelled back. She'd been working with the calf on her days off from the glass factory. The calf seemed just as frustrated. It shook its head and refused to move. Jordan could feel her mother's eyes upon her waiting for an answer. She didn't want to go looking for more trouble with the Barbos, but she didn't feel that she could say no to her mother. Things had been tense between them even before Clay's death and seemed more so now.

"Fine, I'll go." She turned the calf, yelling as it took off toward the pen pulling her along. Jordan slammed the gate and slid into the car where her mother waited.

The Barbos lived in one of the row houses on Main Street. Decades earlier, the mill bosses and their families had lived in those houses, now multi-family dwellings, awkwardly divided with doors and entries. But aside from the grinder shop, there was no commerce in the center; the town seemed frozen in time. Children pedaled their bicycles on the cracked pavement, while men sat on the stoop watching them and drinking beer. They all stopped and watched the Hawkins women climb the steps of the Barbo house.

"I don't think this is a good idea, Mom," Jordan whispered.

But her mother seemed determined. She gave a sharp knock, and a moment later, Mrs. Barbo came to the door, wearing a long baggy T-shirt and a pair of sweatpants that stretched at the top of her thighs. She glared from behind the screen. "What do you want?"

Diane held out the muffins. "Please, I'd like to talk to you."

Mrs. Barbo shook her head without opening the door. "We don't have anything to say to each other." When Diane didn't move, she said, "Please leave."

The children and men moved further up the street.

"But we do," Diane pleaded. "We're both mothers."

"You want to bring me your fancy muffins and talk? You know who I want to talk to?" Mrs. Barbo's voice trembled. "Tony. That's who. Not you." Pain pinched her face.

From the house's dark interior, they heard movement and then Tina's toddler crawled into sight and climbed up Mrs. Barbo's leg. Mrs. Barbo swooped the child into her arms.

Diane's arms drooped. "I'm sorry. But we've heard—"

"You thought you'd come talk to me because you heard I might sue. Well, what did you think? Did you think your boy could kill my boy and get away with it?" Mrs. Barbo said, pressing the baby to her chest. "Is that what you thought? Do you know how he suffered?"

"They all died, for God's sake," Diane cried. "No one got away with anything! Clay didn't kill your son. Please don't do this! We could be helping each other, not looking for revenge." She bent to leave the basket, but Mrs. Barbo hissed.

"Don't you tell me what I should be doing, and don't you dare leave those."

"Come on, Mom," Jordan said. "Please." She steered her mother down the steps with Mrs. Barbo watching from behind the screen and the children watching from the street. They got in the car and drove home. Diane left Jordan, the muffins, and the thermos behind and without a word went into the house. *Fine mess you left us in, Clay,* Jordan thought as she unwrapped a muffin and practically swallowed it whole. She took a second and stuffed it in her mouth, but she had to open the car door and spit it out because she couldn't swallow past the hard knot of anger in her throat.

The next morning, Sam and Jordan finished the milking early. While Jordan fed the calves, Sam loaded Bucky in the back of his truck. "I suppose we should buy her a leather halter and maybe a new grooming brush," he said.

"Isn't this good enough?" Jordan snapped. She was reaching her limit. They had started at five a.m. It was now eight. Barn cleanup waited for Diane, who would be home from the hospital soon. She would have to clean the barn before going off to the farmer's market. The day was just starting, and Jordan was already exhausted.

"We're going right by Agway. I think we'll stop," Sam waited for her to put on her seat belt; he insisted on them since Clay's death.

Sam slowed as they passed the field on Main Street. The corn was now about three feet high.

Before Clay's death, on a rare evening when they were all in the house, the first selectman, Bruce Scott had knocked on the door. That night Diane had made a chicken casserole and the smell of exotic spices, coriander and cumin, warmed the air. Jordan and Clay had cleared the dishes and they were watching *Gladiator*, Clay's favorite movie. Bruce stood in the hallway, looking at the leather-bound set of *Encyclopedia Britannica* facing him on the shelf. He raised his eyebrows as he reconsidered Sam and then got right to the point of his visit. "The town has applied for and received a federal grant for a new school, Sam."

"What's wrong with the one we've got?" Sam asked. He had stepped into the living room to give the man more room and almost blended into the enormous farm scene painting on the wall behind him, where a small boy in tattered jeans stood watching a man, presumably his father, shoe a horse hitched to a wagon full of hay.

"It hasn't been updated in forty years. We need some major renovations, and we need to add some technology. It's not cost effective to keep using the old school. We wonder if you'd consider selling an acre of that piece on Main Street?"

"I'm not really for building a new school when we have one still working fine," Sam said, "but even if I was for the school project, I'd have to ask—can't you think of any better place to put it beside the middle of my field?"

Bruce Scott leaned further into the room and took in the painting on the wall. He paused for a moment. "It's only one acre, Sam. And the price is quite handsome. It's a million dollars."

Jordan looked around the room. Had she heard right? Clay had moved to the edge of the couch, every muscle tensed, and his eyes and mouth open wide. His look of shock and excitement told her she must have.

Diane floated from the kitchen to stand between them. "A million dollars?"

"That's right," Bruce said.

Sam shook his head, but his voice wavered when he spoke. "Doesn't sound like a good idea putting kids near a field with heavy machinery. I couldn't sell that land and stay farming. It's at the center of my field crops."

Bruce Scott tried to reassure Sam that the town would put up a barrier fence and make a plan for minimal disruption of the field. Diane stepped closer to Sam and put a hand on his arm. "Sam?"

Sam shifted and squinted at the painting, his gaze sweeping over the farmer holding the horse's hoof up, with a look of contentment on his face. Sam took a deep breath and drew himself up, turning back to the selectman. "No. Once you develop the land, there's no going back. I intend to keep farming and I need that field to feed the cows." Bruce Scott was not even out of the driveway when Clay turned on him.

"Are you crazy, Dad? A million dollars? I could go to woodworking school."

"Did you hear anything I said, Clay? Selling that piece would be like plucking the heart right out of the body. The farm wouldn't survive it. You'd have no future on it. Besides, you haven't picked up any wood to carve in months."

"What do you mean? I don't want to be a farmer, Dad! And maybe I don't care because I don't have any time. Mom could quit nursing. She could get the farmstand going like she's wanted." Diane stormed back to the kitchen, slamming pots in the sink.

The fighting intensified. Sam told Clay he didn't have any clear sense of direction and Clay shouted back. He hated farm work. Sam squared his jaw and announced that farming was a family tradition and Clay should feel honored to carry it on and one day he might just appreciate what he was being given. Now that he was gone, Jordan wondered if there could have been a middle ground. Jordan didn't remember her mother speaking up that night. Had she?

The town found another building lot, but the threat of development remained.

Her father's voice brought her back to the present.

"Doesn't look like anyone's been in the corn," he said.

Sometimes, kids partied in the field, parking their cars along the back edge.

A group of teenagers stood smoking on the concrete bridge spanning the Quanduck River and when they saw the Hawkins' truck, they stopped and stared. Sam returned their stony glares and one of them flicked them the finger.

"Damned fools," Sam said. "Not one of them's got any gumption."

He drove around to the back of the Agway building, pulled two twenties from his wallet and held them out to her. "Get the best halter," he said. "And don't take all day."

Jordan hurried around to the front of the building and climbed the stairs to a holding platform stacked with 50 lb. bags of corn and oats. Three men wearing flannel shirts, holding steaming Styrofoam cups of coffee, leaned against the burlap sacks. Jim Tyson owned a chainsaw repair business. He was a friend of Sam's and with his round, pleasant face, and full beard Jordan thought he looked like Santa Claus.

He greeted her and addressed the two other men. "You know, her brother was quite a good woodworker. We got a pair of his cherry candlesticks on our table. How's your dad?"

"He's okay." Jordan moved toward the door. She heard one of the other men say Clay's name.

"He was a little wild—"

"Yeah, but you remember yourself that age?"

Jordan heard Jim. "He was a good kid. It ain't right, if she does—"

"Who you talking about, Jim?"

Sam had climbed the steps without the men hearing. Jordan turned and saw her father's anger rippling under his flat expression.

"Sam! Why, I was telling them Clay... I—I was only saying—"

"You were only saying—?" Sam took in the other men, too. "I'd appreciate it if you didn't say anything."

Tyson drained his cup and tossed it in the garbage can. Yellow jackets flew up. Neither man moved. Then he said, "Not everyone is against you, Sam." He jumped down off the platform and the other men broke away too, heading down the stairs past Sam.

When the last man had disappeared around the corner, her father turned to her. "You gonna get that halter or do I have to?"

"I'm going," she said.

Jordan went in, found the most expensive halter and a brush, paid for them and hurried back out to the truck.

Sam shut the thermos tight and tucked it back under the seat. He gripped the wheel and started the truck as if summoning his last strength. A fairgrounds worker directed them to the livestock barn. One of the local farmers, Lou Dupree, was leading cows two at a time into the barn. He owned a farm in Stonyfield and his cows were sure to take blue ribbons; they always did. Sam had never been the kind of man to stand around talking with other farmers, and Clay's death made him even quieter. He nodded to Dupree and led Bucky to a stall at the other end of the barn. Jordan followed with a sleeping bag. Folding cots and blankets were spread around the barn.

"I better not get fleas," she muttered.

At that Sam smiled, and to see her father's chin softening, the old laugh lines etched around his eyes, moved Jordan.

"We'll bring home a ribbon, Dad," she said.

Sam patted the calf's rump. "I doubt it. I'm not expecting a ribbon."

"Well, what am I here for?" Jordan asked.

"It was Clay supposed to be here and you in college." Because Tyson's words had already cut him, she remained silent. "Try to have some fun while you're here," Sam added. "I'll pick you up Sunday morning." He gave Bucky a final pat and left.

Jordan looked around the barn. She recognized some of these kids as the Ag kids who hung out at one end of the high school, wearing jeans and work boots, smelling of hay and grain, driving trucks to school, talking animals and tractors. She'd dropped out of the Ag program her sophomore year, as it impinged on her college prep courses.

Now, her old classmate, a boy named Dale Thomson saw her. He'd been picked on in high school and called gay for wanting to be a florist. Jordan hadn't picked on him, but as Dale gave her a warm smile, she regretted that she hadn't stood up more for him.

"Jordan Hawkins? What brings you here?" His companions looked up. The Dexter twins, Laura and Lynne. As the three of them came toward her, she remembered how she'd snubbed them when she switched to the college track. College track kids made fun of the aggies for their clothes and mannerisms and the cars they drove. Ag classes were held at one end of the high school, out of sight. Jordan hadn't made fun of her old friends after she switched, but her grief over Clay was like a mirror now at odd moments, showing her herself.

"What are you doing here?" they took turns hugging her.

Jordan pressed the grooming brush into Bucky's hide. The animal jumped.

"Showing this worthless piece of shit."

The three friends exchanged glances.

"She's got good lines," Dale said, regarding the calf.

"My mother wanted me to do this for my brother. She was his calf."

Jordan waited for the uncomfortable silence her peers always gave her now, but these three seemed focused on the task at hand. Bucky swished her tail and Laura caught it, combing the coarse strands with her fingers. "You didn't shave her. You've got to have her shaved if you want any chance of a ribbon." Lynne ran her hand over the cow's neck. "Here too," she said. "It's all got to be shaved."

Jordan glanced over at the stall where Laura and Lynne's

cows lay on clean hay, coats shining and the shaved areas along the spine spiked up neatly.

"I don't think she'll let me do that. She's a nervous animal," Jordan said.

"You got her nice and clean," Lynne said, dropping her tail, "but if you don't shave her, you won't have a chance."

Laura and Dale excused themselves. "We're judging a kid's poultry show at three."

"Let me help you," Lynne offered, grabbing her grooming kit, with brushes, combs, and shavers. They brushed Bucky, shaved her tail, cleaned her hooves and eyes and sprayed her for the flies that inevitably flocked to the barns. Lynne took a picture of Jordan with her arm around Bucky's neck and pinned it to the front of the stall.

"Wow," Jordan said, admiring the difference. "But she still won't place. She can't follow a lead for shit."

"Sure, she can," Lynne said. "You have to be more confident." She grabbed the halter and led the calf to the ring, once again giving Jordan instructions, this time on how to stop and start the calf on command. Bucky's performance improved.

That night, Lynne and Laura and Dale invited Jordan to cook dinner in the Dexters' RV, but Jordan decided to work Bucky in the ring. When she finished, she found a plate of stir-fried veggies and a note waiting in the barn. It said, "You go, girl." She rolled out her sleeping bag and went to sleep feeling just a little happy.

The next morning, Dale and the Dexter twins brought her a cup of coffee and they walked their calves together to the judges' ring. The judges called the first two entrants forward. Jordan watched a girl her age walking in circles with her calf.

"Don't do that to me, Bucky," Jordan said, patting the calf's neck.

The judge called her name, and Jordan waved to her mother in the bleachers as she and the calf glided forward.

A clean-cut student from the state university, wearing a

white shirt, khaki pants, and a blue tie, walked around Bucky and one other calf, talking into his microphone.

"Not as much size and scale in this one," he said, referring to the other calf, then as he looked over Bucky, "Lots of angularity and directness here. A little more width through the front for balance over the shoulders."

A group of teenagers crowded up to the fence. Jordan recognized Tina Barbo balancing her toddler on her hip.

"Heh! Don't give her a ribbon," one yelled. "You know who that is?"

"Who's the cow? Moo!" They cracked up laughing.

Jordan recognized the kids from the bridge. The Dexter twins and Dale rushed over to the fence. Whatever they said was effective; the hecklers moved away.

But Jordan's face burned with shame as she retreated from the judging circle. A woman she didn't know patted her arm. "Don't let them get the best of you, honey. These kids have nothing but their own misery." A little Chihuahua wearing a purple bandana around its neck yipped at the kids as they disappeared into the crowd.

The judge conferred with two other judges sitting at a table and then he called out names. Jordan heard her name called for third place.

"Mom! A ribbon," she yelled.

Lynne and Laura got second. The Duprees, as expected, got first.

The judge handed Jordan the ribbon. "Work that calf a little more and next time she might take first. She's got potential."

Jordan thanked him.

"I'm sorry about those kids, honey," Diane said coming up beside her. "Maybe this was a bad idea. I'm sorry I forced it. It's just going to take more time, I guess. Try to stay away from them. We don't need to pour any fuel on this fire."

"Do you want to walk around with me?" Jordan asked. She couldn't remember a time her mother had apologized to her.

"I can't," Diane said. "I've got to get back and help Dad

feed the calves. And I need to pick some more veggies for the booth. Cassie and Jane are selling them here."

"Dad said we wouldn't get a ribbon." The edge in Jordan's voice brought her mother's attention back.

"Hey," her mother said, "you did well. Just focus on that."

Her mother's acknowledgment made Jordan feel better, although she wanted to remind her that she hadn't wanted to do this at all, that she'd done it because they'd asked her to—for Clay. She didn't want to be at the fair without Clay. But she knew better than to say so—she gave her mother a wave and led Bucky back to the barn.

"I owe you guys a big thank you," she called over to the twins who were tying their prizewinner in the stall. "What did you say to those kids?"

"Doesn't matter," Lynne answered. "You got him a ribbon."

But it did matter. "Tell me," Jordan snapped. "I want to know."

Dale stepped between Jordan and the twins. "Don't let them ruin your day," he clapped his hands like a camp counselor. "Who's hungry? What do you say we go out on the midway and get some food?"

"Good idea." Lynne started to move away.

"Do you want to come with us, Jordan?" Dale asked.

"No." Jordan knew she was behaving badly, and it only made her feel worse, but why wouldn't they tell her what they'd said to Tina's friends? She slumped into her folding chair and watched them disappear into the crowd.

About an hour later, Tina Barbo appeared with the child still on her hip and this time her mother was with her. Mrs. Barbo glanced into Bucky's stall at the ribbon hanging on the nail, and she glared at Jordan. Tina put her daughter down and the little girl began poking the animal's eyes.

Jordan closed her eyes and counted to twenty, waiting for them to move away, but she felt Mrs. Barbo's hostility radiating toward her, getting stronger and when she opened her eyes she turned and saw Bucky straining at her rope, trying to escape the child's prodding fingers. As calmly as she could, she said to Tina, "Could you please tell your daughter not to do that?"

Tina reached to pick up her daughter and Mrs. Barbo stopped her. "These animals are on display, aren't they?"

Jordan jumped out of her chair. "Don't poke her eyes! Would you like someone to poke you in the eyes?"

The little girl started to cry. Tina swooped her up.

"Don't speak to my granddaughter that way." Mrs. Barbo pointed a finger at Jordan. "When you put yourself above people, you're bound to have a hard fall." She pushed past and the three of them disappeared into the crowd.

Any joy Jordan felt at winning a ribbon evaporated. How was protecting Bucky's eyes putting herself above people? It wasn't her fault that Tony Barbo died in an accident with Clay. He was one of those hard-drinking kids on a destructive path. Clay had not been that kind of kid. It wasn't fair. She slipped the ribbon around her neck and escaped from the barn. She simply couldn't take one more confrontation. She consoled herself with a bacon burger and fries as she strolled alone past the game booths and the attendants.

"Ball toss! Take your chances!"

"Pretty lady! You look like a winner!"

"Only top shelf prizes here!"

Every year she and Clay had gone up and down the midway playing games. But the ball toss they'd loved above all others. Clay had taught her how to throw a ball so that her arm didn't flop out to the side like a wimpy girl.

She stepped up to the booth, put down her money and took the three balls. She could almost feel Clay beside her, the solid energy of her brother coaxing her on.

Jordan licked the last bit of grease off her fingers, weighed the ball in her hands, adjusted her grip around the stitches as Clay had taught her and whipped the ball. Three tosses and she walked away with an enormous St. Bernard with sad, felt eyes.

The fair was heating up. Lights flashed; music pounded; screeches filled the air. Couples strolled, kids darted from ride to ride, and Jordan looked to the end of the midway. There, straddling one of the motorcycles on display, sat Win.

Jordan headed toward the bikes. It was something she would normally have steered clear of, bikers. She wasn't looking for trouble, not really. But she thought he should know about the Barbos and the threat of being sued and, if she was more honest, she had to admit that over the past weeks, whenever she caught sight of a long haired man, a flood of feelings stirred, like a river breaking a dam, hurling sticks and rocks through the water.

Win didn't see her until she put her arm around him and slid her hand into his back pocket. "You thinking about buying this thing?"

He looked startled.

"Because it would be a step up from that piece of shit you call a truck."

The men standing around snickered. Win swung his leg over the seat and stood. He was half a foot taller than her. She leaned into him, and he smiled and with one finger brushed the furry head of the St. Bernard. "You got lucky, huh?" he asked.

"Wasn't luck at all. I have deadly aim."

He threw his head back and laughed. "That, I believe." He blocked her from the view of the other men and touched the ribbon. She liked the feel of his hand there.

"What'd you win the medal for?"

"It's a ribbon. Wouldn't you like to know?"

"I would," he said, taking her arm and moving her away from the men.

"Are you inviting me for a romantic stroll?"

He smiled. "You'd wait for an invitation?" He took her hand out of his pocket and held it. The men were laughing, but she told herself that whatever they were saying, she didn't care.

"You'll walk right out there on the midway with me? Don't care what people say?"

"Like what? You're ruining my reputation?"

He squeezed her hand. "I could get used to you," he said. "But I'm going back tomorrow."

"Back where?" she asked, trying to hide her disappointment.

"Maine."

Jordan stopped in front of the ticket booth. "You want to ride the Ferris wheel with me?"

Win looked up. The Ferris wheel, lit with white lights, looked like a spider web against the sky. "The Ferris wheel, huh?"

"Unless you would rather start with the roller coaster." She pulled out money and bought eight tickets, what it would take for two to ride.

"I don't do roller coasters," he said. "I'll do this though," he said. The line was short, so they got on the first round. Jordan slid next to Win and put the St. Bernard on her other side.

When the attendant lowered the bar in front of them, he looked hard at Win. "You Tim Hatch's cousin?"

"Yeah." Win answered. "What of it?"

The guy looked at him again, and then at Jordan. "Strange, seeing you two together." He pushed the button and sent them up out of his view.

"Asshole," Jordan shouted. She flinched at the harsh sound of her own voice. "What exactly do you think he meant by that?"

"I'm not sure," Win said. "But don't let it get to you." Win stared out to the fairground throbbing with music and lights and people. One side of his face was cast in yellow light, and the other in shadow. "People think blaming someone solves the problem."

"There's a rumor the Barbos are filing a claim against our family and Tim's estate, too, since it was his truck. Have you heard it?" Jordan asked.

The Ferris wheel spun them again and Win grabbed the bar, white-knuckled. "Yeah, I heard. That won't bring them back though, will it? Way I see it, some things are just gonna happen, no matter how hard you try to prevent them. Call it accident or mistake or fate."

"So, what do you call it? Do you believe it was fate they were going to die?" She'd thought about these questions since Clay's death, but she had no one to talk to.

"Smart people don't believe in fate. But I believe in it. I've seen too many things that weren't fair, happening to good people. And sometimes people could make good things come of it and sometimes they couldn't. There must be some reason for them, I guess." The wheel spun and swung them further up in the air.

"Your brother was driving Tim's truck because he was in better shape than Tim and Tony. Still, the accident happened."

"If it was fate, that would make God a pretty mean son of a bitch, wouldn't it?" Jordan kicked their little car and sent it swinging. The St. Bernard almost tumbled out of the seat. She grabbed it back.

Win gripped the bar again. "The worst thing that ever happened to me also saved my life."

"What's that?" Jordan asked. She nudged him with her elbow, until she saw the way he pursed his lips together. That made her feel soft toward him again, that and the fact he didn't share in blaming Clay. She put a hand over his. "I thought about you. Did you think about me?"

"You got a hell of a way of showing it," he grinned. "Yeah, I thought about you." He studied her for a moment. "You're even prettier than I remember."

"You're just afraid to get me mad, with this ride going," Jordan said, sliding closer to him on the seat.

Win put his arm around her. He smelled like hay and onions. Jordan breathed him in. She rested her head on his shoulder and he smoothed her hair down, letting his hand travel down to her breast. She liked the way he made her feel, even if it was just for a moment.

Jordan tipped her face up and Win pressed his lips to hers. His hands moved down her body, caressing heat into her hips and thighs. She felt the base of the music in his pulse. His beer breath tasted warm and sweet, then it turned bitter, and she had to tell herself she liked it that way too.

She wanted to ask him to sing again for her, but she felt stupid, out in the open fairground, like a baby wanting a lullaby. When the ride stopped, she held Win's hand and carried the St. Bernard under her arm as he threaded behind the rides and the RVs, to the edge of the field. He took off his flannel shirt; Jordan thought it might have been the same one he had been wearing the night they met, and he laid it on the grass, then he sat down and pulled her down too. She put the St. Bernard beside her.

"So, what do you want from me, Ms. Jordan Hawkins?"

"I don't know," she said, looking down at her sandaled feet, swinging like a child's next to his man-sized ones tied tight in work boots.

"You don't strike me as the kind of girl who would be interested in a guy like me."

Jordan looked away. The old her would never have met him, would never have gone near the bridge that night or stayed for a beer—or what came after. But she wasn't the old her and this new her was a person she couldn't explain.

"Hey," he pulled her toward him. "I'm not saying no, but—"

"Maybe I'm trying to find out what kind of girl I am," she said.

Win took the St. Bernard and propped it behind her as a pillow. A dark sky and the RVs blocked them from view, but the fair lights sent up faint arcs of red and blue and golden light. Win slid his hand under her shirt, undid her bra. Jordan pulled away. The first time she was drunk, but what was her excuse now?

"What?" he asked. "Are we all set?"

"Yeah, we're set," she said, even though they weren't. "But can you sing that song to me?"

Without the beer or the storm or the cover of the shack, Win sang and ran his hands over her breasts, strumming the chords of her stomach, along to her wet spot, where he coaxed the heat up from her and it took a little longer now without the alcohol, but there with the stars overhead, she felt the dam of herself breaking and then his mouth covered hers, and he stopped singing, thrusting himself in her now, and she knew this was the stupidest thing she had ever done, even stupider because it was the second time with no alcohol to blame. She wanted the sex and she wanted it over at the same time. When it was, she pushed him off.

Win propped himself on one elbow and peered into her face. "What's that for?"

Jordan stood up and felt the semen leak down her leg.

Win pulled up his own pants. He looked confused. "You decided you don't like me?"

"I like you."

He tucked a loose strand of hair behind her ear and touched the ribbon on her chest. "I know," he said. "I know what the trouble is. Clay."

"I told you not to say his name!" To hear Clay's name here at the fair without him really being here—it was more than she could take. Jordan flung the St. Bernard and the surprise of it knocked Win off balance. He took his eyes off her for a minute to pick up the animal and because she didn't know what came next or what should come next, she turned and ran toward the barn.

Crossing the midway, she saw Lynne and Laura, arms around each other's shoulders, waving up to Dale and some other kids on the roller coaster, as they whipped around the curve, arms extended overhead, laughing. At that moment, Jordan understood how everything had changed forever, because she could never go back to that kind of moment where gravity itself could be laughed at and maybe suspended, as if it was a thing you could trick. She knew better, now.

She started for the barn and found herself face to face with Sister Rachael. She glanced nervously around for Brother Michael, who she assumed could not be far off, but he was nowhere in sight.

"Don't be afraid," Sister Rachael said. "I have something to tell you—about your brother."

Jordan hesitated. Was Sister Rachael going to say something ridiculous like Clay had died a sinner? If so, she was going to punch her, because she was at that point, but Sister Rachael rushed on.

"The night of your brother's accident, we were in the park when some boys pulled into the lot near the old Riverside site. It was your brother with the other two. They disappeared up the hill with a crowbar. A few minutes later we heard them up there whoopin' and banging on metal."

"So what? Lots of kids go up there," Jordan said crossly. She tried to move past, but Sister Rachael stepped into her path.

"No, listen. Your brother and his friends—"

Whatever she said after that was drowned out by the distance Jordan was putting between them. "Stay away from me," she called over her shoulder as she hurried to the barn. When she reached Bucky's stall, she hung the ribbon back on the nail, grabbed the grooming brush and began brushing the calf's already gleaming hair.

"Sister Rachael is crazy," she whispered in Bucky's ear. So, what if they'd been at the Riverside site before going to Gravity Hill. Plenty of kids messed around there because there was nothing else to do in town. And how would Sister Rachael know anything anyway? She was hardly a reliable witness. Jordan laid the brush on a bale of hay and climbed into her sleeping bag; but she was still awake when the band finished its last song and the cleaning crews had gone through with their tractors. Only the crickets' chirping put her to sleep.

Jordan woke in the early morning. She opened her eyes to see a furry blob by her feet. She jerked them away from the St. Bernard staring with its sad eyes and shivered at the thought of Win standing over her as she slept. A crumpled piece of paper hung from its collar. *Winthrop Hatch, East Mountain Road, Purgatory, Maine. If you ever get to Maine, look me up.*

Jordan crumpled up the paper and shoved it in her pocket. Purgatory, Maine. Was that a joke?

Sam arrived at seven. Jordan was already outside the barn

waiting for him. He backed the truck up, dropped the ramp, and Jordan led Bucky up into the truck.

"You in a hurry to leave?" Sam asked as he pinned the ramp back up. He gave it a shake to be sure it was secure.

Jordan tossed the St. Bernard on the passenger seat and climbed into the cab. She handed her father the ribbon.

"I underestimated you and this animal, I guess." Sam hung the ribbon over the rearview mirror and shifted into gear. He looked more tired than usual.

"How'd things go at home without me?"

"All kinds of activity," Sam said. "A visit from Martin. He came back to get those water and soil samples from down by the river. He says the fern is definitely under some environmental stress," Sam sighed. "He's annoying."

"The environment's a big concern for our generation, Dad. We've got to live with the mess your generation made."

Her father looked at her sideways. "He's not your generation."

Jordan pulled the St. Bernard onto her lap. "Okay, good point."

Sam hesitated. "We got the letter from the insurance company. Mrs. Barbo filed a claim."

Jordan groaned. "This is getting worse, not better. What does she want?"

"Money. She's going after Tim's estate too, but it was Clay driving and he was covered under the farm policy. That's the only money there is," Sam said grimly.

Jordan told him about the confrontation with Tina and Mrs. Barbo. "She seems to really hate us."

"Jordan. I don't think that's true."

"Yes, it is! What's her story, anyway?"

Sam shrugged. "He's quite a drinker I hear, but I don't know anything about her."

"There's got to be more than that," Jordan muttered, "and I'm going to find out what it is."

"Never mind that," Sam said. "I need you to clean the machines and the tank when we get home."

"I'm taking a shower first." When they arrived home, she helped unload Bucky, who limped coming down the ramp.

"What's going on here?" Sam asked. "How long's she been limping?" He lifted Bucky's foot. A piece of gravel wedged tight between her toes. Sam pulled out his jack knife, talking soothingly to the calf. "It's okay, girl, Hold still now." He propped his hip against the calf to help steady her as he pried the gravel out from between her toes with the point of the knife blade.

"I didn't see her limping at all," Jordan said. She watched her father and the calf walking toward the barn and then she went to the house to shower. A large pot simmered on the stove. Tomatoes and basil, garlic and olive oil. Two baskets of ripe tomatoes sat on the counter. Her mother bent over a cookbook, a wooden mixing spoon in her hand. Clay had carved that spoon for her.

"Can you help me peel these tomatoes?" she asked.

"I can't," Jordan said. "I've got to help Dad."

Diane slapped the spoon onto the counter top. "I can't keep up with all these vegetables. I committed to this when I thought we were going full steam to develop the farm stand. Now I'm stuck making sauce between hospital shifts. I'm exhausted and you and Dad aren't supporting me at all."

Her mother's words stung. "Well guess what, Mom? I don't feel supported either." She stomped up the stairs, her mother's words following her.

"Well, it's not all about you, Jordan."

When she came down, showered a few minutes later, Jordan heard her mother in the living room on the phone with one of her friends. She slammed the door to let her know she was still mad and marched to the barn, expecting her father to take her side, but he said, "She's right. We should pitch in to help her more."

Jordan couldn't find the words to speak, she was so angry. Couldn't they see everything she'd already sacrificed? What about her?

A week after bringing Bucky home from the fair, Sam entreated Jordan after milking one night to help him deal with a sick heifer. He led Bucky from her pen to the front of the barn, lit by a floodlight. Her limp was so severe she was almost lame.

"What happened?" Jordan asked.

"Footrot." Sam instructed her to hold Bucky's foot while he washed it gently with hot soapy water.

"Have we had this before?" Jordan asked.

"Nope." Sam's fingers probed around the hairline of the swollen foot as he washed.

"Smells awful," Jordan said.

"That's the infection," Sam muttered. "It's a bad one. I should have been paying better attention."

"What caused it?"

"That gravel punctured the skin, I guess. Then standing in manure in the pen let the bacteria in." Sam dabbed the foot dry with a towel from the house.

"Mom's gonna kill you, using her good towels."

"This calf deserves the best, don't you girl?" Sam crooned as he took a strip of gauze, soaked it in some solution and flossed between Bucky's toes. Bucky mooed softly. "I know girl, I know. Steady." Working quickly, he soaked a thick gauze pad with more solution, wrapped it tight around Bucky's foot and wrapped surgical tape to hold it in place. He put all the waste into a bag, knotted it and handed it to Jordan, along with the pail of dirty water. "Dump this water over the back of the stonewall," he said. "Then wash your hands good. Bucky, you come with me—I got you all set up."

"Where are you taking her?" Jordan asked.

"Built her a lean-to," Sam said, turning the heifer with his hip, and leaning in to provide balance on her lame side. The geese followed along on Sam's other side, and the rooster brought up the rear. They would normally have been locked safely in the barn by this time to protect them from night predators, but they made an odd procession in the moonlight—Sam, the lame Bucky and the feathered fowl, clucking and strutting as guards. Jordan shook her head, wishing Clay could see this with her. She disposed of the bag in the garbage and tossed the dirty water behind the stonewall as her father instructed, then out of curiosity went around the side of the barn. When had her father built this? The lean-to, framed in with a screen door to let in air and light, was covered with heavy construction plastic above and a floor of dry hay. Bucky rested on the hay and Sam sat beside her, offering grain from the palm of his hand. "You got to live, girl. You got to do this for him, you hear?"

Jordan wished she could back away unseen; she didn't think her father would want her to see this moment or hear him talking to Clay's calf this way, but he sensed her there and looked up. "I'm going to try to get her to eat a little more. You go on up to the house. I'll be the one to take care of her. We already decided that, didn't we, girl?"

They each had their own ways of considering Clay, and saving Bucky was her father's. For Jordan, Sister Rachael's words at the fair—that the boys had been vandalizing something—nagged at her that whole week, pursuing her in the quiet moments before sleep and in the solitary hours of work. People were already mad enough about the accident; she couldn't bear more criticism of Clay. The old Riverside site had been closed to the public ever since the toxic waste had been cleaned up years before. On her next day off, Jordan decided to check out the hill where Sister Rachael had claimed Tony, Tim, and Clay had been the night of the accident.

The site was just across the street from the general store, so Jordan waited for the breakfast rush to be over before she grabbed a shovel from her truck bed and sprinted up the hill. Why allow herself to become alarmed by Sister Rachael? She was so gullible! Clay had always told her that. But still, she crisscrossed the ridge in a methodical way, and just as she was making her last sweep at the highest point, she spied a mound of freshly dug dirt and clay; a half-exposed drum oozed oil, and a pool of rainbow colors sat on the surface. Jordan didn't want to touch the barrel or risk spilling the remaining contents. What was she going to do?

"Damn it, Clay!" What had the boys been up to? Why would Clay and the other boys puncture the barrel? That was just plain stupid, but she was sure they had. Before Jordan could think any further, she was shoveling dirt over the mess. When she finished, it still looked suspicious because of the fresh dirt and the uneven mound, so she put loose stones in a pile over the heap, hoping it would look like one of the boundary markers that dotted so much of New England's secondary forests. One barrel will make no difference in what's already a toxic site, she reasoned. There was not much else she could do for Clay or his memory, not much but this.

Over the next few weeks, Jordan helped her father mend more fences and repair sections of a stonewall. The corn sprouted and waved golden tassels in the air. Jordan saw how it helped Sam to be working in the fields again, with one of his kids at his side—and it would have helped her too, except her period was late. She told herself it was just a day or so—she never kept track and she shouldn't be too worried. She saw the problem three ways: HIV, STDs and/or PREGNANT. She tried bargaining with God over which punishment she deserved, because although she'd told Win at the fair she didn't believe he handed out cruel fates, she thought he probably would in this instance, given her stupidity.

The next day, Jordan's period still hadn't come. She was helping Sam milk and they were finishing the last switch when the milk room door swung open. Dave the breeder was a middle-aged man, with small intent eyes that darted around a room no matter how many times he'd been in it. He wore a short-sleeved buttoned-down Oxford, with a patch on the chest that said DAVE and underneath it IBA, for International Breeders Association. He'd been breeding cows for more than twenty years and he knew his farmers like family, some were closer than others. Sam and his kids were among his favorites. He often brought them snacks and treats, like today. He was carrying a box and a tray with three large coffees from Baker's Dozen.

"Time for your union coffee break," he called cheerfully. He came down into the pit and set the box on a plastic crate, along with the coffees. He'd already put their names on each cup, and he handed Jordan hers. "Milk, no sugar. And, Sam, milk and two sugars."

Sam smiled and took his.

"Jordan, I got you a low-fat blueberry muffin." When he opened the box to get her muffin, Jordan saw there were only three donuts in the box, not the dozen he used to bring, and she thought of the way Clay ate Boston crème donuts by sucking out the custard first. She felt like one of those donuts with all the life sucked out of it.

"Jordan?" Sam turned down the country music. "Why don't you go tie up those cows Dave needs?"

Jordan knew her father was going to tell Dave about the Barbos' claim. Since receiving the Barbo's letter, the insurance company's attorney had replied to Mrs. Barbo's attorney with a letter that Sam and Diane had approved, one that was filled with legal defenses 1) the rain may have contributed to the road conditions, 2) a clarification that alcohol-related death did not necessarily mean alcohol-caused death, and 3) that a full investigation of the vehicle needed to be made. The lawyer said the company would do its investigation quickly and that Clay had been covered by the policy, but the policy coverage was for $500,000 and that was the limit. He ended with a personal appeal to Mrs. Barbo. "Please do not let your actions be driven by revenge." He'd told Sam that Tony Barbo hadn't had any insurance coverage at all and neither had Tim Hatch.

Jordan went out into the holding pen with the halter

looped and ready and went after the quieter of the two cows in heat. She tied the heifer in a stall, and went to deal with the more aggressive cow, who shook a long stream of snot that landed on Jordan's arm. Jordan reached over and wiped it on the cow's side. "No wonder you're havin' trouble." The cow had been inseminated the month before. "You're too mean to take."

The cow regarded her, wild-eyed, its nostrils flaring in and out. Jordan wanted to feel sorry for her, but all she felt was mad.

"You want to mess with me? Really?" She threw the rope over the cow's head and pulled, the loop falling perfectly. She tugged and the cow yanked its head up and away, but Jordan wrapped the rope around the nearest stall, so that the cow almost knocked herself over with the force of her own protest.

"What are you doing?" Dave came down the aisle, with the long plastic glove up to his armpit and the syringe full of semen. "If your father sees you rough-handling these cows..."

Jordan cut him off. "What's he gonna do? Fire me?"

Dave cocked his head and regarded her. "You've got a point. You regretting sticking around for this year?"

"No."

"You sure?"

"Not really."

"Can you get your scholarship back?"

"I'd have to reapply."

"Are you thinking you'll stay closer to home?"

"I guess I'm not thinking, Dave," she said.

"Well, that's obvious," he shot back. He stepped around her to get to the cow. He held the vial high, so the cow couldn't swish her tail or kick it out of his hand.

Jordan couldn't take her eyes off the milky fluid. Dave didn't talk now; he focused on the cow and his job. He grabbed her tail with his ungloved hand, and then he took his gloved hand and the syringe with the semen and eased it into the cow's vagina.

Jordan was standing at the cow's head. The cow's hard, wild-eyed look softened. She mooed softly.

"Shit," Jordan muttered. She stomped down the aisle, away from him and the cow in heat.

The bell jingled when Jordan entered the General Store. She had known Maxine since kindergarten when Maxine was her bus driver.

Now, Maxine looked up from the cash register. "Italian grinder coming right up," she said. Maxine prided herself on knowing the orders of her regulars before they actually ordered.

"You want blue fish or cod this year?" Maxine brought the Hawkins family a fish every year from her deep-sea fishing trip she took with her husband. She'd first taken a liking to Clay, and now extended herself in the same way to Jordan.

"Cod, I guess. You heard about the Barbos?"

Maxine nodded. "Clay's insurance will take care of it, though? Right?"

"He was covered under the farm policy for $500,000," Jordan said. "He didn't have his own insurance. It was cheaper that way, but Mrs. Barbo's asking for a million dollars." Jordan watched the implications of it settle on Maxine's face.

"A million dollars!" Maxine exploded. "That's outrageous. No disrespect, but Tony Barbo was a bum. The whole Barbo family... a bunch of bums." She shook her head. "She's a piece of work."

Jordan knew that Maxine's disgust with Mrs. Barbo and the lawsuit was genuine, and that Maxine would pass on the information to every customer entering the store, which might help shift the tide of public opinion against Mrs. Barbo instead of the Hawkinses. Jordan wanted more than that, though; she wanted Mrs. Barbo to drop the lawsuit.

"She had quite a singing voice," Maxine said. "Wanted to go to Nashville. But next thing we knew she was engaged to Barbo, and we thought for sure she must be pregnant. But Tony didn't come along until years later. I don't know what else to tell you."

"What about Tim Hatch's cousin? The guy who sang at the memorial service?"

Maxine folded the hard salami on the oiled bread before she answered. "Win? Yeah, I knew him. Before he got in trouble." She rolled the grinder onto a square of waxed paper and began to wrap it tightly.

"What do you mean... trouble?"

Maxine pushed the grinder across the counter at her. "Armed robbery."

Jordan gripped the case. She felt her feet sliding out from under her.

"Don't lean against that. I just cleaned it. He was supposedly doing drugs or something. That's why he came to live with Tim's family... to get away from those influences. Nobody got hurt. At least that's the story I heard."

"Who did he rob?"

Maxine sighed and swept the loose strands back into her untidy bun. "I don't remember, Jordan. It was a long time ago. Went to jail, I remember that. But I heard he really pulled himself together after he moved. Oh, I think it was a convenience store. Works for the power company now, up there in Maine. Is Barbo going after him too?"

Jordan nodded. She thought about Win saying the worst thing that ever happened to him also saved him. But prison? Armed robbery? The door jingled and two customers entered. She slid a five-dollar bill across the counter and slipped out.

Jordan crossed the street and stood on the bridge that spanned the river. A small boy hung on the swings at the playground. Where was his mother? The river cut a deep channel through town with no fence around it. Jordan waited a moment; then as she started to approach the child, a voice called out.

"Willie?" A young woman called from the porch of a shabby house on the edge of the park. "Come here, honey. Time for lunch."

The little boy eyed Jordan. She wanted to tell him not to

get too close to the river, but he scurried off as if she, not the river, were the danger.

On her way to the factory, Jordan pulled into the Stop & Shop. She'd planned she would ditch the pregnancy test if she saw anyone she knew, but she encountered no one, so she bought the test and tucked it into her purse, trying to ignore the heavy feeling in her body as she began her shift. She worked four hours and just before break, Tilchek came over to her with a box full of broken glass.

"A dozen defects." He frowned. "What's going on with you tonight, Jordan?"

She couldn't give him her full attention as the bottles continued to whip by, but as if to prove his point further, Tilchek reached in and plucked off another split neck.

"That's enough," he exclaimed. "Go take your break and when you come back, switch off with Gary and finish packing for the rest of the night."

Jordan went straight to the bathroom and tore open the packet. The wand shook in her hands as she squatted over it and held her breath. How could some little cotton swab decide such an important thing? She rested the wand on her leg because the instructions said it should be held level and she couldn't get her hands to stop shaking.

Please, she whispered. Please, please, please. She waited. It felt like an hour passed, as she watched the cotton changing color under the double plastic windows. A pink line in one of the windows meant not pregnant. A line in each meant pregnant. Jordan's vision blurred as the second line appeared. Two pink lines? She slumped onto the toilet, closed her eyes and on the screen of her mind flashed an image of a wet dark uterus, a part of her body she had carried with her for eighteen years but had never, not once, considered and now, just like that, there was a baby in it? The reality of it hit her in waves of nausea and dread. Jordan Hawkins, pregnant? The girl who everyone said would go away and do Asheville proud? Pregnant? And not even by some gorgeous high school jock or a brainy college boy but by some guy who committed armed robbery. This wasn't possible.

"You stupid fuck." She must have spoken out loud, because then Betty Olson, one of the older women on the shift, was knocking on the stall. "Hey? Who's in there? Hello. You all right?"

Jordan hid the wand in the bottom of her purse and emerged from the stall.

"Jordan! You're white as a ghost. Are you all right, hon?" Betty put her solid arm around Jordan and guided her to a chair in the corner. "I'll just go get you a cup of water and tell Mr. Tilchek you need to go home." But when she opened the door, the roar of the lines, the dank heat of the sand being fired into liquid glass, the bottles clanking down the conveyor, all pressed together, spinning wildly, snapped Jordan back to the present moment. She couldn't go home. Not yet.

"Wait, Betty. I'm fine. Really. It was just something I ate, I guess." Jordan brushed by her and went and took her place packing bottles. For hours, she tossed bottles into boxes and slammed them onto the conveyor belt that ran to the warehouse. She begged Tilchek to give her a double. He did. Toward the end of the second shift, she got so tired the room started to spin around her, and when she turned to heave a box onto the conveyor belt, it slipped from her grasp and crashed to the floor, sending broken glass flying everywhere.

She dropped to her hands and knees and started picking up the glass, when one of the supervisors came running.

"Young lady, where are your safety glasses?"

Jordan shrugged.

"I've got to give you a warning. You're lucky you didn't hurt yourself or somebody else."

"Real lucky," Jordan said.

The supervisor didn't respond; she watched Jordan sweep up every last shard, and then ordered her to clock out, even though there were thirty minutes remaining on the shift. "We don't need any more accidents tonight," she said. "Go home and get some sleep."

An early morning haze stood over the cornfields. Jordan rolled down the windows and heard the crickets chirping. The air smelled of dew and corn. The golden tassels poked up through the haze, catching the morning light. Her mother was not yet home. Country music floated from the barn, the pulse of the compressor on the air behind it. Her father would be almost done with the milking. She tried to imagine sitting them down and telling them that she was pregnant. She felt so ashamed. How had this happened to her?

Jordan pressed her foot to the gas and drove on. Before she turned the curve, she looked in the rearview mirror. The sun shone on the barn roof, gleaming on the emerald green insulator panels, then the corn field filled the mirror with a more tender green, and then she rounded the corner and the farm disappeared from sight.

Chapter 6

The last morning of Clay's life, Jordan had sat at the kitchen table reading over her senior project on Gravity Hill. Across the barnyard Clay had been trying to teach Bucky how to drink from a bucket. Bucky's mother had slipped on the cement and broken her leg. The butcher had been called for the slaughter. Clay hated farming, but he hated slaughter most of all, especially Santos the butcher with the loose sideboards of his truck rattling a death knock on the air. At the sound of his truck, the dogs slunk away and even the rooster, prone to attacking visitors, scurried off into the woods and stayed until dusk when the fox chased him home. There was no escape for Clay, though, and as he waited for Santos to arrive that morning, he slipped a rope over the calf's head, opened the gate and tugged her out into the barnyard. Jordan strained to catch a glimpse of the more carefree Clay who'd disappeared when full-time farm work landed on his shoulders.

His scowl lifted when their mother pulled into the driveway. She got out of her car, straightened her nursing smock and went to hug Clay. She had been hugging him a lot now that Jordan's college acceptances were arriving. She grinned as she ran her hands through his dark curls, and a look of appreciation crossed Clay's face and her mother's too... their expressions like the bones of their faces, exactly the same.

Then the barn door banged, startling all three of them and Sam, hands on hips, his tall, lanky frame rigid, said, "Feed the other calves, Clay." Annoyance seeped through his voice.

Clay muttered something under his breath. Diane released him and shot Sam a hard look. He bowed his head and disappeared into the barn. Only when he made a full retreat did she enter the house and bang the door behind her.

She barked at Jordan. "You didn't get up to milk? You are so selfish, Jordan."

"Dad didn't wake me," Jordan answered defensively, but her response didn't address the real problem, the unfair workload Sam placed on Clay to lighten Jordan's load while she got her college applications and now her senior research project done. Before her mother said another word, Jordan hoisted her backpack over her shoulder and let the door bang behind her.

"Hey, I'm dying for a cigarette." She approached Clay as he latched the calf pen. "Want to go have a quick one at Gravity Hill before I go to school?"

Clay didn't answer but got in her truck and started flipping through CDs. He put in Garth Brooks.

"Thanks for milking this morning. I really appreciate it." Clay said nothing. "Don't you ever get tired of hearing him?" Jordan asked.

Clay shook his head. "How about you buy me breakfast?"

"Okay, after we go to Gravity Hill." She planned to tell him what she'd learned while doing her senior project, but she could tell it wasn't yet the right moment.

Clay stared out the window as they passed the river. He rubbed his hands over his face. "Today's Senior Skip Day, isn't it?" he asked.

She nodded.

"You're not going?"

On Senior Skip Day, most of the senior class went to Misquamicut Beach in Rhode Island.

"I don't know," she said.

"Who the hell will care, Jordan? You're graduating."

Jordan's knuckles paled on the steering wheel, but she made no reply as she pulled the truck off the road near Gravity Hill. No houses stood there; people respected the strange phenomenon, and no one wanted to disturb it. In their small town where nothing seemed to happen, the mystical power of

Gravity Hill gave purpose to their solitude and isolation. So many times when she was younger, Jordan had begged Clay to bring her to this hill and he had. She admired her handsome brother. The sun streamed through the window catching particles of dust like a halo around his head. In those early days, before Jordan could drive, Clay would give the signal and she would reach over and shift the truck into neutral at just the right time to start the smooth, slow motion that seemed to defy gravity and inch up the hill.

But on this last day, Clay hopped out of the truck and stomped into the clearing before he turned to see if she was following. She was. She picked her way around the cigarette butts and broken glass and clambered up the boulder worn smooth from decades of climbing. Clay offered her a cigarette and a light. They blew smoke around each other. Jordan wished she could get things to be the way they used to be between them.

"Hatch is skipping," Clay said. Tim Hatch, Clay's best friend, had flunked a bunch of classes the year before and so was doing the year over. "You could hang out with him." He handed her a twenty-dollar bill. "Go to the beach and buy a six pack to share with Hatch." He was always giving his money away, buying little things for her and all his friends.

She pushed the money back.

"Hatch says Garth's coming to Foxwoods. He might get us tickets. You wanna go?"

"Garth Brooks? No."

"Yes, you do." He jabbed her ribs. "A concert date with Hatch? You know you would."

"Would not," she shot back.

"You're blushing!" Clay laughed. "It's okay, Jordan. He thinks you're hot, too."

"Clay! I don't—" She felt flattered, but it was seeing Clay laugh that made her really happy. Like most mornings, Clay's hair sprang willy-nilly everywhere, and hair stubble sprouted on his chin, showing the man that had formed against his will.

"I did my senior report on Gravity Hill," she said. "I

found this scientific article that explained it so clearly. The hill creates the optical illusion. Something about a hilly landscape surrounding the road on both sides, and the road being curvy and there not being any horizon."

Clay took a long drag from his cigarette. "You always think some book can answer all your questions, Jordan."

"But the article included maps and measurements and everything, Clay. The scientist *proved* it," she insisted. The sun lit up his long lashes. Energy seemed to be leaking from his skin; he looked so vulnerable to her.

Clay held the smoke a long time before blowing it out. "It's always the things you can't see that are hardest to explain."

She thought he would be interested in anything about the hill, but he was barely listening. "It was just incredible to see our little town written up in this national journal," she continued. "Did you know a farmer discovered the hill in the early 1900s when he shifted his tractor in neutral for a moment? He said he felt 'a shocking experience of an earth without gravity.' The next time you and your friends come up here you'll have to tell them that. I think we should get the town to make a plaque explaining it."

Clay flicked his cigarette away and slid off the rock. "Why do you always have to take the fun out of things, Jordan? I've got stuff to do. I'll catch up with you later."

Wisps of smoke curled up from the direction of his discarded butt. Clay headed for the woods, and Jordan jumped off the rock to smudge out the smoldering spot and turned to find herself alone.

"Clay," she called after him. "What about breakfast? I thought you were hungry."

She listened to the twigs snapping... he was walking toward the river. As she climbed into the truck, she spied two sheets of paper folded on the floor... Clay's application to an advanced woodworking program at the technical school, empty except for his name, and a blank application to the glass factory.

At the far end of the Region 17 High School parking lot, some kids crowded around a shiny black Mustang. Tim Hatch's Mustang. A couple of the guys stood near the front wheel and Tim leaned against the hood. He waved to Jordan when he saw her. He was tall with blue eyes and long hair and the way he stood, legs spread, his jeans tight, he oozed sex, sex, sex, and that was all Jordan could think about when she saw him. She could swear he raised his eyebrows at her, dropping for a moment the I-don't-care-what-anyone-thinks attitude, the one that disguised the fact that he and his gang huddled in the corner of the parking lot because they didn't fit in anywhere inside the school. For a moment she was tempted to walk right over there and ask him to drive her to the beach, but then the school bell rang, and she went in.

Jordan was one of the few seniors in school that day, and all day she thought about Clay and how often he closed his bedroom door when they were the only ones home and how the marijuana smoke seeped beneath the door anyway, so why did he bother? Was that what he had gone into the woods to do that morning? Get high? The day seemed to drag on forever with these thoughts weighing her down and she was relieved when the bell finally rang. She drove home wondering if Clay had gotten home before their father found him missing. But she no sooner pulled into the barnyard, when her father came out of the barn.

"Where's Clay?" he asked.

"How should I know?" Jordan pulled her backpack off the seat and started for the house.

Sam wrapped his knuckles against the hood of her truck.

"I wanted to get the rye cut in the west lot," he said. "We need the feed for tonight."

Cutting rye for night feeding also meant cutting enough for the next morning. At least two hours of work, hours Jordan didn't have if she was going to ace the next morning's chem quiz.

She told her father so.

"Well, Clay will milk for you tonight," he said. "You can study then."

Jordan didn't argue although she knew a fight was brewing. She changed into her barn clothes and read the note her mother had left on the counter tucked under a pan of brownies.

"Don't eat all the brownies. I'm grocery shopping. Tacos for dinner." Diane always shopped on her day off from work and cooked one of their favorites. Tacos were Clay's.

Despite the homework waiting for her, Jordan enjoyed driving the truck with the cut rye grass flying in the air around her, and her father happy on the tractor in front of her. The chopper hummed and belched, humming as it sucked the crop into its blades and belching as it blew the chopped fibers up and out its Brontosaurus neck. When they finished chopping, she pulled the tractor up to the barn, climbed off the high seat and went into the milk room to sanitize the machines.

Sam came in after he dumped the load of corn feed into the cows' trough. "What are you doing?" he asked.

"I'll help you start milking."

"You just going to come home from college whenever he screws up?" he asked. "You keep covering for him and he'll never grow up."

Jordan said nothing.

"Maybe you think you're helping the situation, but you're not."

Clay appeared at the milk room door hours later when they were more than half done. He wore the faded jeans he had put on for morning chores, but someone else's jean jacket, signed in permanent marker with crosses and names of people he never mentioned at home. A day's beard covered his face and beneath it his skin glowed from a day in the sun. Jordan almost didn't recognize him.

"You look like a bum," Sam said. "I'm not even sure I want you in the milking pit. You'll scare the cows."

Clay looked at Jordan and the understanding passed between them. She hadn't told their father anything, but now she was sure: he'd gone to the beach with Hatch.

"Fine." Clay said. But it wasn't fine. Jordan saw how those words wounded her brother.

"Hey, you get down here," Sam yelled.

Jordan beckoned to Clay, her eyes pleading for him not to escalate the argument.

"I can finish, Dad," she said. "Go on up and eat, Clay. Mom's got tacos."

"What did I tell you before, Jordan?" Sam turned on her.

So did Clay. He taunted her in a way he never had. "Go, Jordan. Go ahead. Why don't you just go right now and run off to college."

"That's enough," Sam interjected. "You have something better worked out for your future, Clay?"

Clay grabbed one of the milking machines and then slammed it back on the hook. The cows jumped. "I guess not. Not that you'll listen to."

"You can't even get yourself home for chores. Where were you all day?" Although he spoke evenly, he kept dipping and wringing the washing rag in the bucket of hot water.

Clay and Jordan had exchanged glances. "Don't," she mouthed, but Clay was too much like their father. He wouldn't back down.

"I went to the beach, okay? How many times have I told you? I don't want to be a stupid farmer."

"You think it's stupid?" Sam took the stairs in two strides to stand over him.

"Yes, I think it's stupid," Clay said, thrusting his chest out.

Sam backed off, jaw clenched. Jordan thought he might hit Clay, but he didn't. "There is no shame in farming, Clay. And you should be grateful."

"I want to go to woodworking school," Clay said.

"There's plenty of wood to work here, fences to mend and a calf barn to build." Clay mumbled something under his breath. But Sam was hurt, that much was clear. "You think figuring nutrition and breeding schedules and crop rotations is for stupid people, you try doing it."

Jordan was afraid they would come to blows. It had happened once before, and her mother had come between them. But Clay backed down and so did Sam.

Clay pulled out his cellphone and dialed. "Hey, Tim. Come pick me up, will you?" He spun out the door. Sam let him go.

After milking, Jordan went to her room and pulled her senior report up on the computer. Above her desk an army of Clay's wooden animals peered down at her. Whales, seals, penguins, and dolphins. Animals he'd carved, but not one farm animal among them. He hadn't given her a new one in months. The cursor pulsed on the conclusion to her report: "No matter what, some locals will not reconsider how gravity could possibly pull a car up hill. But after examining the facts, despite appearances, it is clear to me that Gravity Hill is nothing more than an optical illusion."

Jordan's fingertips caressed the keys as she erased the line and typed, "The mysterious pull of Gravity Hill is hard to explain and yet it is as real as the science debunking it. It is always the things you can't see that are the hardest to believe."

She took comfort that she'd made the change before the police cruiser came to the door. Now, months later, she no longer knew the girl who'd written those statements, or what she truly believed. Because what she'd heard Clay say—under his breath—was not a curse but a question.

Why don't you give me a chance to figure it out, Dad?

Chapter 7

Jordan couldn't go home. Going home meant facing certain facts she wasn't ready to face. She had friends, but they'd stopped calling. She couldn't blame them; they'd tried, and she had ignored their calls. She felt so alone. Sometimes, she and Clay had gone to the ball field at the school when they needed to get away from the farm.

It was late morning, and the summer school kids had been dismissed to the buses, some screeching and jumping from seat to seat, others slumped, staring out the windows with vacant eyes. The kind of despair Jordan had so desperately wanted to escape.

She pressed her cheek against the steering wheel and squeezed her eyes shut. Maybe if she just counted to ten—but when she opened her eyes and looked in the mirror, she still saw her shocked self staring back. She opened the glove compartment and grabbed her glove. The leather was stiff from neglect. She took off the rubber band that had secured the hardball into the pocket to help the glove keep its shape and started working her hand into the glove. She got out of the truck and walked toward the field, tossing the ball and catching it with the thwack of leather meeting leather. When she'd worked up a good sweat, she went to splash some water on her face from the fountain at the back of the school. She came back around the front of the building, slumped on a bench and started to cry. "Fuck," she muttered.

The bench was placed there as part of a memorial to a girl Jordan's age who'd died from cancer twelve years earlier. Cindy had been Jordan's best friend in kindergarten and first grade. Her family had moved a few towns over, to Lisbon, shortly after Cindy's death. She didn't remember seeing them at Clay's memorial service.

What was she going to do? Keep the baby? Give it up for adoption? Have an abortion? None of the options seemed like good ones. She couldn't possibly keep a baby and go to college. Go through with the pregnancy and give it up for adoption? No, she would have to walk around town pregnant, facing everyone she knew wanting to know who, how, and why. Because although she could probably hide it for a number of months with baggy clothes, sooner or later it would show, and Asheville was a small town. She couldn't live with the shame.

Have an abortion, then? An image of a furry sac came to mind. Whenever the cows spontaneously aborted a fetus, they stood over their stillborn young, trying to lick life into it. She'd already gone through so much loss, losing Clay. How could she stand anymore?

Jordan snuffled and brushed some dried leaves away from the stone. She wasn't sure what to do or even how to figure out what to do and sitting in front of Cindy Pascal's memorial stone wasn't giving her any answers. Her whole life she knew herself and her family one way: with Clay. He had understood and believed in her, encouraged her to follow her dream, to go to college and become a teacher. He was always telling her what a good teacher she would be. Even though he and his friends partied at Gravity Hill, he never would have let her get into the situation she was now in. And without him, she wasn't sure how to get herself out of it. She struggled to her feet, got in her truck and headed for home.

When she arrived home, she was shaking. She felt as if a hole had been blown right through her.

Her mother stood in the driveway. A van plastered with stickers, "No farms no food. Buy Local. CSA." was just backing out.

"I sold every single bushel of tomatoes to Agnes and the

others for their market!" she exclaimed. "They can't keep up with the demand. Next week they want even more tomatoes and two bushel of squash and all the lettuce I've got. I don't know how I'll do it, but at least I don't have to make endless batches of sauce." Her mother pushed her hair out of her eyes. There was such strength in her. She wasn't religious but she believed in life and even though she was broken by Clay's death, she seemed broken open, not down. Jordan wanted to ask her, "How'd you do that, Mom?" Or maybe even more, she wanted to ask, "Can't you help me, please?"

Sam, looking very much broken down, scuffled across the yard with a bucket of grain for the calves banging against his leg. "We'll help you," he said.

Diane gave him a long look. "How, Sam? You can't keep up with milking and chores as it is."

"We will," Sam promised, setting down the empty pail and climbing on the tractor. "We'll get it done. Won't we, Jordan?"

"Sure, Dad." But no one seemed to notice her sarcasm or if they did, they didn't react to it. Her mother tossed some empty cartons in her back seat, which was already packed with bushel baskets and crates.

"I stopped at the general store to see if I could sell some produce there and Mrs. Barbo was telling people that we don't value Tony's life because we haven't agreed to pay her a million dollars."

"Mrs. Barbo's evil, Mom."

Diane turned. "Jordan, don't say that. You don't know her pain. What she's doing might be the wrong way to express it, but I understand her grief. Let's just concentrate on something positive, like getting these vegetables ready for market." She got in her car and drove away.

Jordan shook her head as her father escaped onto the tractor. She felt frustrated; they always wanted more of her. Why couldn't they understand what Jordan was going through?

Diane's car disappeared around the bend as the Toyota

Tercel came into sight. Martin looked around for the geese before he even got out. The geese honked but this time they didn't leave the nest.

Martin came toward her. "Is your father around?" he asked.

He was so cheery that her weary-to-the-bone feeling lifted a little.

"He just went down to spread a load of manure," Jordan said. "He'll be back in about twenty minutes. Would you like to see something interesting while you wait?"

Martin raised an eyebrow. Jordan took that as a yes. She hopped into her truck and gestured for him to climb in.

"It sure is a beautiful day," he said as he buckled his seatbelt.

Jordan laughed. "You're a lively conversationalist."

Martin looked surprised. "How old are you?" he asked.

"Old enough, but sometimes surprisingly stupid for my age."

"That's harsh. You should be a little kinder to yourself. Words are powerful, you know. Where are we going, anyway?"

"Have you heard of Gravity Hill?"

Martin shook his head.

They'd reached Main Street. Jordan drove the truck up over the hill, turned around at the intersection, and pointed the truck back in the direction they'd come. She shifted into neutral and watched for his reaction as the truck started to move up the hill.

"Holy shit!" he said. "This is crazy. What's happening? How does it do that?"

"Magic," Jordan said. "You can Google it. Before I could drive, I used to beg my brother to bring me here."

"You have a brother?"

They'd reached the crest of the hill, with the empty horizon before them. Jordan wanted to tell him she felt Clay right there, still beside her, but she didn't. "He died this spring. Car accident. Right through those trees." Tall grass had grown up around the crosses. Someone had removed the dead flowers.

"I'm sorry for your loss," Martin said. "That's tough. It explains some things."

"Yeah? Like what?" When Martin shrugged and it was clear he wasn't going to say more, she went on. "Sometimes it doesn't feel real. Sometimes, it feels like he just walked out of the room, so to speak, but he'll be right back."

"I get it. Sort of," Martin said. "My cousin died two years ago in a skiing accident. We were best friends." He picked at a callous on his hand.

Jordan shifted the truck back into gear and they started downhill. "How'd you get through it?" she asked.

"My parents got me someone to talk to. A counselor. That helped. She let me talk it out and she gave me some activities, like doing something to honor him. My parents helped me set up a scholarship at his ski school. And time helps. It's a cliché, but it's true. What about for you?"

"Nothing so positive," Jordan said. "I've been doing the kind of things Clay would do—stupid things. Things I would never do before."

Martin gripped the dash as she put the truck back into gear. "That probably doesn't feel good, being out of control."

"No, it doesn't."

"Well," he said, "There's a simple solution." When Jordan looked at him, he said, "Just stop doing *that*... being out of control. If you know better, be better. You going to college or what?"

"That was the plan."

"Not was," he corrected her. "Is. That is the plan. Say it." He nudged her arm.

"College. That's the plan," she said. And, the truth was, just saying those few words helped. She *did* feel better. Even though she couldn't see how with the mess she'd made of things in just a short time, but still, she felt better. They pulled back into the barnyard as the old John Deere approached with Sam sitting in the seat and the manure spreader hitching behind.

"Not too many like him left," Martin offered. His face held a look of admiration. "He's a strong man. He'll be fine."

Jordan grunted and Martin looked at her questioningly, but she held her tongue as her father parked the tractor and came toward them.

"Young man. By God, I am glad to see my tax dollars hard at work. We're all going to sleep better tonight knowing that fern's so well looked after."

Martin looked taken aback, but he squared his shoulders and took a deep breath. He stuck his hand out and waited for Sam to shake it. Jordan had to admit that she admired the way he rebounded from her father's rudeness.

"We got the test results back." Martin waved a piece of paper in front of Sam. "Not the water or the soil yet. Those will be back next week," he said, "but the tests on the fronds themselves. The leaflets are suffering from ash particulate in the air."

"The tire burning plant," Sam said, pointing the high stack of smoke on the horizon. "I thought to tell you about it after your first visit and then I forgot." He nodded. "I'm not surprised. You can see it on the corn leaves down in that field, too. Of course, they claimed the plant would have state of the art environmental controls but ask anyone in the center and they'll tell you they find ash on their gardens in the summer."

"It's the world's largest tire-burning plant," Jordan said. "It burns ten million tires a year."

Martin shook his head. "Well, I can have a talk with the state regulatory board. I will do that. But there are a couple other things we could talk about. There has been some destabilization of watercourse banks and some sediment from the fields washing into the wetlands down there. Would you be open to doing some cross-slope row cultivating this fall?"

Jordan looked at her father, who was regarding Martin with a different look. "Mr. Martin, you surprise me. What's your background?" he asked. "What makes you do this job?"

Martin ran his hands through his tight curls and Jordan watched him pull as the curls snagged around his fingers.

"My grandfather owned a dairy farm over in Torrington." Jordan was beginning to understand his admiration of her father.

"Is that right? What was the name?" Sam asked.

"Martin," Martin said. "My father's family." Sam shook his head to indicate he didn't know the farm. "It was a small place," Martin admitted. "You might not have heard of it. There's a Martins Estates there now. Whole new development. Thirty houses."

"Humph," Sam grunted. "He didn't want to hold on to it? For you?"

"Wasn't a choice," Martin said.

The two men stared at each other for a moment, then Sam said, "Sure, we can talk about cross row cultivation."

Martin nodded, pleased with the commitment he'd gotten, and Jordan was glad her father hadn't voiced judgment of his family's development decision.

He stuck his hand out and this time he didn't have to wait for Sam to shake it. "I'll contact the regulatory board about the emissions, and see if I can get some action here," he said as he climbed into his car. He drove away, but not before giving Jordan a wink. "Stay out of trouble now."

Sam cocked his head and looked at her. "Was he flirting with you?" Jordan shrugged. "Well, he's too old for you. Don't even think about it."

If only you knew, Dad, Jordan thought. They started milking and to fill the silence she turned on the radio. She missed Clay terribly. Mostly, at this time of night, during milking. Taking Eugene Martin to Gravity Hill and talking about Clay only made it worse. They'd had some of their best talks while milking cows, sometimes they hadn't talked at all, just worked side-by-side singing every song that came on the radio. She didn't sing anymore. She couldn't imagine ever singing again.

"What's the matter with you?" Sam asked, coming into the milk room, guiding the next switch of cows into stations.

Jordan looked at her father. She wished she could tell him. But she thought about how he'd handled Clay and doubted he'd give her the kind of support she needed now. Clay. That was who she wished was there. He would have helped her figure it out.

"Nothing, Dad. Nothing's wrong. Maybe I don't want to be in this barn listening to country music and dodging the cows peeing on me! Maybe I'd like to be able to walk around town without that old hag Mrs. Barbo telling me that we're going to pay for the fact that her son died in that car with Clay." She imagined Clay in the room with them. Her heart ached with missing him.

Sam leaned against the milk tank, his arm braced against the shiny stainless steel, which reflected his body in a distorted image, bent and broken. "I didn't ask you to give up college this year, but you insisted and now you want to blame me for your decisions."

It was worse than that, though she couldn't say it. She was pregnant and she had no one to blame but herself. She kept working until they got to the last switch of cows and then she brushed past her father and headed for the house. Her mother wasn't home. Perhaps she was working second shift. She'd left a pound of hamburger in the fridge. Jordan made a big hamburger patty, fried it quickly in the pan, plopped it on a roll and wolfed it down. She made another, cut it in half and sat at the table eating more slowly. Was she already feeling extra hungry because of pregnancy? Could it happen that fast? She pushed the thought away, drew the mail toward her and sat staring at the handwriting on one of the envelopes addressed to her. She knew that handwriting.

> Dear Jordan,
>
> We were shocked and deeply saddened to hear the news of Clay's death. Jim had an extended business trip to Seattle and from there we went to Alaska on a family vacation, so we

*didn't know anything about the accident until
we came home last week.*

*We are anxious to hear how you are doing.
We would love to see you and to be here in any
way we can. You know we understand a few
things about getting through the grief of losing
someone. So, we have you in our thoughts and
prayers and hope you will call us. We'd love to
have you come for dinner.*

Love, Jim and Ellen Pascal.

Jordan went to her room and drew the bundle of cards
from the box in her closet. Twelve cards. Twelve years the
family had been gone from Asheville. Each card contained
a picture of the family, Mr. and Mrs. Pascal and their two
sons, Jed and Nelson, big strapping men now who even in
their teenage pictures looked much like Mr. Pascal. The boys
had been five and seven years older than Cindy, so the first
cards captured them during the rapid changes of adolescence
and teen growth... from pimples and braces to the handsome
men of recent years.

The most recent card included Jed's wife and infant
son in the family photo. Each year's card gave an update of
family activities: vacations to Hawaii and winter ski resorts
in Colorado, the boys' academic and athletic achievements,
Mrs. Pascal's return to school to become a massage therapist,
Mr. Pascal beginning his own business. And each year's card
issued an invitation for Jordan to come and visit them. She'd
visited on occasion and always sent a card at the holidays with
a few lines of perfunctory news about school or farm changes.

She put the newest card on top of the stack in the box, put
the box back in the closet and turned on her computer.

How often do pregnancy tests fail? Before she'd finished
typing the words, Google had filled in the search question,
and she clicked on the link to the Mayo Clinic site. "Taking

a home pregnancy test can be nerve-wracking, especially if you're not sure if you can trust the results." She scanned the article until she found it... if the test was taken according to package directions and at least a week after a missed period, the tests claimed 99% accuracy. Jordan slammed the computer shut. She could hear her father in the barn running the vacuum pump, cleaning the milk lines. The ceiling fan above her head whirred in a lazy and rhythmic way. Without bothering to change into her nightgown she got into bed and pulled a pillow over her head.

Chapter 8

How could she be pregnant? Two times with Win and pregnant? She didn't need to go to a clinic. She'd taken a second test and gotten the same result, and more importantly, she just felt different. She was sure she was pregnant. And now that she was sure, the shame of what she'd done was like a fuzzy veil over her thinking. Could she keep the child? No, absolutely not. She thought she would die if anyone found out. The wands were in her purse, and she'd checked them a hundred times. She needed to tell Win. She needed his strength and his experience. Her father had warned her to stay away from Martin, but what would he think about Win? Yet, Win was older and had seen more life. He could help her figure it out. If she decided to have an abortion, she wanted Win to go with her and hold her hand. If she decided to have the baby and give it up for adoption, he'd have to give his permission as well. But what if he tried to convince her to keep the baby. What would she do then?

She'd gotten the directions to Purgatory, Maine on Google Maps. She dug into her pocket for the scrap of paper with Win's phone number.

Win answered on the second ring. "Hello?" Even one word spoken with his rich timbre calmed her.

"Win? It's Jordan." She pressed her back against the bedroom door; she'd closed it even though she was alone in the house.

"Well, hello, Jordan." He paused. "How are you?"

"Hey, I'm on the road and I'm going to be passing through your neck of the woods. Any chance we could get together? Are you free today?"

"Passing through Purgatory, today?" He chuckled. "Good luck with that."

She looked at herself in the mirror. She was frowning.

"I'm only kidding you, girl of the fairgrounds. We can get together. It's Saturday. I don't work today. How long do you have?"

She was working third shift at the glass factory, so she needed to get back. "Not long," she said. She wasn't sure she would have GPS when she got that far into Maine, so she'd bought a map when she filled up with gas and she traced the route now with her finger. "Can we meet in Colridge around 2? Right off I- 95? Is there a McDonalds or Burger King there?"

"A BK," he answered. "But wouldn't you like a proper date? I can afford more than Burger King."

"I appreciate that, Win, but Burger King is good."

"All right then, Burger King it is. Drive safe."

That was sweet of him, telling her to be safe, but how would Win react to the news of her pregnancy? Telling him was the right thing to do. She knew that. Was she hoping he might want her and the baby? She had to be honest that there was some part of her that wanted him to convince her not to have an abortion. She packed her steel-toed boots, flannel shirt, jeans—everything she'd need later for the glass factory and headed for the highway. Route 95 straight highway driving through Massachusetts. It looked easy on the map, but she'd never driven further than Worcester, and even though she was traveling against traffic both ways, the tractor-trailer trucks on I-495 and I-95 demanded all of her attention. She drove highway the whole way and the landscape lacked personality, making it easier for her to think the farther north she drove. Once she passed Portland, Maine, she started thinking about the conversation with Win. She wasn't going to let Win convince her to keep the baby. She would argue that they were never meant to make a baby or to be together and that she was leaving Asheville just as soon as she got things straightened out at home and that having a child was not in her college plans. She spent the drive formulating what she would say and then what he might say and then what she might say in response, so absorbed in her thoughts that she was dizzy by the time she neared the Colridge, Maine exit.

The Burger King in Colridge was part of a strip that looked like it could be anywhere. How could it be that she could drive so far from Asheville and feel as though she'd never left? She saw that Win's truck was already in the parking lot. As she entered the Burger King, the smell of red meat and French fries coated everything, and Jordan gagged on the odor. She fought it, took a few deep breaths and approached Win sitting in a corner booth. Dressed in Levis and a plaid flannel shirt with the sleeves rolled up, his long legs poked out into the aisle. Jordan slid into the booth opposite him and noticed that his hair, pulled back in a ponytail, was still slightly damp. He smelled spicy.

"Hi Win." She wasn't sure exactly how to greet him. Should she lean over and kiss him? Wait for him to kiss her? Here she was pregnant sitting with the man responsible and unsure how to even say hello.

Win saved her. He leaned over the table and planted a quick kiss on her cheek. "Girl of the fairgrounds, you are a sight for sore eyes. How have you been?" His eyes traveled down to her chest. She wore a black Lycra V-necked top and last minute had thrown a thin cotton cardigan over it and tucked them both into her Lucky Brand jeans.

"I'm good, Win." She pulled the sweater tighter.

"And the sunny town of Asheville?"

"The same," she grimaced.

"Can I buy you a delicious meal cooked by our local chef?" he smirked.

"Just a cup of coffee," she said. Just seeing him cheered her up and bolstered her courage. "And a tossed salad." Sweat started to sprout above her lip. She wiped it away and hoped Win wouldn't notice. There was no line, so he was back in no time with the tray and had only ordered an apple turnover and a cup of coffee for himself. He handed her the food and she thanked him. He slid back into his side of the booth, but with both feet planted on the floor now. He folded his hands on the table and waited for her to say more and when she didn't, he sat up to the edge of the table, and watched her twirl the coffee twizzler around her finger. "What's up, Jordan?"

"Win, I'm pregnant."

Win pushed his half-eaten apple turnover away and pressed his back to the upholstery. He glared at her. "What?"

"I'm sorry. I know."

"You know? Why are you telling me this?"

"Why?" Jordan winced. Win was looking at her as if she were a bug, or worse.

"You're—we—it happened when we slept together."

"Oh, is that what you call what we did? We fucked. Twice. And do you not recall me asking you if you had protection?"

Jordan looked around to see if others had heard. There was no one near them. She dropped her hands into her lap. In all her imagined scenarios, she hadn't thought Win would speak to her like this.

"Did I not ask you that?" His voice held the angry condemnation of a parent, not a lover, not an older wiser gentle man who she thought might help her through this.

"Win—I was hurting." Her voice sounded like it was coming through a tunnel.

"Were you or were you not using protection?" She shook her head. "So, you lied to me and now here you are... what do you want, child support? You're going to be like every pregnant teenager in Asheville extracting money from men who never wanted..."

"Stop it! Win." She pressed her hands over her ears until he stopped speaking. "I don't want to keep it." She couldn't be sure, but did he look relieved? Perhaps.

"So, you want money for an abortion. Is that it? You came to get money for an abortion. How much does an abortion cost these days?" He was leaning over the table, hissing at her, his sexy mouth now twisted in an ugly way she wouldn't have been able to imagine.

"I don't know. I haven't... I came here first. I thought..."

"Well, whatever you thought, you thought wrong. Jordan. You got yourself into this and you'll have to get yourself out of it." He pushed himself out of the booth and stood over her. "I don't even know if I believe you that I'm the father. It's not like you gave me any reason to think you discriminate about who you sleep with, is there?"

And then he was gone.

Jordan stumbled to her truck, pulled herself up into the cab and avoided looking in the rearview mirror. No one had ever talked to her the way Win had talked to her. Her hands shook when she reached to shift gears. She was pregnant, with no one to help her figure it out. And the father of her baby didn't even believe he was the father. Shame glued her to the seat. She drove back to Connecticut, numb. What was she going to do? She had no idea. Win wasn't going to help. There was no one, then. It was too much to think about, so she made up her mind not to think about it. It wasn't a good long-term solution, and she knew that at some deep level, but she figured there was time, and she would just stay very, very busy until the answer came to her.

She hardly saw the roads or the scenery she passed; the yellow line her only focus until she was out of Maine. Back in Connecticut, when she spied the glass factory smokestack, she drew a deep breath, filling her lungs with the hot acrid scent of the smoke. She clocked in twenty minutes early and found Mr. Tilchek in his office. "Any chance of a double shift?" she asked.

"You're in luck," he said cheerfully. "Early bird gets the worm."

She was already walking away, pulling on her gloves to relieve the person on her line. She checked her reflection in the glass. She didn't look different. Nobody could have guessed. If she could just do things as she'd been doing them, maybe everything would go back to being the way it had been before. Somewhere along the way, she packed all her thinking and worry with the bottles and convinced herself that was possible.

When Jordan returned home the next afternoon, she expected to find her father milking. Instead, he was in the field, picking tomatoes with her mother. Jordan grabbed a basket and went to the opposite end of the row where her parents picked, even though she was so tired, she was dizzy. Chestnut wagged his tail and plopped in the dirt at her feet. The vines lay heavy with ripe tomatoes. She breathed in their sweet scent mixed with the damp earth and felt her body expand.

"Don't put them in that basket unless they're perfect," her mother said. "Use a separate basket for seconds."

"Okay," Jordan called. A hawk flew overhead, and the corn leaves shivered in rows beside them. She couldn't hear her parents' words; they spoke in a low tone. She wrapped herself in the cocoon of soft sounds, a balm to help soothe the hurt of the way Win had spoken to her. When they all reached the middle, her mother counted the baskets.

"Five bushels just in this row. Can you believe it, Sam?"

"It's been a good growing season."

They'd already picked the summer and zucchini squash. Diane handed Jordan a tomato and Jordan rubbed it against her shirt before she bit into the sweet flesh. "Just in case there's any ash from the tire burning plant."

"It doesn't come this far," Sam said, eying the plume of smoke from the distant stack. "The crops are fine."

"I think I saw Tina Barbo at the factory this afternoon filling out an application."

"Will that be awkward?" Sam asked.

"Mrs. Barbo is the problem. Not Tina or her dad."

Sam and Diane shook their heads. Diane spoke. "You got a call today from Cindy Pascal's parents. They want you to go for dinner."

"I don't feel very social," Jordan said.

"That's exactly why you should go," Sam said.

Diane grabbed the last empty basket. "Thank you both," she said. "I can get the lettuce. You better get to milking, now." She reached up and gave Sam a kiss. It seemed awkward for them both.

The Pascals lived a mile outside the center of Canterbury. Potted petunias flanked the front door of a modern A-frame house, the deep purple hue of the plants a few shades darker than the taupe color of the house.

Mrs. Pascal opened the door before Jordan even knocked. She was an attractive woman, with a bright smile and black curly hair. The comforting smell of mashed potatoes and grilled meat wafted out to the front porch. Mrs. Pascal drew Jordan into a big hug before inviting her into the house where running water tinkled from a fountain on a table in the entry way. Mrs. Pascal was a believer in feng shui and Jordan had to admit that things just felt different at the Pascals' house. A chandelier with tiny glass prisms threw rainbow patterns of light on the walls. Bare wood floors smelled of lemon oil and a few oriental rugs added color and warmth. From the hall one could see straight into the dining area and out the cathedral window of the backside of the house to the thick woods.

"You look good, honey," Mrs. Pascal commented. "A little thin, but under the circumstances… How are your parents?"

"Fine."

Mrs. Pascal was not satisfied with 'fine.' She watched and waited for more. "My mother seems a little better than my dad."

Mrs. Pascal seemed disappointed, but not deterred. "And how are things on the farm?"

"Good, I guess."

"Did you get the corn in?"

"Yes, but we planted late."

"Can I get you something to drink?" Mrs. Pascal asked her. "Water? Orange Juice? Lemonade?"

"Lemonade," Jordan answered and while Mrs. Pascal went

to the kitchen to pour it, Jordan stepped into the living room to look at the photos. The fieldstone fireplace held pillar candles on the mantel and family photos in silver frames. There was a photo of Cindy—with the family that last Christmas before she died, the little bald head the only thing signaling her illness and another photo of her alone, with her blonde baby curls—before cancer.

Mrs. Pascal came in, handed Jordan the lemonade, and called out. "Jim? Jordan's here."

Mr. Pascal appeared from the interior of the house. He shook Jordan's hand instead of hugging her. He'd always been a more formal man and conversation came hard to him.

"I'm so sorry about Clay. It's such a tragedy. All three boys—leaves a big hole in the town, doesn't it?"

"Mrs. Barbo's suing us for Tony's death," Jordan said abruptly. "And people have turned against us because of the accident."

The Pascals exchanged looks and it was Mr. Pascal who answered. "A lawsuit? When our boys were teenagers, we held our breath every night until they came home. Every parent knows the risks of letting their kids get into a car with other kids. But a lawsuit? I'm surprised at her."

"How are your folks dealing with this?" Mrs. Pascal asked.

"Okay, I guess." Jordan wasn't sure how much to share. "Mom has friends who stop by—people she can talk to—but Dad keeps things to himself."

"It's harder for men," Mr. Pascal said. "He's probably worried about losing the farm."

"Oh, Jim, don't say that! You won't lose the farm, honey." Mrs. Pascal tried to reassure Jordan.

"I didn't mean to worry you," Mr. Pascal said, but he seemed unconvinced as he excused himself to go check the grill.

Mrs. Pascal led Jordan into the kitchen and gave her the task of putting corn into the steamer while she cut vegetables for a salad.

The entire house, the Pascals' demeanor, everything felt peaceful and content. Jordan wanted to tell Mrs. Pascal about the pregnancy but she didn't know how. Would Mrs. Pascal judge her? She had always been so understanding, she decided to risk it. "My life just seems to be falling apart. How did you put your lives back after Cindy died?"

Mrs. Pascal put the tongs down and gave Jordan her full attention. "That is part of why you've come, isn't it?" she said. "Clay's death has set you on a seeker's path." It took Jordan a moment to absorb the words. "Spirit has guided you to us. I'm so glad, Jordan," Mrs. Pascal said. "Cindy's life and everything that happened in her life, including her cancer has brought us a gift—" When she saw Jordan's face, she said, "Yes, I did say 'gift'."

"A gift?" Jordan thought about the way she'd yelled at her father the day before, the way he and Clay had yelled at each other. Mrs. Barbo's fury. The way Win spoke to her when she told him about the tiny seed sprouting in her that she was trying so hard now to deny. How could any of it be a gift?

"Did that happen right away?" Jordan said. "Seeing this gift? Or did it take a while?"

Mrs. Pascal considered Jordan's question. "It was happening the whole time, I guess." She spoke slowly as she tore lettuce. "Although I wasn't aware of it at first—just as I wasn't aware that I could connect with Cindy on the other side."

"The other side?"

"There is but a thin veil between us and when we open ourselves to the reality of a higher spiritual dimension, we become connected to that divine reality and loved ones who have passed, like Cindy and Clay. I believe Cindy is helping Clay on the other side right now," Mrs. Pascal said.

Jordan thought about this. She thought about the night at the river with Win and how she'd sensed Clay's presence. Was he trying to reach out to her?

"When we understand this, we know that there is no such thing as death—our spirit just passes out of this physical form back to Spirit, we don't need to fear so much."

"I was afraid when Cindy was sick," Jordan said.

"That's because you felt compassion for her. You've always been a compassionate girl, Jordan."

That made Jordan feel it might be safe to trust Mrs. Pascal and she was just about to tell her about being pregnant, but Mr. Pascal opening the slider door interrupted them. "Chicken's going to get cold."

"We better eat," Mrs. Pascal said. "Shall we?"

They proceeded to the dining room table, Mr. Pascal carrying the chicken and Jordan, the corn, while Mrs. Pascal followed with the salad. The table shone with the colors of the food, and they pulled their chairs up and Mr. and Mrs. Pascal paused. They did not say a formal prayer, but Jordan got the sense that they were in fact expressing gratitude for their meal. She waited and then when they picked up their forks, so did she.

"Jordan and I were just discussing how Cindy's death helped us connect to a deeper sense of Spirit, Jim."

"Umm." Mr. Pascal ground some pepper on his chicken.

"But I don't understand how Cindy's death or Clay's death could be a gift." Jordan challenged. "I don't understand."

"I didn't say the *deaths* were a gift. I said they brought a gift. Every soul comes here to do its work, to fulfill its purpose," Mrs. Pascal said. "That's what we believe anyway. People getting angry is just because they're hurting."

"Yes," Mr. Pascal said. "But Ellen, you can't make it sound easy. It wasn't easy."

"No," Mrs. Pascal sighed. "I know that."

"I don't see any gift from Clay dying," Jordan said. She decided she wouldn't discuss being pregnant, not with Mr. Pascal present, but she felt more open talking with the Pascals about Clay's accident than with her own family.

"The soul doesn't die, honey," Mrs. Pascal continued. "Just the body. Each soul makes its journey as agreed upon, some longer than others." It was hard for Jordan to think of Clay as a spirit agreeing to a short life beforehand. Had he known how much she would miss him?

Jordan mentioned the lawsuit, the hostility from Mrs. Barbo. "That's what's come from Clay's death. And Cindy was just six years old."

"We always felt we had more love in our life because of Cindy," Mrs. Pascal said. "She was so connected to Heaven, wasn't she, Jim? She taught us not to be afraid and not to take love for granted."

"It's true," Mr. Pascal whispered.

Jordan felt the connection between the two of them. It was hard to doubt them with so much love in the room.

"But we understand that kind of hostility."

"You do?" Jordan finished the last bite of her chicken and Mrs. Pascal put another small piece on her plate. Jordan thanked her and turned back to Mr. Pascal.

"You were too young to remember the mill burning down, but you might have heard talk about it?"

Jordan shrugged. She didn't remember.

"Well, the mill burning put a big hole in the town. It was as if the town lost its soul," Mr. Pascal said. "Barely six months after the mill burned, the tire company officials came around talking about wanting to put in the tire burning plant and the supposed benefits to the town. Three million tires a day," Mr. Pascal shook his head. "How could anyone see that as a benefit?"

"Jim," Mrs. Pascal said. "Jordan didn't come for this."

But Jordan urged him to go on, so he did. "We spent $10,000 of our own money within six months," he said. "We took out ads in the *Norwich Bulletin,* the *Hartford Courant* and the *Providence Journal Inquirer.* We formed a concerned citizens group."

"I didn't know any of this," Jordan said, shaking her head.

"You were too young to remember. You were no older than six at the time," Mrs. Pascal said.

"They understood the population perfectly," Mr. Pascal continued. "They knew most of the working people in town had lost their jobs when the mill burned, and they were desperate for a way to feed their families. After Cindy's cancer, we felt that speaking up was a way to do *something*. We wanted to fight the tire burning plant and we had the resources to do it. But it was a fight we couldn't win without the town. No matter how much money we spent. Most of those protesting were from Rhode Island, the Foster area, near the water reservoir, where the wind currents carry the ash particulate emitted from the stack. They were the ones who had hard science to lobby their cause and a population educated enough, and with enough money to fight the thing."

"But in the end, the Connecticut legislature ruled that the plant caused no danger to public health and the town voted for the plant," Mrs. Pascal said. "And that was the end of that."

Mr. Pascal turned to his wife. "Well, not really, Ellen." He turned back to Jordan. "That night before the vote, we had a meeting to organize the next day's protest. I went out to my car and all the tires were slashed. I should have called Ellen, but instead I started walking home. It was dark; you know how there are no lights on those roads and a car pulled up. I started to run, but there were three of them. They gave me a good beating, to reinforce their message."

"Who?" Jordan asked. She couldn't imagine anyone in town capable of that. "Who would do that?"

The Pascals shook their heads. "We've no idea."

"I was angry for a long time, Jordan," Mr. Pascal said. "We lost Cindy and people turned on us. This other way of thinking—it didn't come easy to me. I struggled. Here's what Ellen got me to understand. Everything you do affects everything else. When the Riverside mill burned, and the town decided to bring in the tire burning plant we tried to warn everyone that the town was replacing one form of pollution with another. We remain convinced that Cindy died as a result of environmental pollution. We started digging into it, trying to find out who else might have cancer. It seemed we were close to documenting a cancer cluster caused by those leaking barrels and buried right under our noses by shady characters who thought the town was just too poor to notice or do anything about it. We had a choice to become bitter. There were plenty of times I laid in bed at night after kissing my little girl goodnight, watching her body waste away, hearing her breathing and I wanted to—" he folded his lips together in a tight seam. "I was on the road to bitterness, but it couldn't bring Cindy back and I couldn't hold that level of anger in my body without it destroying Ellen and the boys—"

"And you too, Jim," Mrs. Pascal said.

Mr. Pascal nodded agreement and went on. "I couldn't love anyone with that anger sloshing around inside me." His fingers worked at peeling the label from his beer. "But I had to work at it. I would have liked it if we could have got some people to listen to us, though. I would have felt like Cindy's death helped the town. But people needed jobs and they thought the tire-burning plant was the answer."

"I would have been mad," Jordan said. "Just hearing this makes me mad." She had never thought about death as being able to help anyone. This expansive way of thinking was new to her. "I still find it hard to understand how a death like Cindy's or Clay's and the other boys… how can that be anything but a tragedy?"

For a moment, neither Ellen nor Jim answered. Jordan looked from one to the other. Jim fixed his gaze on the family photo on the mantelpiece. In the photo, the two boys, who looked like Jim, were about the age she was now, so Cindy would have been gone a couple of years by that time. Ellen followed his gaze to the picture and the two of them exchanged a smile. It wasn't a sad smile or a broken one, it was a smile that started on the inside and found its way out like a door or a window to the open space within them. Jordan thought if she stared at them long enough maybe she could figure it out. But how long would it take? She had the feeling that if they left her to figure it out on her own, it might take her years.

"Just be open to it," Mrs. Pascal said.

"I should get home," Jordan said suddenly. "I have to get up early to work at the factory."

It was hard to hold onto the feeling of peace when she left the Pascals because on the drive home, Jordan started to think again about how Clay's death had brought her entire life crashing down, turned people against them, and how she'd just made her own problems worse by creating the problem she was afraid to think about. But thinking the Pascals' way felt better, even though it challenged her world view, so she kept telling herself to be on the lookout for a gift, hard as it was to believe.

Chapter 9

Even though Asheville was rural and isolated, Jordan and Clay were not the only children on their road. There was another family, the Dyers, who lived a mile or so down the road, although they could have been a world away for all the families saw of each other. The Dyer children watched too much television according to Sam. TV was a sore subject because whenever Jordan and Clay turned it on, Sam turned it off and sent them outside, saying it would rot their brains. For years, Diane had worked second shift at the hospital, leaving Sam to supervise them after school. He made sure they did their homework and chores. If there was any free time left, his agenda did not include television. "You have two hundred acres to roam," he would say as they pulled on their outdoor clothes, reluctantly. They couldn't argue with that. Connecticut was a small state, but their northeastern corner was a world to itself. No gym, no movie theater, limited cell service. The natural world was their entertainment. With fields and forest and the river, there were endless places to build forts and track deer. In this insulated world they were each other's best friends—until that summer, when Clay grew into his man's body and Jordan withdrew into a world of books and faraway places. She made little nests under towering pines, whose branches swept the ground like soft curtains shielding her from the rest of life. Sam never bothered her as long as she was outside, away from the TV and her chores were done. Because Clay didn't hide or fill his own time well, Sam gave him more work to do.

But one Saturday, Clay and Jordan slipped away before Sam could assign the endless litany of chores. Jordan's summer assignment had been to read *The Adventures of Huckleberry Finn* for her high school English class and the teacher had offered extra credit for anyone who chose to do "a related enrichment project." Jordan decided that she and Clay could build a raft.

"Hey, I've got a Hermes project for you, Clay." It had been years since they had played the Greek gods, but Clay went along because he could use his knife to whittle wood for the raft. "And then we'll float it," she said.

They went into the woods and cut some saplings and shaped a frame, using hay-bailing twine as binding for the joints. The whole time they worked, Jordan talked about Huck's adventures, and finished by saying, "He had to light out for the territories."

"What territories?" Clay asked.

"I don't think the territories are a real place," Jordan said as she inspected a loose binding. "It's just the author's way of saying there was no way for Huck to live with the contradictions he saw in society, so he had to leave it."

"How does someone leave society?" Clay laughed. "Where else you going to live?" He lifted the raft on its side. "Now, let's float this thing." He pulled it toward the water, which roared with the heavy rains of the day before.

"Wait," Jordan said. She was looking around for a long, sturdy stick to help them steer, when Clay heaved the raft into the water and hopped on. It slid from the riverbank, tipped and lurched into the current, away from her.

"Clay, no fair!" she protested. "Come back!" But Clay was laughing like she hadn't heard him laugh in a long time, whooping in delight. This was his kind of adventure, filled with enough danger to make it interesting.

"Clay, come on."

The raft moved farther out. Jordan saw Clay's lips moving, he was trying to tell her something, but the water was too loud to hear what he was saying. As the raft caught the torrent and carried him away, his eyes widened in fear.

She turned and ran up the field toward the barn.

"Dad! Dad!"

Sam was running the scrapper, pushing manure down the aisles of the barn and out into a big holding pit. The machine drowned out all other noise, but then, almost as if he sensed something wrong, Sam turned and saw her. He turned off the scrapper and ran to meet her.

"What is it?" he asked.

"It's Clay! We made a raft and he's floating down river."

Sam's jaw clamped shut. He spun away from her, running for the house.

When she reached the house, he was already on the phone.

"Sam Hawkins here. You've got to send the trucks down to the falls. My boy's going down the river in a raft. He'll be there any minute. See you there." He slammed down the phone and brushed past Jordan.

"Wait. Dad, wait for me." Diane was at work and Jordan didn't want to be alone.

"You stay here." Sam ordered, jumping into his truck.

"But—"

"Jordan! I don't know what you two were thinking. If he goes over the falls—"

He was shouting from the truck as he peeled out of the barnyard, spraying gravel and leaving Jordan to fill in the rest of his sentence. She hopped on her bike and pedaled behind as fast as she could.

It was three miles to the falls, most of it downhill. Within fifteen minutes Jordan arrived in Moosup and when she came into town, the fire engines were lined up just above the falls, with their lights flashing and Sam's truck parked behind them, the tailgate down. A group of firefighters stood on a bridge, the yellow reflective bars on their rescue outfits lighting up the gloomy day. A huge red net stretched across the river and secured on the other side. All Jordan could see was a wall of broad backs. She jumped off her bike and ran toward them.

She couldn't get in front of the men, and she couldn't see Sam either.

"I see him," one of the men yelled.

A second later, the other men started shouting.

"Here he comes!"

"Do you think the net will hold?"

"Is the rope ready?"

"Clay, grab the rope."

Then—"He's got it! Pull!"

The men started pulling and others spread out to give them room. Jordan saw Clay's head appear over the rail of the bridge.

"Clay!" she yelled.

Sam still had his back to her as he wrapped Clay in a woolen blanket and then he twisted his head to acknowledge her, just half a turn, without loosening his embrace on Clay. Water dripped from Clay's black curls. His body was shaking, and blue lips outlined his teeth, as if he'd been eating Popsicles. Sam squeezed him close to his chest and kissed the top of his head. Jordan couldn't remember the last time she'd seen her father do that. He carried Clay to the tailgate as if he were a toddler and not a growing teenager and set him down gently. Jordan came up next to them and she could see Sam's face, white, his eyes wide with shock. He held Clay like he was afraid to let him go.

Clay saw her and started to laugh, a wild, uncontrollable laugh.

"Jordan! That was some ride! How did Huck stop his raft?"

Sam turned to her, not understanding at first, but then his eyes narrowed. Fury sparked out of them.

"Do you know what could have happened? Because if you're having a hard time understanding this, take a look at those rocks right there."

Jordan looked over the bridge. A cold spray hit her in the face. Water roared as it fell toward the jagged rocks and broke into frothy caps. She felt faint, imagining Clay getting torn up by those rocks. All she could think was how quickly it had happened. She wasn't about to tell her father that she'd wanted to climb on too. She was afraid to get into trouble. She looked back and saw in him something she'd never seen: fear, almost a prescience that the balance of their lives might be about to change.

"I don't *ever* want to get this kind of scare again! Do you hear me? Don't you two have enough work to keep you out of trouble?" Sam picked Clay up and put him in the truck, then motioned for Jordan to get in too. When he went over to thank the men from the fire department, who patted him on the back, sympathetically—seven or eight kids had died going over the falls and they were all relieved not to add another— Clay said, "Tell him it was your idea, Jordan."

Sam got in the truck and put the key in the ignition. His hand shook. "When we get home, I want you to change into dry clothes and then you meet me down at the barn. Apparently, you need more work to fill your time," he said, looking at Clay.

Clay looked at Jordan, who said nothing, and then he said "What about Jordan? We built the raft together."

"I'm sorry, Dad," Jordan said. "You can give me a punishment, too." Clay was now glaring at her, because offering to take a punishment was not the same thing as owning up to the fact that it had all been her idea and that only a matter of seconds and the river's pull had kept her from being on the raft with him.

"Making a raft and getting on it are two different things. I'll think of something for Jordan," he said, grimly. "It'll be fair."

But they both knew it wouldn't be because things hadn't been fair for a long time. When Clay looked at her, Jordan saw the hurt and confusion in his eyes before a current of anger swept in, like the hard rain driving the river. The dark shadow of it moved across his face and swept it blank—his muscles were tight but flat, his eyes staring calmly ahead as he slammed the door between them.

She hadn't thought about this for a long time. She'd buried it deep down. But the fact of her pregnancy and Mrs. Barbo's confrontations and the Pascals sharing things they hadn't been afraid to face loosened the dark secret. Clay hadn't wanted a life on the farm and more than anything he'd just wanted her to see that, to bear witness to it. She'd been afraid to, in part because she didn't know what to do about it, and because she thought he might ask her to stay instead of him.

Chapter 10

Jordan buried herself in work at the factory and the farm, and each night retreated to her bedroom depleted. She saw no one outside of work and she planned no activities, so when Dale and Laura's engagement announcement and party invitation came in the mail, she avoided opening it until the weekend, when her mother pushed it in front of her. Jordan pushed it back, but her mother insisted she open it and when she did, she encouraged her to attend. "These are your good friends."

"That was before, Mom." Jordan tossed the card to the edge of the table where she and her mother sat eating tuna sandwiches and chips from the bag.

"Before?"

"Before Clay."

"And now, this is after," Diane said gently. Her own friends were always calling her for coffee dates at the farmer's market on Saturdays or for lunchtime walks at the hospital. Sometimes her friends stopped by the farm, too. In fact, a couple of them had just pulled out of the driveway a few minutes earlier. "Come on," she said to Jordan. "After lunch, let's go shopping. I'll buy you an outfit."

"I don't feel like shopping," Jordan groaned, but her mother wouldn't take no for an answer, so Jordan let herself be dragged forty minutes to the mall. She had to admit it felt good to get out of Asheville. The traffic, the stores, the restaurants—she felt herself perk up as she followed her mother into the mall. Diane headed toward Forever 21, Jordan's favorite store. Jordan started in the opposite direction, toward American Eagle.

"It's going to be a real country crowd, Mom," she explained. "People aren't going to get dressed up for this." But her real worry was that she wouldn't fit into the other, tighter styles of the trendier store. As they entered American Eagle, Jordan grabbed a pair of jeans off the rack and a baggy sweater from the shelf and headed for checkout.

Her mother frowned. "You're not going to try things on?" Jordan shook her head.

"Yes you are. Come on." Her mother pushed her to the dressing room and waited outside. Jordan tried not to look at herself in the mirror. The jeans zipped, thank God, but they didn't feel as loose as she thought they should. She threw the sweater on before she stepped out and modeled for her mother. Her mother didn't say anything about the jeans being tight; she'd wanted Jordan to gain some weight. She approved them even though they were ripped in the butt. A thought floated up as her mother threw in a pair of riding boots as well—if the jeans fit, she couldn't be that pregnant. She still had time. She watched her mother pay for the clothes, and the pressure of her secret was almost too much to bear. She thought about spilling it, but to face it brought a wave of fear so big, she shoved it back down.

When they got home, Jordan went upstairs to shower. She washed her hair and put it up in a ponytail with little wisps framing her face and she put on some lipstick and makeup. She came down to model the outfit and found her mother at the front door, deep in conversation with Eugene Martin.

"Oh, hi," was all Jordan could think to say.

"You look nice," he said. "Big date tonight?"

"A party," she said. Her mother was watching the dynamic between them, and she felt it too.

"You got your dancing boots on, eh?"

Jordan wasn't sure how to answer. "What are you doing here," she asked. "On a Saturday?"

"Good question," Martin laughed. "I guess I need to get a life outside of trying to save endangered plants."

Diane jumped in. "That's a worthy cause. Don't doubt it. I'll tell my husband you stopped by, and he should give you a call."

"I've tried calling," Martin said. "Does he have a cell phone?"

Jordan and her mother exchanged glances and laughed.

"Dad's not big on carrying a cellphone. But text me and I'll give him the message." Jordan grabbed her purse and a jacket and motioned for him to step aside so she could get out the door.

"What time will you be home?" Diane asked.

"Not too late," Jordan said. "But you don't need to wait up." She stepped off the porch and Eugene Martin followed her. After Diane closed the door, Jordan said, "Mothers!"

Martin took a long step and caught up to her stride. He grinned. "Teenagers."

Jordan stopped. "Wait! How old are you?" she shot back.

"Twenty-six."

"You don't look that old," Jordan said. "And I'm very mature for my age." She turned toward him and batted her eyes. She was flirting, but still she was surprised when Martin leaned over and kissed her. "Hey!" she said. "What's that?"

"I thought that's what you wanted. Should I apologize?"

Jordan saw the curtain move in the kitchen. "My mother's watching."

"You need watching," Martin quipped.

"Hah," Jordan said. She felt life shooting through her. "You think you're the person for the job?" In the falling darkness, she felt him pull back. "Sorry," she said. "I was just teasing you."

"No worries," Martin said. "I guess I was out of line. I misread the signals."

"No," Jordan said. "There might have been a signal. I think you're hot—it's just my life is complicated right now."

"Complicated?" Martin said. "Well, how about a cup of coffee sometime? That keep it simple enough?"

"Maybe," Jordan slid into her truck, thinking that it might

be nice to have coffee with Eugene Martin, but that it was bound to make things more, not less, complicated.

The American Legion Hall sat one block back from Route 14 and Jordan parked her truck in one of the only spots available. Apparently, it was the place to be that night. Jordan knocked on the door and was let in. The party was a Jack and Jill shower with both men and women there to celebrate the engagement. Dale wasn't the type for strippers jumping out of cakes. He couldn't wait to start his life with Laura. Jordan's heart ached that that kind of love really existed. She paid her fifteen dollars into the cash till, went to the table set up with food and heaped her plate from the tins of pasta salads, lasagna, and tossed greens. She grabbed plastic utensils and looked for a seat. The strobe lights of the DJ shone over the parquet dance floor. Dale and Laura stood together in the middle of the room, their heads bent together. Jordan felt a pang of longing—their love for each other was so palpable. A kind of light shimmered around them and washed out over everyone in the room. All day she'd been thinking about the rough-edged crowd who would fill the hall and yet, here they were, a bunch of characters connected to Dale and Laura's life, eating pasta and grinders at folding tables. The most colorful character was a guy named "Hoss," wearing black cowboy boots and hat and black jeans. He was dancing with Teresa T., who started making out with boys in cars in early high school and now had a toddler girl who she'd brought with her onto the dance floor. But, despite her judgments, Jordan could feel it. Joy in the room. She felt lonely.

Tables lined the walls, each wrapped with red plastic, holding a bowl of chocolate kisses in the middle. Streamers hung from the ceiling with balloons attached. Jordan looked around the room, filled with some of her friends and some older people she didn't know. Laura went to the kitchen where her sister and others were arranging trays of food. Jordan saw Dale at the table of his guy friends. She went over.

"Hey Dale."

"Jordan. Sit down." Dale pulled out the chair next to him and Jordan sat next to a tall boy with a powerful build and a shaved head. He gave her that hungry look and she found herself smiling encouragement. Did she really need this complication? Well, it was a party after all, and he had blue eyes. The music throbbed from the dance floor and someplace deeper within her and she felt quite simply: alive.

Before she'd eaten three bites of pasta, the boy—his name was Jacob, and he was Dale's cousin who'd just graduated from the electrical engineering program of the tech school the year before—heard the first line of the Rolling Stones "Honky Tonk Woman" a song that never got outdated in Asheville and looked at her tapping her feet.

"Would you like to dance?" he asked.

Jordan let him pull her to the dance floor. He placed his hands on her hips, smiled and pulled her close. She could feel every muscle of his well-constructed body and she let herself enjoy the sensation. The hay barn flashed to mind. She'd never taken a boy to the hay barn. I'm in control of myself, she thought. I'm just having a little fun. And when she looked over Jacob's shoulder, she didn't know what made her do so at that moment, there was Win standing inside the doorway.

"Oh my god," Jordan gasped. She pushed away from Jacob. "Excuse me," she said. "Thank you for dancing." As she made her way toward Win, Lynne and one of Dale's brothers were conducting a raffle drawing, getting ready to announce the winners and to present them with items from the table: a basket of bath products, a Mr. Coffee Maker, a Baker's Dozen Donuts gift certificate. Hoss must have won something good, as he whooped and hollered, waving his black cowboy hat, but Jordan couldn't register anything but Win, looking like a lost and overgrown child, even though he wore his signature leather biker's jacket. He was peering at Jacob behind her and then at her face, trying to read it. "Hi. This is a surprise," Jordan said. She felt curious eyes upon them.

Win gave her a look that was more understanding than she thought she deserved.

"Your father told me where I could find you."

Jordan groaned. "You went to my house."

"What's wrong with that?" he asked. "Don't tell me no guys are allowed." He glanced at Jacob again.

"Let's go outside," she said, pulling on his arm. If her father thought Eugene Martin was too old, what would he think of Win? "What are you doing in Asheville?"

"I came down yesterday to get the last load of stuff from Tim's house. It sold and the closing is Monday."

The door closed behind them as the DJ started to play "Nights in White Satin."

"Yes, but what are you doing *here*, right now?"

"I came to apologize to you. I'm sorry for the way I talked to you."

Tears sprang to her eyes. "That really hurt, Win."

"I know. It was a terrible thing to say. I'm only going to ask this once. Are you sure I'm the one?"

She watched the bugs swarming above his head, where one bulb lit the porch. Their motions seemed chaotic, trapped by the allure of the light. "Yes, you're the only one, Win."

Win searched her face and whatever he saw satisfied him. He tucked a strand of hair behind her ear. "How are you feeling?" he asked.

"I'm trying not to feel."

Win raised his eyebrows. "Are you still... Did you...?"

"Yes, I'm still pregnant. I haven't done 'it' if you mean an abortion. Or anything else for that matter."

"Have you been to the doctor?"

Jordan shook her head.

"No visit at all?"

"No."

Win frowned. "You need to go to a doctor, Jordan. You can't just ignore this and hope it will go away."

Hearing him talk in such a mature and matter-of-fact way

helped her to do the same. "I've made a mess of things, Win. And I dragged you right into it." She pulled her arms tighter around herself.

"I know how the path curves. I'm a lot older than you."

"Thanks," she whispered. "That helps."

"And the sooner you face things, the better it will be. No matter what." He pulled an envelope out of his pocket. It was tattered around the edges and Jordan imagined he'd been carrying it around for a while.

"It's too much, Win," she protested without looking inside.

"Do whatever you need with it." He put the envelope in the back pocket of her jeans and let his hand linger there. Then he wrapped her in his arms and pulled her head to his chest. "I'm sorry for things, too," he said into her hair. "Although probably not the ones other people think I should be sorry for." He squeezed her tight. "Go to the doctor, Jordan. Do you promise?"

She nodded.

"Do you want me to stay?"

Jordan thought about taking Win back to the farm, him standing by her side while she told her mother and father she was pregnant, and then going to the clinic, to do... what?

"No. I want to go see the doctor first on my own. And I will. But, as long as you're here would you like to dance? Just one dance?"

"I don't think that's a good idea."

"Please? It's just one dance, Win. I'd rather dance with you than anyone else."

His feet were still firmly planted on the porch.

"One dance and then you can leave. That's what I'm asking." So, Win took Jordan's hand and led her back inside. The DJ was playing "Stairway to Heaven" and the other couples moved away a little to watch Jordan dancing with this stranger in their midst. When Win put his arms around her and pulled her close, Jordan shut her eyes, remembering how she'd gotten into this mess, and how the solid rhythm of

Win soothed her. She wished the song would never end, but it did. She tried to ignore the curious stares as they made their way to the back of the hall. "Are you going all the way back tonight?"

"I've spent more time in Asheville than is good for me. It's a full moon, beautiful night to drive, and I've got to get this stuff unloaded tomorrow so I can return the rental truck. But I expect to hear from you, Jordan." He turned and disappeared out the door and into the dark parking lot. Jordan looked over to see Maxine frowning at her from the buffet line.

"There you are," Dale said, coming up from behind her. "We were worried about you. Who's that guy? Is everything okay?"

"Yes," Jordan said. "Just some legal stuff." It was a half lie, she consoled herself. "But I'm really tired. I need to go home. Hope you guys don't mind."

"You won something at the raffle," Laura said.

"How? I didn't put my name in."

"I put it in for you," Laura grinned. She handed Jordan a basket with perfumed soaps and lotions and a bath sponge. "Every farm girl needs this."

Jordan laughed. "I've really missed you guys," she said, realizing it was true.

"So don't be a stranger," Dale said. "Keep in touch."

Her parents were waiting up for her at home.

"You're home early," her mother said, frowning and looking her over the way they'd often examined Clay.

"Some guy stopped here for you." Her father looked up from the pile of bills he was paying.

"Who was that?" her mother asked.

"Tim Hatch's cousin. He was the one who sang at the memorial. We got to know each other a little this summer and he was back for the closing on Tim's house and thought he'd say hi and see how I was doing."

"You never mentioned him before," her mother said.

"Because there wasn't anything to mention." If her parents suspected anything, they didn't say. Her father went back to the bills and her mother sat down beside him and Jordan climbed the stairs to bed, trying to hold on to the feeling of Win, which was hard to do because she hardly knew him, and thinking about him meant thinking about the pregnancy. She shoved the envelope and money under her mattress.

She couldn't ignore it anymore. On Monday, she made an appointment with the family doctor, saying she had a stomach-ache. She used the soap and lotion from the gift basket, but no perfume product could change the doctor's news when Jordan revealed the real reason for her visit. It was worse than she'd expected.

"You're fourteen weeks pregnant," said Dr. Zita, the woman who had given her every flu shot and childhood vaccination. In the end, Jordan decided she couldn't trust a stranger with something so important, and she'd read that Connecticut was one of the few states that did not require parental consent, so Dr. Zita was bound to keep the whole thing confidential, but she was looking at Jordan now as if she were an alien. Jordan wasn't feeling very supported.

"I don't want a baby," Jordan said. "I want to go to college."

"You can terminate the pregnancy up to twenty-four weeks, but now that you are fourteen weeks, it would have to be a surgical abortion," the doctor replied sternly. She started to explain the procedure, with the opening and vacuuming of the uterus.

Jordan put her hand up. "Stop. I read about it. I know."

"Why didn't you come see me before this?" Dr. Zita asked.

"There's just been so much happening, and I felt ashamed. This, on top of everything with Clay. I thought I had more time. I just can't believe I did such a stupid thing."

Dr. Zita gave her the first sincerely sympathetic look. "I

know your family's been going through a lot. And I know this is unlike you, Jordan. The father, does he know?"

"Yes, and he'll support whatever decision I make."

"Do your parents know?" Jordan shook her head. "You should tell them." Dr. Zita waited for Jordan's response. When Jordan just kept shaking her head, Dr. Zita said, "Jordan, I think your parents will help. It's your choice, of course. You know this. You've showed incredible strength since Clay died. But you're going to need support and you'll be stronger to do whatever you decide if you have their support." Dr. Zita prescribed some prenatal vitamins and gave her the name of a gynecologist, asking her secretary to make the appointment for Jordan before she left the office. "I know you see college as your ticket, Jordan. And I agree. No matter what you decide, don't lose sight of that education. It's very important. Let me know if there's anything I can do to help you."

Jordan thought Dr. Zita wanted to say more, and maybe she would have, but a nurse came in and reminded Dr. Zita that there was a patient waiting in the next exam room and they were already running thirty minutes late.

"Call me if I can help," Dr. Zita said again before rushing out the door.

Jordan finished dressing, went to the front counter and got her ob/gyn appointment for the next week. She felt sure the office staff was whispering about her, even though they spoke kindly to her. She couldn't wait to get to her car. She pulled out her cell phone before she could stop herself, reinforcing herself with Dr. Zita's words. It was true. She'd been strong before. She got the answering machine. "Mom. Dad. I need to talk to you both when I get home tonight." Short and sweet. She knew her tone would signal the importance of what she had to say.

When she arrived home after her shift at the glass factory, she parked at the barn. She gripped the cold metal doorknob and looked out to the field just beyond the pear trees and her truck. Near her feet lay a stack of dirty pails from calf feeding that night and in the middle of the barnyard, in pieces, the corn chopper. The calves slept in their hutches and the powerful aroma of shit surrounded them. A few blanched corn stalks looked like starved bodies from lack of rain. The moon cast it all in silver light. She made herself take it all in. She climbed up to the loft where she'd considered taking Dale's cousin and threw down the alfalfa, broke the bales, spread them in the feed bunk, and watched the cows chew it into cud. On the right side, Sassie the heifer rubbed her head against Jordan's arm and tried to lick her face.

The barn door swung open. Her father looked at her. It was a look she'd never seen before. He was looking at her as if she was a stranger. He blinked at her, disoriented by sleep and worry. She came up the steps and hugged him. "Hi, Dad. Just checking on the cows." He squeezed her; it wasn't a long embrace, but the power of it told her he was worried. Chestnut started barking. It was her mother, arriving home from her second shift, too.

"When did you get home?"

"Just a few minutes ago."

The door swung open again. It hit the wall with a bang. Jordan looked up. Diane's nursing uniform draped her frame. Her hair, cut short, drew attention to her face. She came down into the pit, pulled Jordan to her and hugged her, brushing Jordan's hair back from her face. Diane looked at Jordan. "Are you alright?"

"I'm fine, Mom."

"What's going on?"

"I'm pregnant."

"Pregnant?" Diane whispered the word. "In the midst of everything else?"

Jordan stepped away from her. Even though her mother's words echoed her own thoughts, it hurt to hear. "Really, Mom? You mean, 'how dare I?' when we're on a campaign to clear Clay's name?" She stopped. She had to stay calm. "I know this is a shock. I'm not making any excuses for myself."

"Is it that older fellow—Tim Hatch's cousin? The one who stopped by?" Sam asked, matter-of-factly.

Jordan was surprised at his calm. "Yes."

"And what now? Are we going to look into an abortion? You have college to think about." So, that was his tactic, calm logic.

"I've been to the doctor. It's too late for a pill. I'd have to have a surgical abortion, where they vacuum out the uterus. I have a lot of thinking to do. I'd like to take some time to figure it out and to help with the farm in the meantime." She knew she could out-logic him if she kept her temper in check.

Diane stepped away and folded her arms. "Since when?"

Jordan's strong armor fell. "Mom?" she whispered.

"You never stepped forward. You let Clay—"

"Hey," Sam tried to stop her, but Diane went on.

"Sam. Let me speak! As long as we're being honest, as long as we're talking about mistakes… you made him take on the whole burden. It didn't matter how late at night he finished or how early he had to start, or—" Now she was looking at Sam and her eyes flashed the anger her voice carried, "or what *he* wanted to do. It was all about *you*, Jordan and what *you* wanted."

"That's enough!" Sam took his wife by the shoulders. "You stop right there. He would have come around."

Diane looked past him, over his shoulders to where Jordan stood, then she narrowed her gaze. She was trying to calm down, Jordan could see that. "I just want to say what's true. For him, Sam. I should have been more vocal with you. Clay was never going to come around to a life of farm work, and we all know it."

Sam was shaking his head. "He was."

"No, Sam." Diane's voice rose again. "And I should have stuck up for his interests, the way you stuck up for what you thought were Jordan's. I've got to live with that, and you have to live knowing."

"No." Sam spun away. "I say he would have come around. He was young, is all. And we have other things before us now, Diane."

Sam glanced at Jordan. "Are you okay?"

"No, she's not okay, Sam. She's pregnant. One more thing we have to deal with."

"I'm sorry, Dad," Jordan said. "I'm sorry for everything."

"It's not your fault," he said, trying to hug her, but she pushed him away. The pregnancy was her fault, no one else's.

Only once before had Jordan's parents disagreed like this.

Clay hadn't been in the ground for more than two weeks when her acceptance came from the teacher's college in Boston. Jordan tore it open while standing at the mailbox although she knew the minute she saw it because it was a big thick envelope. She scanned the words.

"Congratulations... you are among..." as she looked for the cold hard numbers that would make the difference between going and not going. A President's Scholarship, a full scholarship. Every bit of tuition, room and board paid as long as she kept a 3.0 average.

"Yes." Jordan jumped up and down, waving the letter in her hand, and then she stopped. How was she going to broach this subject with her mother? She knew her father wanted her to go, but her mother had been very quiet as the acceptances rolled in and Jordan wasn't sure what she was thinking now that Clay was gone.

Jordan headed to the house where her parents waited for her to have breakfast. Pancakes, which was a Sunday morning after milking tradition. Her mother didn't help with the outdoor chores. On Sunday mornings she put together the remaining boxes of winter vegetables to deliver to her customers; mixed up the pancake batter, brewed the coffee and waited for the signal from them at the barn that milking was finished.

Jordan stepped into the house. Boxes of butternut squash, potatoes, turnips, and onions lined the wall. Later in the morning, after pancakes, Diane would load them into the car and deliver them to her customers, savvy local people who'd always lived by the land and planted summer gardens themselves, as well as some city transplants that could barely be considered townspeople except for the taxes they paid. Their long work hours and commutes took them in the dark morning hours to Providence and Hartford and back same way in the evening, in the dark.

Jordan fingered the envelope in her pocket as she accepted the cup of coffee her mother handed her.

Her father bent over his pancakes, shoulders slumped.

"Hey, Dad? Mom? Guess what?"

Jordan pulled the envelope out and waved it. "Lesley College. I got accepted." Sam's head jerked up. "A full scholarship. The President's Scholarship." She handed the envelope to him. Diane stood at the sink. She banged the skillet down and opened the faucet full blast. Sam and Jordan turned to stare at her, but she kept her back to them running her hands under the dishwater.

"Mom?" No answer. Jordan tried to read something from her father's expression. He frowned and went back to reading the acceptance. He smoothed it down with his big rough hands as he read.

When he finished reading, he folded it up and handed it to Jordan. "This is quite an honor. Only the top two percent of the incoming freshmen get a President's Scholarship. It's worth $45,000 a year."

"I know," Jordan said. "I can't believe it. What do you think?"

"It's obvious," he said. "You'll go."

Diane dropped the skillet into the sink with a bang and snagged the dish towel off the hook.

"What the hell is the matter with you?" Sam asked.

"Really?" Diane pressed her back against the counter. "What about Clay?" She choked his name out and Jordan felt she could see Clay there, standing beside their mother, scowling beneath his knit hat, his arms folded across his chest.

"Clay's gone, Diane."

"I know that."

"So, who's going to help you keep this place running, Sam?"

Sam moved a forkful of pancake across the plate, sweeping up syrup with it. "We've been trying to plan for Jordan to go to school and nothing changes that."

"Really?" Diane snapped, pushing herself away from the sink. "Really, Sam? Your son dying doesn't change anything? I shouldn't have worried so much about keeping the peace with you. Maybe if I'd spoken up sooner, Clay would still be alive."

Sam put down his fork and pushed his plate away. Diane stood over him, but Sam didn't look up into her face. He muttered. "Clay dying changes a lot of things. But it doesn't change Jordan going to school like we planned."

Diane pointed at Jordan. "You're so selfish. I cannot believe you!" She threw down the dish towel and swept out of the kitchen, picking up one of the boxes and carrying it to the door. She balanced it on her thigh, opened the door and let it bang behind her.

"Mom?" Jordan called.

"Let her go," Sam said, but Jordan barely heard him. She picked up a box and hurried out the door behind her mother. "Mom, please. I'll go with you."

Diane raised her head from the inside of the car trunk where she was arranging and rearranging items to make room for the boxes. Her eyes flashed in anger.

"I'm sorry, Mom. It wasn't a good idea to bring this up." Jordan set the box down and turned toward the house to get the next one. Her father came out the door with a box and put it in the trunk.

"Diane, come here." He reached for his wife's arm, but she skirted around him. Sam stood watching her retreat from him. He gave a loud sigh and scratched his head.

"Whatever," he muttered. He jammed his hands into his pockets and slumped back to the barn. Jordan watched her father go. And then, because she didn't know what else to do, she went back to the house to get another box of produce. She and her mother crossed paths, making trips back and forth, and when Jordan went back into the house to check for any remaining boxes, she heard the car engine and looked out to see her mother backing out of the driveway. Diane jammed the car into gear and peeled away without looking toward the house or waiting for Jordan who was hurrying down the steps toward her.

That night no matter how many pillows Jordan put over her head, she couldn't block out her parents' fight.

"No, Sam. I'm not going to help you milk those cows!"

Her father's voice was a mumble Jordan could not make out.

"No, Sam. You're not listening to me. I have a full-time job. And I'm trying to get my business going. If I stop now…"

There was something again murmured by her father and then, a long silence and then the words that shattered the silence.

"Goddamned you, Sam. That's it. I want a divorce!"

Jordan slid the pillow off her head and put her feet to the floor. She crept to the hallway and stood as close to her parents' room as she dared. But there was not a word, not a sound. She waited there, crouched until her legs cramped and the cold settled into her bones. She heard her father snoring and her mother weeping, and she went back to bed, but she saw the sky change to a melon color before she fell into an uneasy sleep. When she woke, her father was at the barn and her mother had gone to the hospital, just like every other day but it was not like every other day. Jordan turned on her computer and sent an email to the admissions office of Lesley College. She could not bear to speak to a real person on the phone. Thanks, but no, she would not be able to accept the college's offer of a presidential scholarship this year.

"Mom's right, Dad," Jordan told her father now. "It wasn't fair to put so much pressure on Clay."

To see the way her parents stood, both thin and gaunt and bending in toward each other, brittle as two jagged halves of a broken dish, scared her. Too many years of not speaking the truth made it come out in shards, but at least now it was coming out. Clay had been trying to speak, too, but nobody was listening. Jordan followed her mother up to the house. She stepped onto the porch and around the broken grill that had never been removed to the dump. The screen door squeaked when she opened it and the house was dark inside. At the kitchen table, Diane's face showed white behind the laptop computer screen.

"Mom?" Jordan said. Diane typed something on the key-board. "You were right. What you said at the barn." Jordan went and stood behind her mother. On the computer screen was a brochure Diane was creating explaining the benefits of organic produce. Jordan marveled at the way her mother was trying to stay focused on her goals, no matter what. Jordan turned the light on, knelt down beside her mother and hugged her. "Mom, I'm so sorry."

Diane stroked Jordan's hair. "I know, honey. I've been so angry. I hate to hear myself speak to you that way. It comes out when I least expect it, and it's not fair to put that on you. Have you told the father?"

Jordan pushed herself away and went to the cabinet, searching for some crackers. "He knows about the pregnancy." She realized she was speaking in a detached way, as if this was someone else's problem, not hers.

"Morning sickness?" Diane asked.

Jordan shrugged. She craved her bed.

"I had it with you. Just for the first trimester though."

Jordan saw the dark circles under her mother's eyes and felt a little stab of fear. "Are you and Dad going to be okay, Mom?"

"We're going to make it be okay, I guess. Won't we? Isn't that what your father says? Where there's a will, there's a way."

Jordan looked into her mother's eyes; she wanted the

reassurance of their steely resolve. "I'm tired. I'm going to bed now."

"That's probably a good idea. A good night's sleep helps everything."

Jordan crept up the stairs and went to use the bathroom. She sat on the toilet to pee and in her distracted state, it took her a moment to see the drops of blood on her underwear. She looked into the toilet. A few more drops swirled, turning the water pink.

Her body broke into a sweat and then chills started. She rolled some toilet paper into her underwear, fixed her clothes and stared at the pink splotches. The bathroom filled with steam from the shower she'd turned on. Would taking a shower make the bleeding worse? Should she get in the shower and encourage her body to release the little life within? Jordan turned off the shower and made her way to the bed. She propped her feet on some pillows. She fully intended to keep the spotting to herself, but some surge of emotion, a force greater than her own determination kept prodding and poking at her consciousness until she got out of bed and opened the door. "Mom?" she whispered.

She could hear her parents in the living room, their low voices. "Mom?" she said a little more loudly.

Her mother climbed the stairs and appeared at her door. "What is it, Jordan?"

Jordan pulled her inside. "I'm bleeding."

Diane stepped inside and closed the door. "Maybe it would be best if there was no baby, honey."

"Mom! Help me, please."

Diane searched Jordan's face. "How heavy is the bleeding?" she asked.

"Just a few drops," Jordan whispered.

"Are you cramping?"

Jordan thought. "Maybe." She had not been aware of it until now.

"When you woke up this morning?"

"I think so," Jordan whispered.

Diane frowned. "Is this the first incidence of spotting?"

Jordan nodded.

Diane led her by the elbow to the bed and instructed her to lie down. She put another pillow under her feet. "Let's keep your feet elevated." She put her hand on Jordan's forehead. "No fever. That's good. Would you like some tea?"

Jordan shook her head and caught her mother's hand. "Mom, I'm scared." Tears welled up in her eyes.

They held hands. "Take some deep breaths. Close your eyes and breathe." Diane turned off the light and returned to her bedside. "I'll sit here with you until you fall asleep. Fill your body with breath and if you can, put a pleasant picture in your mind."

"A picture?"

"Something that gives you a complete sense of wellbeing. It can be a scene from nature, a lovely field or the river—"

Jordan's first thought was of the Hartford Fern, its delicate hand shaped leaflets clinging to the vine near the river. That's the image she held in her head, the little embryo as a fern. She gently separated Eugene Martin from the image.

"There, now just breathe deeply and let air fill your body, washing it clean of all the stress. And breathe out. Just imagine the stress leaving your body. That's right—"

The best thing was her mother's soothing voice chanting —breathe—breathe—breathe.

Jordan woke to sunlight streaming into the room. She walked gingerly to the bathroom to check the pad. There were just two faint spots of blood. Jordan felt relieved. She could still feel some cramping, although it was better than it had been the previous evening. She peed and flushed and tiptoed back to bed. A few minutes later, her mother came to the door with a tray.

"Are you hungry?" she asked as she set the tray on Jordan's lap. "How's the bleeding?"

"Almost gone."

"And the cramping?"

"It's still there, but very faint."

"That's a good sign," Diane said. "I called Mr. Tilchek and told him you needed to take a few days off. I didn't say why."

"Thank you."

Diane gave her a hug. "I did a lot of thinking last night, honey. I wanted Clay to fly, not you to be held back. Both should have been possible. I never meant for you to feel it was your fault, or to punish yourself like this. Maybe we both can try a little harder." Her eyes misted over. "I don't want to lose you, too."

Jordan could see it cost her mother something to let go of her anger. And she had to wonder if that was what she'd been doing, punishing herself.

"I'm sorry, Mom. I was afraid Clay would ask me to stay and that I'd never get to leave Asheville."

Diane adjusted the plates on the tray. "Eat your breakfast now and let's take one day at a time. We'll get this all figured out."

She left the room, and it was such a relief, to have told them, and to have her mother say they would figure it out together, that Jordan ate all her food, set the plate aside and fell back to sleep.

Chapter 11

Jordan spent a few days in bed. Between waking and sleeping the past and the present mixed and split and mixed again. She lay with her hands on her belly and imagined the baby growing inside her. She wondered what it would look like. Was it a boy or a girl? She imagined giving it up for adoption, handing this part of herself over to some strange couple and never seeing it again. Could she do that? Her mother hovered in a way Jordan had never remembered. Did she want someone else to be doing that for her baby? It seemed that whenever she opened her eyes her mother was there looking worried and worn, with fresh fruit and broth and whole-wheat toast. At day three the cramping and bleeding stopped so her mother proclaimed her fit to get out of bed.

Jordan went downstairs in her PJs, and her mother put a plate of scrambled eggs in front of her. Chestnut sidled up to her chair and put his head in her lap. The phone rang and her mother took it in the other room, but Jordan could hear her talking about the lawsuit and the insurance policy. When she came back into the room she asked, "How do you feel?"

"Better," Jordan said. "What was that about?"

Diane explained that the insurance company had decided to settle the claim for the limits of the policy, which was $500,000 but that Mrs. Barbo was still insisting on a million dollars and threatening to take the matter to court.

"Are you kidding?" Jordan set her teacup down and liquid sloshed over the side.

"Jordan, you need to stay calm. Your body is highly sensitive to stress right now. You have to do this for the baby. Dad and I can take care of this."

"What if the court agrees with her, Mom? How would we come up with the other $500,000?" Jordan asked. "Would we lose the farm?"

"Just eat your breakfast and let us worry about this, honey," Diane said. "Let's not overreact. The attorney seems very good. He said Mrs. Barbo's grief is still raw and complicated by her seeing Tony in pain, but alive after the accident, and that makes it harder to let go. He's going to do everything possible to help her see that pursuing this further just prolongs the agony. Let's try to think positive."

Jordan didn't believe positive thinking was going to have any effect on Mrs. Barbo. After a bit of pleading, she was given the day off from chores and got permission from her mother to drive to the General Store to buy bottled water.

The bell jingled, just like always when Jordan opened the door, but everything looked different in light of her pregnancy and the latest news of the lawsuit. Maxine looked grim behind the cash register.

"Well, look what the cat dragged in," Maxine quipped.

"Max, don't be like that. I have something to tell you."

"Oh, God," Maxine said. "You'd better let me sit down. I don't like the sound of that."

"I'm pregnant."

Maxine stepped away from the cash register. "I was afraid of something like that when I saw you and Win Hatch on the dance floor—" Maxine picked up the bottle of Windex and started to clean the counter. "It's him, isn't it?" Jordan nodded. Maxine looked away and then went back to rubbing the glass. "He never brought anything good to this town."

"Max! Why do you say that?"

"He always had an eye for pretty girls, and you already know he was in prison."

"But you said yourself that he got straightened out when he moved to Maine."

"Well, there's more I should have told you about him."

"What's that, Max?" Jordan stood with her hands on her hips and now Maxine did the same.

"Like that people thought he was the one who burned the mill down."

"Win? Really?" Jordan thought about the tender way he tucked her hair behind her ear. No, it wasn't possible. But then she thought about the way he spoke to her when she told him she was pregnant. She couldn't say for sure exactly who Win was, after all.

Maxine was watching her think. "They never pursued it," she said. "There was no evidence but anyway—you're going to be just like these other girls, stuck here with their kids and no future? You have choices."

"I know that."

"You going to tell him?" Maxine challenged, holding Jordan's gaze.

Jordan looked away. "I already did."

Maxine relented. "Don't be like these other girls, honey, with a baby and no future. You have the chance to get out and do something with your life. You had a vision. Hold on to it."

Jordan had expected more support from Maxine, but she didn't know how to ask for it. She set two gallons of bottled water on the counter and handed Maxine a five-dollar bill. Maxine rang up the water and gave her change. As Jordan moved toward the door, Maxine added, "God gave you a good brain. Now's the time to use it."

Jordan closed the door and stood on the steps. It was a fine fall day. She crossed the bridge to the old mill site. The river ran slowly so that she could see the silt and rocky bottom before it dropped off to the deeper channel. What was it about that mill? Something about it held a grip over the town. She thought about Clay and Tim and Tony up there with the barrel. And now, Win had been suspected of burning it down?

Chapter 12

A few days later, when she had a day off from the glass factory, Jordan told Sam she needed the day off from farm chores, too. He asked her if she thought working on the farm came with a vacation plan. But Jordan didn't answer, instead she filled the gas tank of her truck. She considered packing an overnight bag.

She waited until her mother came home and then told them both. "I need to go see Win." If she could have decided on an abortion, she would have called and told him and then never seen him again, but now that she wanted to go through with the pregnancy, she would have to deal with whatever reaction he gave her, and despite his kind words at the Jack and Jill shower, she expected him to be angry.

It was her mother who spoke. "You don't want to promise your life to a stranger. Marriage is hard enough when you love a person, Jordan." Diane squinted, watching Jordan's face. Maxine had already tried to taint Jordan's romantic thoughts of Win. Had her mother and Maxine been talking? In her gut, Jordan didn't feel that Win was capable of burning down the mill, and their future was for the two of them to decide.

Purgatory, Maine was a real town 230 miles from Asheville. Jordan drove under a slate gray sky, skirting Boston, making it in less than four hours, entering into the thick pine forests of Maine before noon, although the clouds obscured the morning light making her think of horror movies. A dusting of snow covered the hollow of the pine forest. What if Win lived with someone? What if Win was married? What did she really know about him, except that he was Tim's cousin and he'd slept with her, and he'd been in jail and now, supposedly, had straightened out?

A cluster of buildings formed the town of Purgatory. A small grocery, the post office and a pharmacy under one roof, the hardware store across the street, a video store and a pizza restaurant further down the street.

Jordan stopped at the convenience store/gas station, and the air, thick with the acrid scent of pine pitch, filled her nostrils. She brushed the cracker crumbs from her lap and then she pumped her tank full and went in to pay.

At the register, she asked the cashier, a middle-aged man of medium build, wearing a John Deere hat, for directions to East Mountain Road.

"Who you lookin' for?" he asked. His question contained the same wariness the people in Asheville reserved for strangers.

She paused to let him know she had reason to be wary, too. "Winthrop Hatch," she said.

"Won't be home, now," he said, opening the register to get her change. The clock on the wall read 10:30 a.m. "He's out cuttin' logs. He stops in here every morning for coffee."

"He's… he was already here?"

"Hours ago, now."

She thought about how dark the woods must be on a day like this. "Do you know where he's cutting?" she asked. She couldn't afford to wait for him to finish a day's work. The cashier said nothing. That was good, if he was protecting Win, it meant Win had friends who cared about him. Or did it? She didn't know.

"How do you know him?" the guy asked.

"I'm a friend of his from Connecticut," she answered. "I need to see him. It can't wait 'til the end of the day." Dropping syllables equaled dropping one's guard in the New England woods. The clerk noticed.

"You can't go there by yourself. It's too dangerous. Trees fall on guys all the time. That's why they go out in pairs." He paused. "But they're just down the road a bit. If you promise to be careful, I'll take you there." She hesitated. "You want to follow behind me?"

She shook her head. "No. Just give me a minute to lock my truck." She went out and locked her truck and he locked the entrance door and pointed her to his car, an old model Pontiac with body rust around the doors. He moved some CDs and a stained paper bag from the passenger seat and dumped them in back where food wrappers covered the seat and floor.

"Name's Dewey," he said. "Sorry about the mess."

"Hi, Dewey." She shook his hand. "Can you get in trouble for leaving work?"

"It'll only be ten minutes."

They bumped along the narrow road in silence and when Dewey pulled into an open space a few miles down the road, Jordan saw Win's truck. Her heart beat faster. Her palms were clammy. At that moment, the idea of calling him or writing a letter seemed better, but she'd thought it important to see the look on his face. The look would tell her things words could not. She wiped her sweaty palms on her pants and stuck her hand out to thank Dewey for driving her.

"I'm not just gonna leave you here," he said. "I told you it's dangerous. I'll take you in there."

Jordan got out of the car and followed him. The woods were dark and deep. She could see her breath on the air. She could barely keep up with Dewey, he walked so quickly.

When they could hear the whine of chainsaws, he said, "Win's in there. If you want, I'll go to the edge of the clearing and let him know we're here. That way if they're about to fell a tree, they'll know enough to wait."

"No," she said. "I'll go." She paused. "You're sure it's him, though? You're sure he's the one who's out here?"

He nodded.

She pulled out a ten-dollar bill. "For your gas and your time," she said.

He waved the money away. "Watch the trees," he said. "If you hear a yell, that's a warning. Be ready."

She moved in the direction of the chain saw. She turned and saw Dewey waiting, watching. Pine needles snapped underfoot. The chainsaw motor whined, then purred as it bit into wood. She saw Win before he saw her. She turned and waved Dewey off. He returned the wave and stepped back onto the path. Win held the chainsaw braced against his body and she understood now why he was so strong. The massive trees resisted his efforts and the burning smell of metal grinding wood, the flying sawdust, the gas exhaust, attested to the protest. It all made her a little dizzy. Win turned, as if he sensed her presence. His fingers slipped off the throttle and the chainsaw stalled. He flipped the safety glasses up on his head and pushed away the protective ear pads he wore. The saw blade gleamed blue as he worked it out of the gouged tree that lay across the clearing.

"Jordan?" The baby was like a root between them, pulling her here and she felt a little unsteady. She braced herself against the pine behind her. Win was walking toward her. He reached her and put an arm out, but she pushed herself off the tree and stood straight, right up to him. "Is everything okay?" he asked.

She felt the knot tightening in her stomach. She wanted Win to open himself up to her, to say he was happy to see her, but he wasn't saying that. "I'm not going to have an abortion, Win," she blurted it out. She hadn't rehearsed what she had to say. She didn't think it mattered how she said it.

"Shit." Win jammed his gloves into his pocket and then brushed the wood chips off his face and the front of his clothes. He smelled of pine and fresh air and she wanted him to hold her. He didn't. He said, "You waited too long?"

"I waited too long for the abortion pill. I could still have the surgical kind, but I don't want to do it, Win. I don't know if I'll keep it or give it up for adoption. I'm not asking anything of you," she said. It wasn't true, of course, but she didn't like the way he looked at her, so disapproving. "I just thought you should know."

"What do you mean you're not asking anything of me? Why are you here, then?" he said. "If you don't want anything from me."

"My parents want me to consider adoption. I haven't decided about it. I just want you to be prepared, because if I do that, you'd have to sign away your parental rights."

He looked at her and when she looked into the depth of those eyes, the pale blue seemed to have changed; she wasn't sure if it was the lack of light in these dark woods or something else. She thought of the night in the shack and felt that quickening in her body. Perhaps it was still possible. She tried to suppress her thoughts, but he watched her, and nothing was lost in his gaze.

"What about college?" His anger seemed blunted.

"Yes."

"What about college?"

"I don't know. Maybe I could do college part-time," she said.

"So, you're going to have a baby and stay on the farm, now?"

He let his hand rest for just a moment on her shoulder, brushing away pine needles.

She stepped into him and the feeling of him touching her. "I have to figure it out."

He turned away and disappeared, the way he had that first night. She stood riveted to her spot, wondering how it could be that after some months and so little time together, one touch from him could make her body feel hot, then cold, but not neutral. A minute later, he came back. With one hand, he grabbed his chainsaw, and with the other her hand, he started leading her out of the woods.

"I had to tell my partner I'm leaving," he said. "He can't be in here by himself."

"What about your work?"

"We've got enough timber downed; he can cut lengths all day. I'll work a longer day tomorrow," he said. His face looked so matter of fact, she couldn't read it.

"I parked at the convenience store. Can you take me to my truck?"

"Dewey brought you out here?"

"Yeah, Dewey. Is he your friend?" she asked.

He didn't answer her. His concentration moved to another place. She followed him to his truck and got in. It was neat and clean inside. She could see nothing of him in the truck. When they got to the road where she knew they should go left to the convenience store, he went right.

"Wait," she said. "My truck."

"I'll take you to get your truck, later," he said. "You're not leaving yet." They were going only ten miles per hour. She thought that she could jump if she wanted. "I want to show you my house," he said. "I want you to know where I live so you can have your questions answered." He looked at her and asked. "You okay with that?"

"Yeah," she said, then after a moment's pause, "I went and got tested. I got the results this week. Everything came back clean."

"I could have told you that," he said.

"You spent time in prison," she said.

"I know my mistakes," he said. "They're part of me, but not the whole story." He didn't say those words with pride or shame, but something closer to humility. "Like I told you before, if you live through your mistakes, you can learn some things."

She debated questioning him about the mill but decided against it. She didn't want to make him defensive right off the bat. "What do you think I need to learn from this mistake?" The words came out and then she vowed never to say them again, now that there was going to be a baby.

He'd been driving up a steep gravel road and he pulled in now to a small cabin, with a porch and a cord of wood stacked there and stairs leading up to it. A wisp of smoke curled out of the chimney. Jordan held her breath, wondering who else lived with him. "I leave the wood stove low," he said, following her gaze. "I don't like to come home at night to a cold, dark house."

She thought then about his emptiness, how big it must be, maybe big enough to fill these woods once he cleared them. Maybe that's what he was doing, clearing forest and trying to leave his emptiness there. He still hadn't answered her question. Jordan followed him up onto the porch and into the cabin. A braided rug covered the bare pine boards in the living room floor, matching a shabby plaid couch and chair and a coffee table and lamp, all of pine framing. The walls' knotty pine darkened the cabin although windows cast light from the bathroom and from the kitchen at the back of the house. To the left, Jordan saw a bedroom with a lumpy quilt covering the bed. Win followed her gaze.

"You want something to drink?" he asked, going into the kitchen.

The kitchen held a green Formica table and four red plastic covered chrome chairs. A stack of mail sat neatly piled by the toaster on the table. The stove and refrigerator were old, but clean and a simple pair of yellow curtains covered the one window looking out to the back of the mountain. No beer bottles overflowed trashcans; nothing was as Jordan had thought it might be. Everything about the place indicated a person living a quiet life, fully in control of himself. So, what did that say about the fact that he'd slept with her so easily, not once, but twice? Had he sensed her emptiness? Or was he such a hermit that she presented him with an easy opportunity?

He opened the refrigerator and poured some root beer into a coffee cup and set it down in front of her. Jordan hated root beer, but she drank it.

"You hungry?" he asked, going to the cupboard and opening the door. There was a box of Ritz crackers, some cans of soup, fruit cocktail and an assortment of canned vegetables: corn, beans, peas and spinach.

"I didn't expect this," she said as she watched him open a

can of peaches and dump them into a bowl, which he brought her along with a spoon.

She severed the chunks into smaller pieces and ate them, while he watched her.

"You expected me to be wild like Tim."

"No, not like Tim."

"You're lying," he said. "And I don't know why, because I don't think you're really a liar." He leaned over the chair opposite her and braced himself on its back. Everything about him, even the way he stood, said that he was a man, not a boy.

"Well, we were drunk," she said.

"Not that drunk. And not the second time."

"I never would have done it the first time if I wasn't drunk."

"You're fooling yourself." He said. "Yes, you would of."

"I never would have before Clay died."

"Maybe not."

"Clay dying changed things."

He slid into the chair opposite her. "Life does that. You look older, but it looks good on you."

She wiped her face and looked at him, trying to read his emotions. His eyes went from scanning her face to her breasts and then her stomach. She wanted to see if he could see more of her than that. She needed to know. When he looked into her eyes, the light in his eyes made her trust him. "You said you believed in fate. Do you think this is fate?" She wanted to feel connected to him, but his guard was back up.

Win brought over the rest of the peaches and dumped them into the bowl. They glistened in the syrup.

"You live here all by yourself?" She lifted the sweet pulpy flesh to her lips watching Win watch her.

"Yes."

She could tell he was remembering being with her, but what was he feeling?

"Win, I'm trying to think of what's best. Mrs. Barbo told me Asheville would kill my dreams."

He reached to clear her bowl from the table. "I don't know

if a place has that much power. I think it's the people in the place that do."

She brushed his hand away and stood. She could smell the pine on him. "I can clear my own mess," she said.

"I got it." He reached for the bowl and brushed her hand. She drew her hand back and he caught it and held it against his side, folded into his own. "You have to give me time to get used to this. You come up here and just spring this on me. I didn't expect it. I wasn't looking to become a father. You throw this word 'fate' at me hoping I'll swallow it, because you know I believe in it, but you lied to me. Fate's not about lies."

"You're right." Jordan started to cry. She saw he was not a man to play games and that he wasn't going to treat her like a child. She brushed the tears away. "I lied." She had no defense. She stepped closer, "but could you come to Asheville and we could try to see if we could love each other for this baby?"

He shook his head. "Jordan, love doesn't sprout up like a corn seed just because you want it to. There's more to it than that." And she sensed that Win had had his fair share of love. "What about college?" he asked again.

"I know. I'm trying to figure it out, Win. I'm staying at the farm. I could do school part-time. But If I decide to keep the baby, I want it to know its father. I missed you, Win. I'm not looking for any promises, but I barely know you and I'd like to get to know you. Is that too much to ask?"

He let go of her hand then and caressed her face. She pressed her cheek into his palm, and she saw light pulse into his eyes, mixed with desire. His lips parted and his hand traveled down her body, to her stomach, where he opened his palm and laid it flat against her skin, slipping it into her jeans and just letting it rest there. Heat bloomed from that spot, but he didn't kiss her, he didn't try to press himself closer. He seemed to want her and yet he seemed unsure about it. They stood that way, and then Jordan shivered and took a step toward him. "You going to invite me into any place beside the kitchen?"

"You really think that's a good idea?"

"Maybe not, but what's the worst that can happen?"

He took her hand and she followed him back through the living room to the bedroom. A weak stream of light came in the window; it was soft and gray like the underside of a morning dove. Win pulled off her shirt and she reached around to unlatch her bra. He kissed her nipples, already darkened by pregnancy and the icy heat of his tongue covered her. But she couldn't concentrate on the feeling. She pushed him away.

"What?"

She picked up her shirt and held it over her chest. "I came here for more than this. You want honesty? I have to be honest about that."

Win picked up her bra. It looked like nothing in his hand. "I know. Let's give it a chance then." He tried to kiss her again.

She wanted to, but she used every bit of resolve to pull herself away, again. "A chance for what?"

"A chance to know each other, to see if we could do this…"

"By this—do you mean just sex, or…?"

Win tossed her bra on the bed and took a step toward her. "You want a written contract?" Jordan thought of what her mother had said. Don't ask for a permanent commitment from a man you don't even know. "Plenty of people start like this, because of a baby," he said. He brushed her hair back from her face as if he was seeing it for the first time and then he pulled her in so that her head rested on his shoulder.

Jordan could tell that this was a new role for Win, and that he was trying as best he could. She let her shirt slide to the floor, and she didn't protest when Win unzipped her jeans. She still felt unsure, but she let Win undress her. When she was naked, he stepped back and looked at her.

"You're a skinny thing," he said. "We've got to fatten you up."

She'd never seen him in proper light, and he'd not seen her pregnant. Now, she wanted to feel like she belonged to him and so she took his comment as commitment. There would be more time for talking and learning about his past. This was about now.

Jordan slid under the covers and waited for him. He got in and kissed her.

"You taste sweet," he said.

"Like honey?" she asked.

"More like peaches."

Whereas the other times their coming together had felt like ice burning its way through grief, Win touched her now with a sense of responsibility, she could feel it in the way he brushed her hair away from her face and then ran his thumb along her cheek, gestures more tender than sexual. His hug was protective, pulling her tight to his chest and holding her there. She could feel their hearts beating together and she inhaled the scent of him, running her hands up and down his strong back, until she felt the pulse coursing through him and the response of his body to her, which was thrilling. He was careful this time when he entered her even though he was engorged and full, and sex this time lasted until together, they flowed over the small bed.

After they were through, Jordan ran her hands down Win's back, feeling the wood shavings and smelling the fresh pine on him. He pulled her into the curve of his body.

She'd never actually slept with a man after making love. She nuzzled into Win, and he put his hands over her stomach. She fell asleep.

When she woke, sun streamed through the window. She'd slept through the night. Win had left a note on the kitchen table, along with a clean bowl, a spoon and a box of Cheerios. The note said, "I've got to make up for yesterday's time off. I'll be back by four. I'm glad you're here."

The first thing she did was go through his closet. Shirts hung on hangers, an old velour bathrobe, a blue suit still wrapped in the cleaner bag, a pair of beat-up sneakers, corduroy slippers, a heap of dirty laundry in the pile on the floor, but no bundles of love letters from old girlfriends, no photo albums, no secret past. Under the bed, dust balls. In the medicine cabinet, aspirin, a broken thermometer, mouthwash, dental floss, cold tablets. She searched the house. But if he had any secrets, they weren't in the obvious places and the little cabin had no real attic or basement. She decided the reason she could find no secret was because there wasn't one to find, and she felt guilty for suspecting him. He'd said no lying. She had to believe him. He'd offered to give things a try. If she wanted him to come back to Asheville to help with the baby, she would need to trust him.

She ate cereal, washed the bowl, found the broom and swept the floor, which was already spotless except for those dust bunnies under the bed and couch. She went out looking for the paper, but there was no paper box. She turned on the TV to fill the house with sound. When she got hungry again, she ate the crackers she'd seen in the cabinet the day before and opened a can of soup. Then, she sat down to watch soap operas. It exhausted her, keeping track of all the characters' problems and she must have fallen asleep, because when she woke, Win was sitting in a chair next to the couch, his hair freshly washed and pulled back in a ponytail. He was dressed in a pair of brown corduroys, a cable-knit sweater and a pair of moccasins.

Jordan sat up and stretched. She kicked off the afghan. "How was your day?" she asked.

Win's gaze slid off to the corner of the room, now in afternoon shadow. "Pretty good. Listen, Jordan. I have a meeting," he said.

"Meeting?"

"Yeah. At four-thirty. I'll be back a little after five-thirty."

She'd waited all day and now he was leaving again?

"AA," he said.

"AA?"

"Alcoholics Anonymous."

"I know what AA is." It was hard to clear the fog in her brain. "You're an alcoholic?"

"Not anymore," he said. "I've been dry for five years, except the slip back in Asheville."

She ignored the fact that he referred to Asheville as a slip.

138

"What am I supposed to do?" She felt a little angry. He was going to leave her stranded there, without her truck.

"Watch TV or something," he said. He was already getting his coat out of the closet.

"I watched as much TV as I can stand. Win?" she asked, jumping off the couch and moving toward him. He turned. "Do you have to go tonight? Can't you just stay with me?"

"I'll be back soon," he said.

"Do you need to go because of me? Is it—? Did I do something wrong?" How was she ever going to get him to open up and talk to her if he kept retreating?

He jammed his arms into his coat and moved toward the door. "No." He stood with one hand on the doorknob and the other gripping his keys. He saw her face and came back to give her a kiss, but it was a dry, nervous kiss. He closed the door, leaving her alone.

Why was she upset by him going to a meeting? Part of his appeal was that he was a man, not a boy, and wasn't he being a man to admit his problem? If he needed to go to meetings, then he should go to meetings. She decided she would make him cookies. Let him come home and see what he had to look forward to if he came to live in Asheville. She thought she would create a warm environment, one he could see and taste and maybe they could sit at the table, eat warm cookies and really talk. There were no chocolate chips, so she had to make peanut butter. She found some old tin baking sheets and all the ingredients, a bowl and measuring spoons. She mixed the dough and tasted it. She hoped Win liked peanut butter cookies. She got out a fork so she could press it into the cookies and then she measured even amounts onto the sheets and she stood bent over the oven; peering in at the interior light to be sure she took them out at just the right time. She began to feel that it had been the right thing to come, after all. She imagined herself with Win, milking cows, plowing fields. An hour passed and just as she was putting them on a plate to cool, Win returned.

"Hey," she called, cheerfully. "I made you cookies. I hope you like peanut butter." He came into the kitchen and tried to smile, but his mouth stayed closed, and his eyes looked troubled. He seemed farther away from her, even though he was standing right there. "What is it?" she asked. "What?"

Win sat down heavily in one of the chairs and moved it forward to close the space between them. He'd taken his hair out of its ponytail, and it fell loose around his face. He lifted his head and pushed his hair back. "If you want to get to know me, we have to take this slow, Jordan."

Jordan held the spatula high in one hand. "What do you mean?"

Win was shaking his head as if trying out the various ways he could explain it and discarding each attempt as insufficient. "Asheville was a bad place for me," he said.

"But you said—?"

He shrugged. "I know... I said we could give this a try. And we can. But it doesn't have to be Asheville. You could come here."

"Here?" she cried. "But Asheville is home. Things would be different with us there."

"No," he said. "Not for me, Jordan."

She felt her stomach knot. Was Win getting ready to confess that he'd burned down the mill? "But you said a place can't destroy a person."

"It's what I did in that environment."

"What did you do, Win? Tell me the truth."

Win looked puzzled. "What do you mean? I went to an AA meeting. I told you. I talked to my sponsor about you and me and the baby."

Jordan took a deep breath. "He told you to say that?" Jordan pushed the cookies to the back of the counter. "Because those words don't sound like you, Win."

"Stop," he said. "Just stop. You can't say what sounds like me, Jordan, because you don't know me. And I don't know you. The meetings make you look really deep into yourself.

That's why I go to them. I'm not saying yes yet to the responsibilities of being a father. You haven't even decided you're keeping it."

She started to cry but he went on. "That's not criticism, Jordan. It's fact. And that's the fact we have to start with. This is all coming as a big surprise if I can remind you of that. And I'm trying to figure out the best way to handle things. Would you like to move in here with me? You could get to know me here. Where my life is." He'd removed the sweater in the heat of the kitchen, revealing a clean white T-shirt underneath. Just the way he moved forward on the chair, caught her breath. She loved to look at him. But would that be enough? Could it last long enough for something deeper to grow between them? Is that what she wanted? To move to Purgatory, Maine and live with Win and raise their baby?

"Why not Asheville? I have family there, support. Here I'd have no one but you."

Win was shaking his head. "It's the way people know me. The whole Hatch family. The ghosts jump on my back there and I become the last one. The Hatch family—boozers and losers. If we want to give anything a shot, I need to be able to have a solid base, so I'm offering for you to move here," he repeated, holding her arm.

She had to know the truth. It was now or never. "Win, did you burn the Riverside mill down?"

He released her arm and stood up. "What? What are you asking me?"

"Did you?" She stood to confront him.

"Jesus Christ, Jordan! Where is this coming from?"

"It's a simple question, Win. Yes or no."

"Who told you that?"

"Did you?" she asked again.

"What has this got to do with anything?"

"It has everything to do with everything," Jordan said. "The night of the accident Tim, Tony and Clay were there at the old mill site, and they dug up a barrel of old chemicals."

141

Win's face paled. "How do you know that?"

"Sister Rachael told me. That night at the fair. She told me and then I went there myself. I found the barrel and I reburied it. Then, Maxine told me you were a suspect when the mill burned."

"She's right that they accused me. But the answer is no. I didn't burn the mill down and that's why there was no evidence against me, Jordan."

"So why did you leave?"

Win stared over the top of her head to the wall. His eyes seemed vacant. "Since I already had a record, it was easy for people to believe I was guilty. Only I wasn't." He shook away the memory and she realized that she'd wounded him.

"I'm sorry, Win. I had to know."

"But why didn't you tell me that Tim and your brother and the other boy were there the night of the accident?" Win asked.

"What difference does it make?" Jordan asked.

"I think Tim was trying to uncover evidence to clear my name," Win said.

"What?"

Win continued. "After his mom died and he was alone, he wanted me to come back and live with him. I said I couldn't, and he wanted to know why, and I told him the story. No one ever had. I think that may be why they went there that night. I'd talked to him just a week or so before."

"I don't get it. I saw just one barrel. How would digging that up clear your name?"

"It wouldn't," Win said, "because there wasn't anything to clear."

Jordan frowned. "Well, if you didn't do it and there was no evidence what made you come all the way up here?"

"Sometimes an unfounded accusation is just as bad," he said. "That's the kind of thing that can happen in a small town, right? The shadow was cast over me. Mr. Z helped me," Win added. "He had contacts up here and he used them to get me out and help me get on with my life."

"Mr. Z?" Jordan whispered. "He tried to help Clay too.

And he paid for some of my college applications." She no longer doubted Win's story at all. If Mr. Z had lined up to help Win, Win must be innocent. "Did you know about the barrel? Or anything else about the mill burning?"

Win shook his head. "No. I don't get it… if they were looking for clues, why would they think they could find something when the police never did? I think it is just an unfortunate coincidence, them being there and dying the same night in a crash. Can't we just figure out you and I?" Win went to the sink and took down a glass and poured water from the tap and drank it. The way he tipped the cup and swallowed made Jordan think he was craving alcohol. He offered her a sip and she took it. The water tasted sweet.

"You're right," Jordan said. "We can't take this too fast. We're just strangers who had sex." There were tears in her eyes again. The room was so quiet they could hear the tick of the oven cooling, and wind whipping through the trees.

Win put the cup down and put his arms around her. She stood stiffly. He released her. "We're more than that, Jordan. And we have them—Tim and Clay—they keep us from being strangers. And the baby."

She grimaced. "I guess."

"You asked me before what you needed to learn; maybe this is what we both needed—to figure out ourselves, what we want, and our limits."

Jordan fought back the tears.

"You won't be alone in this no matter what. I promise you that," he said. "Can I give you some more money?"

Jordan waved her hand to stop him. The discussion of money was distasteful. She just wanted to go home.

"It's too late," Win protested. "Wait until the morning." He put his hands on her shoulders and tipped her face up to look at him. "I'm lonely too, Jordan. My bed is always empty; it would be nice to have someone to hold. This is as new to me as it is to you. And I want you to know you're the first person to ever see me as the man I want to be."

His words sounded nice, but she didn't want to spend the night just to spend another night. She wanted to go home. "Take me back to my truck, please," she asked.

They drove without speaking. When the silence got uncomfortable, Jordan told Win about Mrs. Barbo insisting on the million dollars. "Did you settle with her?" she asked him.

"It wasn't as complicated," Win said. "Tim's house wasn't worth much; it was the only asset. I paid her $20,000." He didn't seem angry, only resigned.

Her truck sat underneath the one light lighting the convenience store parking lot. Win pulled up to it. He put both hands on the steering wheel in front of him. "There are no guarantees in life," he said. "Lots of people start out in a better position than us and they get it wrong all the time, you know. Like I said, I don't think it's a coincidence we met that night and made this baby. That might be fate, but how it gets raised and by who and what it does, there's the destiny part. Maybe it's you I've been waiting all my life for."

She leaned over and kissed him goodnight.

Win waited as she climbed into her truck and pulled out onto the road. When Jordan glanced in the rearview mirror, she saw how his body filled the cab, casting him in darkness. He's part of me now, Jordan thought. Because of this baby. And while she'd been drawn to his suffering, the little spark of life they created was something entirely different. For the sake of that spark, she was glad that Win was innocent.

Chapter 13

In Asheville, the slivered moon shone down on the fields and the little white house, all shut up because Sam didn't believe in leaving lights on and Jordan didn't need them anyway, although coming back in the dark made her feel her disorientation more acutely. She didn't want to live in Purgatory, Maine. But what was she going to do now? Jordan climbed into her bed and stared at the ceiling trying to imagine her future. Who was she going to reach out to? She thought of Mr. Z, her eighth-grade teacher. She hadn't seen him since one day when she'd bumped into him at the donut shop, but now Jordan wondered more about him, and not just because of Clay but because he seemed so committed to all the young people. He'd always believed in her. Win had mentioned him as one of his only positive influences in Asheville. If she was going to stay in Asheville alone, she was going to need some support.

The next morning, she woke to realize she didn't feel nauseous. Not one bit. She went to the barn for milking, and Sam said, "You came home so late last night, I thought you might sleep in."

"We have a lot of work to do," she said.

"How are you feeling?" he asked.

"The nausea is gone," she said. "I didn't need to eat any crackers this morning when I woke up."

"I remember your mother ate a box a day. If she ran out, I had to go right to the store, no matter what else I was doing." The memory of it lit his face. "You were quite a kicker," he said.

"I don't feel anything like that, yet," Jordan said.

"So, are we going to see him?"

"I don't think so, Dad," she said.

"Jordan, will you please check into adoption? You have your whole life ahead of you."

"Stop, Dad. Give me a chance to think about things for myself, will you?" It was the line she hoped having heard from Clay he might finally listen to from her. They stood watching the cows eat their grain and they let silence say the rest. Even though Jordan didn't want to discuss things with her father, it didn't mean she wasn't thinking about her decision. Now that she'd decided to go through with the pregnancy, she thought about little else. When she wasn't working at the glass factory or farm chores, she was online reading the stories of couples waiting to adopt a child. Their stories touched and saddened her. The adoption websites were well-organized with videos of couples hugging, holding hands, showing closeness, looking eagerly into the camera as if they could see the pregnant woman who was seeing them, trying to communicate in any way possible the love they would give the child should she choose them as the adoptive parents. Couples walking along beaches, playing with nieces and nephews in parks, strolling through their neighborhood, in front of the home in which they would raise her child. There were currently six couples in Connecticut waiting to adopt a child and over the next week Jordan read their bios and watched their videos and tried to imagine placing her baby with each of them. As suggested by the American Adoption website, she closed her eyes and tried to envision the ideal environment her child would see. But she didn't see a skyscraper. Or a beach. Or a neighborhood filled with playgrounds and kids. She saw nothing that the current Connecticut families offered. And she couldn't imagine sending her child to another state. What she saw was a farm, their farm, fields and animals and annoying geese and Holstein cows. She took the online quiz *Are You Ready to become a Parent?* She made good money at the glass factory, and she had her parents. Her baby, if she chose to keep it, could have her father as a father figure. She couldn't say about Win, but she couldn't say he was out of it, either. He'd left a couple of texts, which she hadn't answered. She wasn't sure what to say. If Win wasn't willing to come to Asheville, where did that leave them? As she drove around town, or to the grocery store, she watched mothers with their children. Sometimes they looked happy; other times they looked stressed, but they always looked as though they belonged together.

Asheville School held grades kindergarten through eighth grade in one neat brick building with white trim, in the middle of an old cornfield bordered by an eight-foot chain link fence meant to keep kick balls and baseballs and Frisbees out of the neighboring properties. Jordan noticed as she sat in the school parking lot that the two portable classrooms recently erected to address the overcrowding interfered with the stretch of open space she so clearly remembered from recesses of running and never seeming to reach the border of the school playground.

She waited for the lunch bell to ring and then walked around the back of the building—she knew that if she went into the school, there would be no way to avoid the watchdog, Mrs. Bennett. Asheville School didn't need buzzers or metal detectors or mirrors as long as it had Mrs. Bennett. That woman had a sixth sense. Jordan could hear bits of conversations floating from the windows of the classrooms she passed and voices she'd heard all of her childhood, including that of Ms. Fay, the beautiful blonde-haired teacher, who was one of ten children and had returned to teach in Asheville. The local men stared wherever she went but were too afraid to approach her. Jordan had wanted to be just like her, only far away from Asheville. She pressed herself against the rough brick for a moment, let it offer strength and grounding, then arranged her face and stepped out onto the playground amidst the shrieking children and flying balls.

"Jordan?" There was Mr. Z, as usual, not huddled with other teachers at the end of the field as if they couldn't wait for recess to end and couldn't be bothered with the children's demands, but instead right in the thick of the kids, today the eighth graders. All the kids loved him, but it was with the older kids he looked most happy, and they looked happy too.

"Hey," she said, blinking away the dark image of those who were no longer there. There were places she could still feel Clay. This was one of them. Mr. Z came over and put his hand out. She shook it, holding on to the big rough feel of it for a little strength.

"Jordan. It's good to see you. How are you?"

She paused. She'd rehearsed this scene in her head the night before. But it didn't make the moment any easier. "I'm pregnant," she said. "I…"

Mr. Z closed his eyes, opened them and rubbed his head as if the news had caused him an instant headache. "I'm sorry. It's just you were the last person I ever expected to hear say this."

"I know. There's nothing you can say that I haven't already said to myself. I know you're disappointed in me." She felt shame color her face.

"No," he said. "I'm disappointed in us." He gestured around the field, "The whole town. We aren't reaching you kids." He looked devastated.

"It's not your fault, Mr. Z."

"No, but it is. Well, not directly, of course, but we keep losing kids in the gap. That's why I took this job…" He stopped. "Sorry, of course you didn't come here for that. I guess if you're telling me, it means you're keeping it?"

"I'm looking at adoption, too. We'll see," she said.

Mr. Z rubbed his head. "Well, in the Jewish tradition there's a belief that when one life ends, another comes in to take its place."

This was exactly why kids loved Mr. Z. "That's what I've been thinking," Jordan said.

"You know it doesn't mean you have to be its mother," Mr. Z said. "That's for you to decide. No one else."

"Thank you for having faith in me to figure it out."

"And the father?"

"Do you remember Win Hatch?"

Mr. Z took a step back and looked at her a little differently, she thought, now that she'd said Win's name.

"Tim Hatch's cousin?"

"He was here for the memorial service; he sang, remember?"

"Of course. I remember Win," Mr. Z nodded.

"Win told me you helped him too, long ago."

"He was a kid who needed help, believe me. But I guess I didn't help him get far enough away." The look on Jordan's face stopped him. Tears filled her eyes again. "I'm sorry. He wasn't a bad kid. He just didn't have anyone he could rely on. Both his parents died before he was out of high school."

"Why did people think he was the one who burned down the mill?"

"Rumors," Mr. Z said. "You know how vicious the rumors in this town can be."

"But who? Who would start a rumor like that?"

"I have my suspicions, but what is all this about?"

"Well, there's something about that mill..."

"There isn't a mill anymore, Jordan. That's old history."

"I know, but it haunts us, somehow. See, the night of the accident," Jordan recounted to Mr. Z the string of events, starting with Sister Rachael telling her about the boys being there and ending with Win's story of his phone conversation with Tim just one week prior to the accident.

The bell rang then. Mr. Z shouted for the kids to line up. Jordan realized she'd done all the talking and that Mr. Z had offered nothing at all. But why did she have the feeling he knew something? Jordan could see that Mr. Z was disappointed with her on more than one level. That wasn't what she wanted.

"Mr. Z, could you use a volunteer in the classroom?" He cocked his head, considering her from that angle. "I still want to go to school," she said. "It's just going to be slower, I guess. And I thought if I could just be in the classroom a little, then

I could keep that reminder in front of me... of you know... what I want to do. And I could help. You know I helped Clay."

Mr. Z considered before he spoke. "If you want to come in a couple times a week, let's say Tuesday and Thursday afternoons, you could help the special needs kids in reading circle. The school can't pay you," he said, "but I have a small discretionary fund... just a few dollars—"

"No, no," she said. "It's enough just to let me come in. Thank you so much."

"Jordan?"

She braced herself.

Mr. Z shifted his gaze to the far trees swaying in the wind. Leaves floated on the air, and then spiraled to the ground without a sound. "Even if the boys were acting like amateur detectives, that doesn't change them getting drunk and Clay crashing the truck. You have to accept that and move on."

She didn't feel it was a good idea to contradict Mr. Z. "I really think being in the school will help. You won't regret this. I promise."

The following Tuesday, on a day off from the factory, after Jordan helped her father with morning milking, she went up to the house, took a shower and stood in front of her closet. Fall was her favorite season. It had always been the season of new beginnings for her. Stacked in the corner of her closet was a milk crate with old pencil cases, hardly worn from use. She could never bear to throw them away after a year's worth of memories. Now she took them down and counted. How many? She unzipped the pencil case from first grade, a giant plastic yellow pencil with the zipper just below the point and slid out a plastic ruler, two hardened erasers and a Bic pen that still worked. Then a Care Bears case with a pink sharpener. Eight pencil cases in all. She thought about the kids in the kindergarten class. Surely, some kids had no case at all. She stuffed them into her backpack and went back to regarding her wardrobe. Her favorite sweater was a moss green argyle sweater with white stitching around the scoop neck. She put on her bra, rolled on some deodorant and put on the sweater. She remembered wearing it with a tan corduroy skirt, but when she tried the skirt on, it wouldn't zip. She took out a jean skirt. It still fit so she put that one on. She picked up her phone and thought about calling Win. It was a big day and she wanted to share it with him, but he hadn't been in touch since she'd ignored his two vague texts. *How are things?* So vague, she was almost insulted. Was he mad at her now? She didn't have time to find out.

She'd spent a little time each day reading the texts Mr. Z had told her the remedial kids were reading. As a group they were reading Lois Lowry's *The Giver.* Jordan found it a spooky book with such a dark outlook on life, but she read it because she wanted to be able to help build connections for them, as she had done for Clay. *Reading is not just about being able to understand the meaning of a sentence, you know,* she used to tell him. *There's a whole life under the surface.* When he closed off access, she'd tried to use the image of the river, the thing that had always connected them. *It's like all those fish living under the surface. They're the life of the river, right?* And that always got him hooked enough for her to continue: *So, these words, they point to an idea and the idea… well, that's the life of the story under the surface.*

She wanted to reach these kids, really reach them. *To do for them what I couldn't do for you, Clay,* she thought as she brushed her teeth, and combed her hair back. It snapped and shimmered with electricity. She regarded herself in the mirror. She'd never looked so alive. How strange was that? She hoisted her backpack on her shoulder, enjoying the weighty feel of it, and took the stairs with a bounce in her step and headed for the school.

In addition to having read the book, Jordan had formed some discussion questions. Just in case Mr. Z asked her to help the kids think about the meaning she wanted to be ready, and a small part of her, well, more than a small part, wanted to show him that she wasn't a failure. When she stopped into the office as Mr. Z had told her to do to pick up her visitor's badge, Mrs. Clark, the secretary, looked up from her computer screen and gave Jordan a big smile.

"Jordan, how *are* you?"

The familiar smell of the office, the faint and mingled odors of coffee and paper and books and perfume, Mrs. Clark's greeting of concern and love; it was like walking into a warm kitchen. "It's good to see you," Jordan smiled. She put the bag with the pencil cases on the desk.

"What's this?" Mrs. Clark asked, peeking inside.

"I thought maybe some of the kindergarten kids could use them?"

"Well, aren't you just the sweetest thing," Mrs. Clark said. "You always were though, weren't you?"

Jordan felt happy as she walked down the hall.

Mr. Z's room was a buzz of activity. The kids stopped talking when she walked into the room.

"Hey, Jordan," Mr. Z greeted her, covering the room's silence. "Come here and let me introduce you. He pulled her over to stand near his desk. "You're going to do fine," he whispered. "You look very professional. Just like a teacher."

"All right, listen up people," he said, shifting his attention to the class. "You remember I mentioned that Ms. Hawkins was going to come in a couple times a week. She'll circulate around and help me keep this motley crew under control." A couple of the kids made fake noises of protest. They all loved Mr. Z because he loved them.

"Jordan, we're just breaking into reading circles now. Why don't you start with the group in the back?" It was a group of four, three boys who looked like they should be graduating from high school. Hair sprouted above their lips and muscles bulged beneath their shirts. She immediately felt drawn to them, and to the one girl, a tiny thing with petite frame and limbs fragile enough to be wings. Her eyes stayed downcast. Jordan asked them each to read a page of the chapter assigned for that day. They stumbled over words more than two syllables and hesitated periodically, as if to signal that the meanings weren't clear.

After the group had finished reading the chapter, Jordan asked, "So what's going on in this chapter?"

Holly looked down as if the worn tiles held the answer and it would be revealed shortly if she just concentrated hard enough.

For the first time in months, Jordan felt exactly like herself. She forgot that she was eighteen and pregnant, and far from being the college graduate she would need to be to teach these kids. In that moment, everything made sense to her. She took her notebook out of her backpack, with the copies of the questions she'd prepared and began handing them to each student, explaining that they would discuss the questions together to try to come up with the bigger picture, not to worry if it didn't seem to make sense yet, it would. She took a sip from the bottle of spring water she carried with her everywhere now. It was all she drank, that and raw milk.

She looked up and Mr. Z was smiling at her with a look on his face that said just maybe she was going to be all right. Seeing the look on his face made her believe it more too.

The sharp rap on his classroom door made them all jump. There stood Mrs. Bennett, the principal, a woman in her late fifties who had been there for years now, but still couldn't compare in popularity to the principal before her, whom the entire town loved. Mrs. Bennett wore a blue suit... no one in Asheville wore suits, unless they were commuter families traveling to the cities—either Hartford or Providence—for work, or to bury people, and in it she looked even more severe than Jordan had remembered. Mr. Z was still smiling as he approached Mrs. Bennett though, so Jordan decided not to pay too much attention and went back to the students and the questions regarding the chapter.

"So, Luke, what do you think Lowry is saying about the power of memory?"

Luke shrugged, silent, but Jordan knew from years of

helping Clay how to allow silence like a lever to crack resistance into interest. Out of the corner of her eye, she saw Mr. Z glance over at her, then shift so that whatever Mrs. Bennett was saying, Jordan couldn't see or hear, because now Mr. Z's back blocked her view.

"Holly?"

"I don't know," Holly said. "Maybe that a lot of times we try to cover it up because it scares us?"

"Bingo!" Jordan said, and maybe it was too loud even though she was excited. Holly had given such a good answer and to the first question, too. Now both Mr. Z and Mrs. Bennett were looking at her and Mrs. Bennett said something more. Jordan saw the effect of it on Mr. Z's face as he snapped, "You don't have to do that."

And Mrs. Bennett replied with an even, authoritative tone that made it clear power resided with her. She called to Jordan. "Ms. Hawkins, may I have a word with you, please?" Jordan got up from the low table and started toward the door, when Mrs. Bennett said to her, "Bring your backpack, why don't you?"

Jordan's euphoria, set in motion by being in the classroom with the students and having the attention of these reluctant readers as Mr. Z called them enough attention that they had already answered one question correctly, crashed. She could hardly move her feet forward.

"Come along," Mrs. Bennett repeated.

Mr. Z shook his head. He came toward her and picked up her backpack and handed it to her. "I'm going to protest, Jordan. I will fight it. But for now, she does have the authority... I'm so sorry." Jordan slid the offered backpack onto her shoulder, grabbed her water bottle and slipped out the door before he could see the film stinging her eyes.

Mrs. Bennett was saying something about liability insurance and background checks and starting a precedent of unofficial volunteers in the classroom. "... if our classroom assistants are not certified, we open ourselves up to a very vulnerable position," she said, "and then when parents call and demand to be in the classroom, we'll have no way to control or even shape these interactions if they hear that you were given different treatment."

"I just want to be here in the school," Jordan whispered. She felt devastated and ashamed that her presence might be questionable. Did Mrs. Bennett know that Jordan was pregnant? Did she consider her a bad role model? It was a painful thought. "I just wanted to help Mr. Z with the kids," she said again.

Mrs. Bennett looked at her carefully brushed hair, the argyle sweater, and polished brown shoes. "Those pencil boxes?"

"I brought them for the kindergarteners," Jordan said.

"Well, we appreciate that." Her glance slid away. "Please understand we have to be careful about setting precedents."

Mr. Z had come up behind them. "Listen," he said, "why don't you arrange with Mrs. Clark for a background check—we can't promise, mind you, but Principal Bennett and I can discuss it after that. Would that be all right, Principal Bennett?"

Mrs. Bennett frowned but gave a quick nod. "I'm not promising. Don't get your hopes up." She spun away.

"Mr. Z?"

"Don't worry. It may take a few weeks, but I think we can get you back."

A few weeks? It wouldn't do. "Mr. Z, I need to know who started the rumor about Win burning the mill."

"Is that the only reason you came to see me, Jordan?"

"No. But I would like to know. Please?"

Mr. Z pulled Jordan by the elbow down the hall. "I'm going to answer your question. I believe the rumor about Win originated with Angela Barbo. I hesitated to tell you because I know about the lawsuit against your family. I don't want this to fuel more conflict. You don't need to get caught up in her story. Nothing good will come of it and it won't change the fact of Clay being killed or driving the truck. Do something positive for yourself. Reapply to school. Get the background check, we'll get you back here and let's move forward, okay?"

"Okay, Mr. Z."

"Promise?"

"Promise." What else could she do but go back to the farm? The energy drained out of her as she thought about the chores waiting. Calves to be fed, stalls mucked out, milking a herd. None of the work inspired her. And that was what she had to fill her days unless she did something else. At the back of her mind hovered Mr. Z's warning about not getting caught up with Mrs. Barbo; but now she knew that Mrs. Barbo had caused misery to another person who mattered to her. Jordan held her phone, debating. Should she call Win? No, not yet. There was a text from Eugene Martin asking if she was free to meet in Moosup for a cup of coffee. She texted back and suggested he bring the coffee to the playground swings. She wasn't sure why, but it seemed less like a date to sit on the swings at the playground and she didn't want to give the wrong signals, especially after her time with Win. She planned to tell Eugene Martin she was pregnant. When she got to the center of town, he gave a wave from where he was on the swing set.

"You look a little big for that swing," she grinned.

He pointed to the Dunkin' Donuts coffee tray a safe distance from the swing with two coffees in it. "I hope it's not cold." He looked her up and down. "Why are you dressed up? Did you enroll in classes?"

Jordan shook her head. "I had a job helping out at the elementary school—for about ten minutes. Why are you in Asheville today?" She hoped her question would distract him from asking her more.

"I thought I'd come see this tire burning plant in action. Some pretty big trucks come through here. This road, the bridge, they weren't built for that kind of heavy traffic. Didn't the people living in those houses put up any kind of a fight about the plant being built here?"

Jordan picked up her coffee and sipped it before answering. Then she told him the story Mr. Pascal had shared with her—everything except the part about him getting beat up. She wasn't sure why she held that back, but she did. She followed Eugene's gaze to the far end of the street, where a figure emerged, pushing a stroller.

Eugene smiled. "Would you like to come over here and give me a kiss to thank me for the coffee?" Jordan stepped close to the swing and gave him a polite kiss, then skirted away. Kissing him felt like cheating on Win, or worse, on herself. "So, what steps have you taken for your future after this year?" Eugene asked.

"I need to tell you something," she said. Martin stopped swinging. "I'm pregnant," she said.

Eugene moved the swing away from her with his foot and looked at her. "So that's what you meant when you said things were complicated." The flirtatious energy evaporated. Jordan told herself she wasn't disappointed. Eugene Martin was twenty-six, handsome, and college-educated with a passion for the environment, but that didn't make him mature. She didn't think he was more mature than she was, and maybe less. "You definitely need to go to college," he said. "There are a lot of ways to do it. Go to community college for a couple years, get a 3.0. Then you're guaranteed admission to the state university. But no matter what, you don't want to fall victim to your circumstances." He was talking down to her. Victim? She wasn't a victim. She looked away and saw that the figure pushing the stroller was Mr. Barbo. Tina's little girl was struggling to get free from the stroller.

"You should go," Jordan said to Eugene, enjoying his look of surprise at being dismissed. "I've got a lot to do, and I don't need your pity or your judgment. I'm smart; I'll figure it out." She picked up his coffee cup and handed it to him, for the first time believing her own words as she turned to walk away—an action that left her no choice but to walk straight toward Mr. Barbo. He pushed the stroller forward, unaware that the toddler had released the safety strap. The little girl lifted a leg over the padded frame and before Jordan blinked, she was running full tilt away from her grandfather and the stroller, straight toward the road and a massive dump truck full of tires careening down the hill, around the bend.

Jordan dropped her coffee and ran toward the toddler. She heard Mr. Barbo yelling and his granddaughter screeching in delight at what she thought was a game. Jordan lunged and grabbed the strap of her stretchy jumper just as the ground shook from the speed and weight of the truck as it neared. Mr. Barbo could be heard swearing and cursing behind her, and hearing his anger, the child hesitated just long enough for Jordan to swoop her up. The driver shook his head and waved as he passed, as if the averted calamity wouldn't have been his fault. Jordan held the little girl tight and walked back to Mr. Barbo, who stood frozen behind the stroller.

"Goddamn those trucks!" he swore. "They don't care!" He took the girl and hugged her. "God, that was close." He squeezed her again and set her gently in the seat. "You stay right there." The girl looked up at him and started to whimper. "Hush," he said. "You're alright." His hand shook as he tried to thread the safety belt around her. When Jordan reached down and tightened it for him, he said. "You saved her life," He paused for a minute. "My wife doesn't mean anything personal."

"Nothing personal? Then why sue us?" Jordan asked.

Mr. Barbo stooped to check the seatbelt, then stood and wiped the bead of sweat from his forehead. He looked sick. "She's like a hurt animal with all that pain. She don't know what else to do with it. Tony was her whole world."

"I understand—how kids are the whole world to parents, but, if you're not in agreement about it, can't you talk to her?"

"There's no talkin' about it." He turned the stroller and started back the way they'd come. "I tried, believe me. It's been that way since he was born."

He'd given her a clue. Now she knew he didn't agree with

the lawsuit—and him saying Tony was Mrs. Barbo's whole world and had been for *his entire life* meant something, and she was going to find out what. Somehow it fit into the boys being at the mill site with the uncovered barrel. But first, she got online and applied to two community colleges because it was the only way she knew to soothe the burn of her experience with Mrs. Bennett, followed by the salt of Eugene Martin.

Chapter 14

The next day, Mrs. Pascal invited Jordan to stop by and see her newly renovated studio before their already planned dinner and Little League fall baseball game. It worked perfectly as Jordan had an OB appointment in town. It was her second pregnancy appointment, and she invited her mother to go with her. They'd been getting along much better since the big explosion in the barn and Jordan's near miscarriage. Her mother was excited to go and promised not to ask too many questions. They sat together in the waiting room flipping through *Parents* magazines until the nurse called Jordan's name. Jordan weighed in and the nurse praised her for a perfect weight gain, just a pound.

"She's been eating really nutritious foods," Diane said. "This is going to be one healthy baby."

When the doctor came in to do her exam, Jordan reported proudly that she was faithful about taking prenatal vitamins, drinking only bottled water and eating organic fruits and vegetables, but she was still worried about the toxic environment of the glass factory. The doctor reassured her, "Plenty of people have worked at the glass factory and had healthy babies. Do what you can. Keep your thoughts positive, feed yourself and baby good nutrition, get plenty of rest and nature will take care of the rest. There are toxins everywhere, honey. Consider yourself lucky if you know what they are, and you can minimize some of them." She put the cold gel on Jordan's stomach and directed her to look at the screen. Her mother leaned over and held her hand.

"There it is!" Diane exclaimed.

"Mom. Look." Jordan couldn't believe that looking at the screen she could see this flashing image of life growing inside her. There was a sudden blip—Jordan felt it as she was seeing it on the screen.

The doctor smiled. "That was a hiccup," she explained.

"I forgot how amazing this is," Diane said.

"A hiccup? They do that? I didn't know..." The lump of flesh took on a shape to Jordan. She'd been reading so many stories online, looking at so many babies. She started to cry. Her mother took her hand. "I'm keeping him," Jordan said. Three little words and she felt their power, although on some level she'd known when she'd swooped Tina's little girl up in her arms that this would be her decision.

Diane bent close and whispered, "Are you sure? Do you understand what that would mean?" The doctor's back stayed turned, giving them privacy.

"Yes, Mom. I'm sure. I think it's a boy. It feels like a boy."

Diane squeezed her hand again and blew out a deep breath, looking at the monitor where the little heart flashed as a pulse of light. "I understand, honey. I do."

The doctor turned then and swiped a towel over the gel on Jordan's stomach. "Can I ask a question?" Jordan asked. "I read that breathing in microfibers at the glass factory can cause asthma and a chronic cough. I've been feeling a little breathless..."

The doctor smiled patiently. "If you want to wear one of those paper masks while you're at work, you could do that. But I don't think there's anything inherently dangerous about the glass factory." She sent Jordan out the door with an ultrasound picture that showed the baby, a curled shadow with wispy limbs and a light, beating heart. Jordan hugged her mother goodbye in the parking lot and held the sonogram against the steering wheel while she dialed Win's number.

The phone rang and rang and finally Win's voice came on saying leave a message. "Hi Win. It's Jordan. I just went to the doctor, and I have this little picture of the baby. A sonogram.

It's so cute, Win. You can't believe it, but when you look on the screen, the heart is a tiny thing, and you can see it pulsing like a little flash of light. I'm sending it to you in a text." She paused, waiting to see if he would pick up. But he didn't, so she sent the text, slipped the sonogram in her pocket and drove to Mrs. Pascal's studio.

The New Horizons Massage and Body Works looked like a miniature Swiss chalet, built at the back of a quaint shopping plaza with an ice cream shop and taco place. The color was a delicious melon with sky blue trim. An old Ford pick-up was pulling out of the massage center as she was pulling in. The driver was none other than Mr. Barbo.

She locked her truck and hurried up the steps. Under the awning, a wind chime sounded and flyers advertising reflexology and reiki massage, meditation opportunities and relaxation yoga—things Jordan knew little about, fluttered on a bulletin board. A faint scent of lavender and orange blossoms greeted her as she stepped into the studio flooded with light from a large picture window that faced the surrounding hills. She went to the magazine rack where she saw *Wellness, Yoga International, Mindful Presence,* magazines she had never heard of. The glass factory's magazine rack held *People, Star, National Inquirer,* and *Automotive World.* Here, a polished wood table held a pitcher of water with sliced cucumbers floating in it and a bowl of almonds and walnuts mixed together. She took a spoonful of nuts and put them on a paper napkin and poured herself a glass of water. Who ever heard of cucumbers in water? But it tasted so refreshing. She finished one glass and poured herself another. She hadn't realized how thirsty she was. Ellen Pascal appeared in the waiting room.

"Hi," Jordan said.

"You like the cucumber water, I see." Mrs. Pascal seemed amused. "Finish it up. I just saw my last client of the day. No one else will drink it."

"Was that Mr. Barbo? Did he come in for a massage?"

"Yes, a reiki massage. Poor man," she shook her head.

"Why do you say poor man?" Jordan asked, her tone sharper than she'd intended because if there were sides, she expected the Pascals to be on their side.

Mrs. Pascal swept an armful of white sheets into a basket. "Jordan, give the man a break. He's got liver cancer. They've tried everything they know to try. Only then do they turn to the healing arts. It so frustrates me that for some of my clients this is the last resort, but I try to remind them that healing can happen at any time."

"How bad is it?" Jordan didn't like to think Mrs. Pascal saw her as lacking compassion. She remembered that Mr. Barbo appeared sick and out of breath at the playground. No wonder he couldn't chase his granddaughter.

"Near the end. That's common knowledge, so there's no harm in me telling you."

"My parents may have to sell land to pay the Barbo lawsuit. We don't know if we'll be able to keep the farm going. It's hard to feel compassion for them."

"He has a lot of unresolved conflict. I'm not sure it's physical healing in the end that he's really wanting. But the energy healing relieves his pain, he says, so I'm happy to help in that way."

"What do you mean, exactly?"

Mrs. Pascal frowned to warn her off from that line of questioning.

Jordan tried a different approach. "What is energy healing?"

Mrs. Pascal seemed happy to answer that question. She swept linens into the basket as she talked. "When you break down anything—this table—the chairs, the atoms, the sub atoms, down to quarks and even smaller particles, what you find is energy. It's true for the body too, so working with the body's energy system brings the body back to wholeness."

"Sounds interesting. The body as energy."

Mrs. Pascal stopped. "Healing can happen in an instant and yet a lifetime of negative belief can be hard to overcome. I'd say like many, Mr. Barbo's still struggling with that."

"Maybe they should change how they treat other people."

"Jordan, Jim wants to talk to you about this very thing. Let's wait until dinner, okay? He has something to share with you—information that might give you a little more compassion toward the Barbos."

Jordan clamped her jaw shut—to keep from spitting a verbal lashing at the gentle Mrs. Pascal, who in no way deserved one.

"Shall we go?" Mrs. Pascal held the door open, key in hand, waiting for Jordan to step out. "Let's take my car," she said. "Save on gas. I'll have Jim bring you back here afterwards for your truck."

The ride to the Pascals' house took just five minutes, but it was enough time for Jordan to fill Mrs. Pascal in on her pregnancy. She showed Mrs. Pascal the sonogram. Jordan respected Mrs. Pascal and her perspective. It was a lifeline, one she felt she needed now more than ever.

"Wow, you're pregnant. That is news." Mrs. Pascal pulled into their driveway and looked carefully at the sonogram before handing it back.

"You didn't notice?"

"Well, you're just a little bit of a thing. I thought maybe you gained a few pounds..."

"I'm going to keep it," Jordan rushed on. She felt tears coming. This was very annoying. All this crying. She just wasn't a crier. She tried to squelch them, but under the watchful gaze of Mrs. Pascal, the flattening out of feelings was impossible.

"What are you feeling right now, honey?"

Jordan's eyes welled with tears. "Scared."

"Where do you think the fear comes from?" Jordan shook her head. "What are you afraid of, my dear? You have choices you know. You're not locked into one decision."

"It's not that," Jordan said. "Keeping the baby is scary, but it feels like the thing I want to do. It's just that everything is falling apart."

"You're going through some major changes," Mrs. Pascal agreed. She patted Jordan's hand. "Sometimes things do break apart—like families when parents divorce, or a child dies, but things get built up from the brokenness, if you're open to it. New dreams. And our pain has something to teach us. There's always opportunity in everything that happens. And there are gifts—what's the gift? You have to ask yourself. You'll have a child if you want that. And that child is helping to fill the empty place, in some ways, of the lives of those who were lost."

"Mr. Z said that too," Jordan sniffed.

"So, you'll have the chance to love this child and share the wisdom you're developing through this experience. If you want to look at it that way."

"Wisdom?"

"Absolutely. When you ask these kinds of questions and put into action the principles of healing and forgiveness, you show the results in your own life, and you help others learn how to live that way too."

"What?" Jordan asked. "What kinds of questions am I asking?"

"Whatever it is that brought you here."

"But what brought me here was you asking me to dinner. And I wanted to tell you about the baby."

Mrs. Pascal laughed. "Somewhere inside you're following your own guidance. You know why you're here. Or, if you don't, you'll figure it out. Nobody else can."

Mr. Pascal pulled up beside them in his new Toyota truck. He got out and came around to give Mrs. Pascal a kiss. Jordan could tell by the easy way they kissed that they always greeted each other with a kiss, and she admired that. They walked hand in hand to the house, leaving Jordan to follow as if her being there were as natural and frequent a visit as one of their own children.

Mr. Pascal threw hamburgers on the grill and then excused himself. As soon as he left the room, Mrs. Pascal said,

"Do you want to talk about what you're so mad about?" The way Mrs. Pascal said it, the fact of it, couldn't be denied.

"I didn't get a chance to say goodbye to Clay," Jordan swallowed hard. The bitter seed welled up and she tried to push it down, but she gasped out the words. "And I can't go back and make up for what I did."

"What did you do, honey?"

"I was just going to go away to college and leave him there on the farm. He hated it. It wasn't what he wanted. He kept saying that and I think he just wanted me to hear him, but I was afraid if I did, I'd have to stay. I know it doesn't make any sense."

Mrs. Pascal sat back in her chair. "You feel guilty for pursuing your dreams?"

Jordan looked at the ceiling trying to stop tears from spilling over.

"When a sibling dies, a surviving sibling can feel grief in many different ways depending on the relationship. They can even take on some of the problems of the person who died. It can get complicated. And confusing. But one thing I'm sure of—Clay would never want you to punish yourself for his death. If you keep your baby for that reason—"

"No. Once I saw him on the screen, moving inside me, it felt amazing. I fell in love with him. He hiccupped." She smiled and Mrs. Pascal, seeing her joy, smiled back.

At that moment, Mr. Pascal came back into the room dressed in his baseball coach's uniform. He sensed he'd interrupted a private conversation, and backed out of the room, but the moment had passed. The burgers were ready, and they had to eat so they could get to the game. Jordan could hardly have guessed Mr. Pascal's next words.

"Jordan, I didn't tell you this the last time when we were talking about why we left Asheville. Ellen and I discussed it and we felt you might benefit from understanding the Barbos', or at least, Mrs. Barbo's history a bit more, so you could free yourself from all that drama of the lawsuit."

Jordan waited.

"We dated in high school."

"You're kidding." Jordan could hardly imagine the gentle and formal Mr. Pascal with Mrs. Barbo.

"We went out for two years, until senior year. When I applied to colleges, Angela Toulosse—that was her maiden name—got involved with Jimmy Barbo. She was pregnant before the end of senior year. Her parents made her marry Barbo. She started working at the dye factory with him."

He stopped, took a few bites, and Ellen nudged him to continue.

"It was one of those stormy summer nights—she came to see me. I opened the door to find her completely drenched and crying. I don't know, maybe she was still losing blood. She just hurled herself into my arms like a beaten dog, looking for protection. I was someone she thought she could turn to for help. That's the thing I feel the worst about now. Being who I am now I would never say the things I said that night."

"What did she want?" Jordan asked. "What was it you said?"

"Well, she told me she'd miscarried, and she wanted to leave Barbo because he had a temper, and he drank too much. I told her she hadn't been married six months and that marriage was hard work and she needed to go back and work on it. As if I knew at eighteen what the hell I was talking about. She cried bitterly. I couldn't get her to stop. 'But you don't know… What about my dreams?'" Mr. Pascal winced as he repeated her words.

Jordan groaned. She imagined someone saying such a thing to her. She thought about her father trying to force Clay to stay on the farm.

"And when I brought Ellen back to Asheville five years later, we were newly married. We took over my parents' house. Angela and I were in two different worlds even though we lived in the same town. Time to time I'd see her, and we'd wave. But slowly over the years she just seemed to sink more and more into herself." He stopped.

"Jordan has her own news to share with us, Jim." Mr. Pascal waited.

"I'm pregnant," Jordan said.

Mr. Pascal regarded her with the same even expression Jordan always associated with him. "Well, you're not Angela Barbo, Jordan. You have options and a future."

"I hope so," Jordan whispered.

"And the father?"

"He's someone who used to live in Asheville, but you probably wouldn't know him."

"Who's that?" Mr. Pascal asked, politely.

"Win Hatch."

Mr. Pascal put down his fork. "We know Win." He looked at Mrs. Pascal. "Win was friends with our oldest son for a while."

"Until he got into trouble?" Jordan asked defensively.

"No, they stayed friends even then. Win didn't have any guidance as a kid, but he was a good boy. Leaving Asheville was the best thing for him. I think that's when they lost touch." Jordan thought about Win saying he couldn't come back to Asheville.

Mrs. Pascal chimed in. "What a small world."

The conversation ended there, and they cleared the dishes, said goodbye to Mrs. Pascal and headed out in Mr. Pascal's truck for a Little League game. Jordan couldn't help thinking of Clay and Tim and Tony as she watched the game. All three had played baseball. Clay had been a pitcher, Tim, first base and Tony, short stop. These boys looked like young angels out in the evening sun, kicking up dust in a golden glimmer of summer night and she felt Clay and the others' spirits there on the field as parents yelled encouragement not just to their sons, but to all the boys. Jordan felt sure Mr. Pascal had set positive ground rules. She didn't think he'd told her everything yet about Mrs. Barbo, though. He was holding something back and as she thought about it, it struck her again—Mr. Barbo saying that Tony was Mrs. Barbo's whole world. How would that be, if she felt she'd given up her dreams being married to Mr. Barbo and having kids? After the game, won by Mr. Pascal's team, parents served pizza, chips, and soda to the players from both teams. Jordan wondered if she'd get the chance to bring up Mrs. Barbo again when they stopped on the way home to get gas, but Mr. Pascal left her filling the tank while he went in to pay. When she finished, she saw through the window Mr. Pascal standing in the aisle pondering the assortment of snacks. She went into the store to oversee his choice and stopped at the vending machine against the wall to select a soda. Welch's Grape—her favorite. The can shot down just as a man darted by, with Mr. Pascal following behind.

"He's got my wallet," Mr. Pascal yelled.

The guy raced toward the door. It was a baseball reflex—Jordan wound up the pitch, brought her arm all the way back, and launched the can, snapping from the wrist, not the elbow. The soda can didn't spin neat the way a ball would, but it connected, catching the guy on the back of the head and sending him reeling into the doorframe. Mr. Pascal stopped short. The guy slid to the floor, out cold.

"My god, Jordan!"

The clerk came from behind the counter, and they all stood over the guy. He moaned and rubbed the swelling egg on his head. He opened his eyes, regarded them with a puzzled expression. The clerk had pressed an emergency call button; a police car was pulling in, its lights flashing. A cop appeared in the store, his gun drawn. "Stand back," he said as he slapped a pair of handcuffs on the guy. He put away his gun as soon as he had the guy cuffed and yanked him through the door.

"I was just pulling my wallet out when he grabbed it," Mr. Pascal said.

The clerk went behind the counter and picked up his phone. Jordan heard him say, "I'm all right, but I quit. That's twice this month and my luck is running out." When he hung up, he turned to Mr. Pascal. "I'm very sorry. Please, take your purchases for free." Mr. Pascal held up a bag of chips. "Take more," the clerk said.

The cop returned and when he heard the story, he said to Jordan, "That's one hell of an aim you've got. Maybe you need to register it as a deadly weapon." He laughed. "Wait till I tell the guys at the station."

But Jordan had one thing on her mind: Mrs. Barbo. When Mr. Pascal pulled into the massage center to drop her at her truck, she thanked him for the game and dinner and said, "Is there more to the story with Mrs. Barbo?" When he didn't answer she told him about Mr. Barbo's comment on the playground.

"I don't know. Seems unfortunate, but maybe Tony was always her favorite." He shrugged, but the way he looked away made Jordan think he knew more. "I was hoping what I told you would help you let go of it so you could focus on your own life, Jordan. Keep us posted on how you're doing, will you?"

Jordan promised she would. He waited for her to be safely in her truck before he drove away. She saw she'd missed a call from Win; she took the sonogram out of her pocket. How could she explain that in order to go on with her own life and be the person she wanted to be in the future she had to get to the bottom of what happened on Gravity Hill and Mrs. Barbo's past seemed to be part of the puzzle.

Chapter 15

Jordan felt different after spending time with the Pascals. It seemed she could discuss everything with them—Clay's death, her pregnancy, the lawsuit—and while none of the *facts* had changed, her *perceptions* had. The Pascals had known Win and not considered him a terrible person. And Mr. Pascal had dated Mrs. Barbo... that was unexpected. Who could have guessed that the strong, gentle loving Jim Pascal had *dated* Mrs. Barbo and could fill in her history? Jordan couldn't actually bring herself to *feel* Mrs. Barbo's pain, since the woman was responsible for causing so much pain herself, but now she understood a bit more the root of it. The Pascals were good at getting to the root of things, Jordan thought as she drove; they helped her to get to the root of her own self, and the Pascals telling her she was going to be okay gave her strength. Mrs. Pascal was right; keeping a baby was not the big deal it had been decades earlier. And Jordan believed now that the very way she became pregnant with Win at the site of the accident, well, it was no accident. Mrs. Pascal had told her to be compassionate with herself and that doing so would give the baby a good environment. "Be gentle with yourself, dear," That's what Mrs. Pascal had said, and Jordan had never considered such a thing—compassion for oneself.

Jordan didn't go straight home. Instead, she found herself on the highway, then exiting where Glass and Company loomed, a solid tumor on the horizon, leaking white steam. About a hundred cars and trucks and motorcycles sat in the parking lot. Third shift was working. She thought about the bottles and all the work; the sorting, the cleaning, the heating of sand and limestone and feldspar to almost 3000 degrees Fahrenheit. The plant manufactured a million bottles a day, bottles being made and remade until the essence of what they were was all mixed up. The deafening sound of the clash and clank of bottles moved down the line. Tonight, the line held mayonnaise jars. Jordan looked around until she saw Tilchek, his pants neatly pressed as always, his attention on the overhead conveyors leading into the warehouse. He was instructing a maintenance guy on a ladder, who tightened a lug nut, which brought two parts of the rail closer and made the boxes flow forward again. Jordan paused a moment and then shouted to be heard.

"Mr. Tilcheck?"

He turned, saw her and looked surprised. "Jordan. What are you doing here? You're not on tonight." He was used to surprising behavior from the long-term crew. Drinking problems, marriage problems, drugs, the unspoken dramas of a life surfaced as work interruptions, and he was a man who tried hard to help his workers get back on track. Jordan knew this. "Come into my office," he said.

Jordan sat in a chair and waited for him to close the door and sit at his desk before she spoke. "I just wanted to come by and tell you personally that I appreciate that you gave me a job, Mr. Tilcheck, but I'm sorry I have to quit."

"Quit?" He said. "You're quitting? I guess you heard the news, then?"

"No," Jordan frowned. "What news?"

"You haven't? Then why are you quitting?"

"I need to be on the farm and there are some other things going on..." She didn't tell him she was pregnant and that despite her doctor's assurances she thought the factory environment might be bad for the baby. "But what news?"

He adjusted his glasses. "They're phasing us out at this location. Within the next six months."

"Oh no," Jordan said. "When did you find out? Do the others know?" Through a large window, she could look down at the factory floor at Norma packing boxes just like always. She felt worried for her. Where was she going to find another job?

Tilchek took his glasses off and rubbed his face. "They've been talking about it. By tomorrow, everyone will know." Jordan remembered the workers talking outside earlier in the summer. It'd just been a rumor then. "Labor's cheaper in North Carolina," Tilchek said. "That, and automation." He paused. "Can I give you some advice?"

"Sure," Jordan said, even though she didn't really want his advice.

"Go back to school. That little piece of paper changes everything, after that, no matter the bumps—because there will be bumps—you got something." The way he said it made Jordan think he was giving advice he wished someone had given him. "Go upstairs and fill out the termination papers. We'll just need to do the paperwork and get that last paycheck to you."

Jordan did as requested. The process took only ten minutes and then she was walking back out the door of the glass factory. She looked at the workers, those in the shadow of the line bent over the hot glass illuminated by the flashing fire. What would they do when the factory closed? She walked through the door into the cool night air and almost bumped right into Tina Barbo, standing under a floodlight with a book open in one hand and a cigarette in the other.

"Hey, Tina," Jordan said. She wondered what her life had felt like, with Tony as her mother's world.

"Oh, hi." Tina had been caught with her guard down. She closed the book. It was a GED test book.

"I didn't know you started working here, but I thought I saw you one day filling out an application."

"I just started last week," Tina said. "You?"

"I just quit." Jordan debated telling her the plant was closing but decided against it. "You going for your GED?"

"Yeah," Tina said. "I heard the news. How you feeling?"

"Okay."

Tina pressed the book to her chest. "Trying. I have a practice test tomorrow. You know, school's not my thing. I get stressed out."

"I could help you," Jordan offered.

"Really?" Tina shifted the book to her hip. "That would be great. Give me your number." She punched it into her cellphone as the whistle sounded the end of break.

"Be sure you call," Jordan shouted as Tina disappeared into the crowd of workers flooding back inside.

Chapter 16

The next morning Jordan woke up and it hurt to open her eyes. Some days were like this. It hurt to be in the house where she'd grown up with Clay. Some mornings she thought she could hear him pounding up the stairs to his room, to his music, away from chores. Sometimes, life didn't feel real without him.

"Clay? Clay are you there?" She put her hand to her stomach. The baby kicked. If it was a boy, maybe she'd name him Clay. She looked at the clock. Nine a.m. Morning milking would be done. She'd slept right through her alarm and her father hadn't woken her. Jordan rolled out of bed, took a shower, and then went down to the kitchen. Her mother had started leaving notes again—she was off delivering produce before her shift at the hospital. There was no coffee in the pot. The house was eerie quiet, and it hurt too much to stay there. She checked her phone and there as promised, a call from Tina, but no message. She didn't care what their parents might think; she wanted to talk to someone else who could understand what she was feeling.

R U THERE? She pressed send.

Y? came back almost immediately.

Want 2 meet 4 coffee?

Y. Where?

High Point in 20.

When she got to the coffee shop in Moosup, Tina was sitting in her car, a baseball cap pulled down over her face. Jordan parked beside her and opened her window.

"Hey, do you want to go in?" Jordan asked.

Tina shook her head and handed Jordan a medium coffee. "I went through the drive through for us. Cream and sugar, okay?"

"Thanks," Jordan took the coffee.

"If we show up in there, we won't have one moment of peace. You know that."

"I suppose you're right," Jordan took a sip of coffee.

"You okay?" Tina asked.

"This morning, I swore I heard Clay walking around the house. I miss him. I really miss him." Jordan's truck had an old CD player. She put in a Garth Brooks CD and turned the volume up so Tina could hear. "This was Clay's favorite song."

"I get it," Tina said. "Sometimes, it just hits me. Like what you're saying and then other times I just feel numb. That's how it is right now."

"I know that feeling too. It's even worse," Jordan said.

"I can't really talk to anyone. People just don't understand."

"Yeah," Jordan said although that wasn't completely true. She had the Pascals and her parents and Mr. Z, and Win. Who did Tina have?

Tina fumbled with her coffee lid. "You know what I hate? I hate when people say it takes time and it will get better, because when it does, they'll have been dead longer."

They sat drinking coffee in silence.

Jordan asked, "How's the studying going?"

"That sucks too."

"I want to help you," Jordan said.

Tina pulled back her baseball cap. "Why?"

Jordan turned off Garth Brooks. "Because being a teacher is what I always wanted to be."

"You should still do it," Tina said. "Giving up your scholarship was stupid."

Jordan jerked her head back. How had Tina known? She shouldn't be surprised, though. News spread in Asheville. "I just reapplied to a couple places," Jordan said. "We'll see what happens. What about you?"

"Well, with the plant closing—I guess you found that out already—I just want to get my GED and maybe a certificate for bookkeeping. Work in an office. I feel like I could do that."

"Totally."

Tina put her baseball cap back down over her eyes. Her phone buzzed and she looked down at it but didn't answer it. "That's my mother wanting to know where I am."

"Our brothers and Tim Hatch were at the old mill site that night of the accident before they died."

Tina sucked in her breath. "How do you know that?"

Speaking quickly, Jordan told her the whole story.

Tina tipped her head back against the seat. "Sister Rachael. She doesn't miss a thing. What the hell were they doing there?" Tina rubbed at a fleck of dirt off her window. "That place was always a big problem between my parents. It was like some ghost looming over us."

"I went up there," Jordan said. "I found the barrel Sister Rachael said they were digging up. I covered it up again. So, she was telling the truth, I guess."

Tina's phone buzzed. "I've got to go. My daughter's awake, and my mom wants me home."

"Thanks for meeting," Jordan said. "When can I help you study?"

"I'm on at the factory the next three days. Then four days off. So sometime then? Text me." Tina started her car, but before backing out she said, "Sometimes on bad days I talk to Tony, and I ask him to send me a little strength. I find it helps."

Jordan would never in a million years have expected such words from Tina Barbo. She was just getting ready to back out of the parking lot when she heard a sharp rap on her window. She almost jumped out of her skin—Sister Rachael loomed there, leaning on her white staff, almost as if summoned. Jordan didn't have time to put the window up before she spoke. "You're on the right path," Sister Rachael said. "Her parents are at the root of it. Work together and you can help each other. It's not just your brother's reputation to save."

Jordan peeled out of the parking lot, leaving dust to settle on Sister Rachael's white robe. She couldn't deny the woman's power—it was both physical and energetic at the same time. But it spooked her, how the woman just appeared out of nowhere, making her mysterious proclamations. Back home, she went to sit on the picnic table at the back of the house and pulled out her phone. She dialed Win's number.

It was not yet 9 a.m., but she was sure Win would have started his workday already and, if he was in the woods, wouldn't hear the phone over the racket of the chainsaw. Still, she let it ring for what felt like forever and just as she was going to hang up, Win answered.

"Jordan? Is everything all right?"

Jordan hadn't thought that a call might worry him. "Yes, Win, I'm fine. How are you?"

"Fine." His voice went up at the end as if to answer an unframed question.

"I didn't think I'd get you."

"So that's why you called?" he joked. She started to laugh and then before she knew it, she was crying. "You sure you're okay?" he asked.

"Yeah. I miss Clay." She sniffed into the silence. What was it she expected from Win?

"I'm with you on that one," he said and somehow, it was exactly what she needed.

"Yeah. I just spoke with Tina Barbo, and she told me that her parents used to fight about the mill and Tony always had a weird fascination with that place." There was another pause. Win was not a big talker and the phone made that more obvious.

"Jordan, don't get caught up in that. Tell me about you. What's going on with you?"

"I'm going to keep him. It's a boy," she whispered. The silence between them was so deep she could almost hear the echo of the wind in the woods behind him.

"I figured you would, and then when I got your message and heard the excitement in your voice, I knew," Win said.

"If it's a boy, I want to name him Clay."

"So, everything's okay with him and you? You been going to the doctor?"

The way he asked the question made her feel better. "Yes, everything's fine."

"So, I'm going to be a father." He whispered it more to himself than her. A man's voice shouted out in the distance. "I've got to get back to work, Jordan," Win said. "Can I call you later? Will you pick up the phone or answer my texts now?"

"Yes, Win. Call me later."

"Take good care of the two of you," he said then he hung up.

Chapter 17

But Win didn't call her back, that day or the next. Jordan worried that maybe when he thought about it, he decided he couldn't handle her keeping the baby. Or maybe he had gotten hurt in the woods. No one would even know to call her. Because no one in Maine knew anything about her. Should she call him? She decided to wait another day because she didn't want to seem needy. She asked herself what she'd expected when she'd told Win she wouldn't go live in Maine. He'd told her he couldn't come back to Asheville. There were plenty of fall chores to do in preparation for winter and she threw herself into them. In a few days, she'd reach out to Tina again—she could hardly wait.

The hoof trimmer came to work on the cows. It was a job that took most of the morning. When Jordan went to fetch the last stragglers for trimming, she found one of the cows, Eartha, down in the aisle. Sam took one look at her and said, "Twisted stomach. I guess we'll have to call Alice."

Alice was their vet, the only woman vet in eastern Connecticut who worked on large farm animals. The farmers loved her because she never charged them full price. If she had, they never would have been able to pay. Jordan loved Alice because throughout high school, Alice had encouraged her to pursue her dream and praised Sam for helping her along her way. Jordan wasn't sure what Alice thought of her these days.

While they waited for Alice, Jordan cleaned up the milk parlor and Sam finished feeding the cows. When Alice arrived, she rolled up her sleeves, in preparation for the surgery.

"You keeping your father in line now?" she asked Jordan.

"I'm trying."

Alice laughed. "He's a tough one. But seriously, Jordan. Do you have more of a plan than keeping him in line?"

Jordan started to answer, but was interrupted by Dave, the breeder, driving in. He parked his car next to Alice's truck and climbed out.

"How you doin', Alice?" he called.

"Got to turn a cow's stomach," Alice said. "Must be your fault, Dave."

"That's right. Whenever anything goes wrong, blame the breeder," Dave joked.

"Calves come out upside down or backwards. It must be the breeder. Ain't that right, Jordan?"

It was a clear October day. The chopper was still in pieces, despite its cheerful paint glowing in the autumn sun. When they'd bought the chopper, Sam had been interested in it because the previous owners had just put a new head on it. "Not going to have any problems with those blades," he'd said. But a bigger problem existed inside. The seller had disguised it by welding the engine to another piece, so the problem wouldn't be discovered until too late.

After most of the previous day working on it, Sam had it nearly fixed. "Can I blame you for the chopper too, Dave?" he called out cheerfully. It seemed, at the moment, like life was back to normal, whatever normal was.

"Go right ahead," Dave yelled. His little beagle sat up in the front seat of his car.

"We got pie, Alice," Sam called. "Jordan, go get Alice a piece of that apple pie."

"No, thanks." Alice arranged her operating tray on the back of the truck. "Been eating too much lately. Already going to have a hard time getting on and off that bucket."

An overturned five-gallon pail served as Alice's operating stool.

Jordan laughed.

"Don't laugh too hard," Alice said. "You're going to know just what I mean in a few months."

Her face was full of affection and her smile held no re-crimination or judgment. Dave chuckled too, and then he grabbed his barn boots from the trunk and went off to in-seminate the cow in heat.

While Alice pulled things from the back of her truck, Jordan shoveled manure off the cement floor in the barn and set up the wooden gate, separating the surgery area from the rest of the herd. The cows left the feed bunk and crowded cu-riously at the gate.

The foliage was brilliant, some maples ruby red, others a deep garnet, set against oaks of solid gold.

"You ready?" Alice called.

"All ready," Jordan said.

"Where's your father?"

"Right here." Sam came around the side of the barn, put the halter on Eartha and pulled it tight to a post on the wall, tight enough to make the cow's knees buckle. Jordan and Alice stood at Eartha's backend, guiding her weight so that as she buckled, they rolled her gently onto her side, tied her back legs together with one rope and her front legs with another and then rolled her onto her back for full exposure of her stomach. Sam held the front rope fast while Jordan and Alice pulled the back rope, which was fastened to a pulley, lifting Eartha's hooves high into the air. Eartha, looking like a pig ready for roasting, moaned in pain as Alice perched on the bucket and shaved her belly with a battery-operated shaver.

"Amazing how making this cut, even without anesthesia, feels better than a twisted stomach."

Jordan and Sam looked on as Alice removed a sterilized blade from her breast pocket, fit it into the scalpel, put on a sanitized pair of rubber gloves, and made the first cut in the skin, drawing almost no blood, then a second, deeper cut through the ligament, and a final, bloody cut through the muscle. Blood seeped up and covered her hand as she plunged it in, grabbed the stomach, which lay twisted over to the side, straightened it out, sewing it first to the muscle.

"Can't trust the muscle to hold it," Alice explained, as she did each time she operated, as if she had a roomful of new students. "It's an unstable anchor. Now, the ligament. See this flat wall? It'll hold even if the muscle doesn't." She completed that suture, and then did another, to sew up the skin. "There now," she said to the cow. "That's better."

Jordan loved to watch Alice work. Alice knew how to make things right. No one, not even Alice herself doubted her ability. Jordan found her strength inspiring.

They loosened the cow's feet, letting her down gently from her position. Without help, the cow rolled onto her side and sat up.

"Some humans couldn't survive that kind of thing," Alice said, looking down at the cow. "Well, in World Wars I and II we had some pretty gruesome operations, but still." She reached over and patted the cow's head.

"Let me go write you a check, Alice," Sam said. He went off toward the house. The $600 Alice charged to operate on a twisted stomach cost much less than replacing a cow.

Jordan had gone off to get a block of the tender alfalfa they fed new calves, and now she shook it out in front of Eartha. The cow curled her tongue around the dried green blades and began chewing.

"You're a brave girl," Jordan cooed to the cow.

"Bravery has nothing to do with it." Alice said. "She had no choice. You have choices."

Jordan cleaned the sawdust from Eartha's eye, where her face had been pressed into the cement during surgery. Alice was being subtle, for Alice.

"I just quit the glass factory," Jordan offered. "And I reapplied to a couple schools."

"Well, that's a start," Alice said.

Sam came back from the house, breaking their conversation. "There's something else, Alice." He led her around the corner, where Bucky, stood tied to a post, although the rope was hardly needed. The hide that had stretched over her emaciated frame weeks earlier, dipping into every hollow, as if her skeleton itself was ready to collapse, was filled in and sleek, the putrid stench of rotting flesh was gone, replaced by new pink tissue.

"I don't believe it," Alice said.

"Yeah," Jordan glanced at the calf. "She got footrot. It got so bad, the calf couldn't stand but Dad wouldn't let me call Santo the butcher. Look at her now."

Alice bent to examine the healed site of the recently oozing abscess. "Might just make it," she muttered. "There aren't too many more like you, Sam. I mean it."

The red Toyota pulled in. Sam's grin faded.

"Oh Christ," he swore. "I am in no mood to see that guy. How much do you think they pay him to run around defending one damned fern! And he's paying too much attention to you, Jordan."

"Dad," Jordan shook her head, "you don't need to be rude to him. I know how to take care of myself. I already told him to get lost."

"Is that so?" Sam asked.

"What's the big deal about this fern?" Alice asked, trying to change the subject. Jordan felt grateful.

"Like I said before, just using up our tax dollars," Sam muttered.

Whereas the first time Martin had climbed from his car and stood like a misfit in the barnyard, now Jordan watched him look around as if the farm was a place familiar to him, and important. She wondered if saving some little endangered fern had given him a sense of entitlement. He wore his signature khakis, and this time, a zippered fleece jacket and hiking boots. The geese were lying up by the house and they honked but didn't get up from their post.

"Looks like the geese have accepted you," Jordan said.

Martin looked at her, wary. "I wouldn't go that far. Respectful acquaintances, maybe."

"To what do we owe the honor, Eugene?" Sam interrupted.

Martin took a deep breath. "Mr. Hawkins, you probably only associate me with bad news."

"Oh, don't take it personal," Sam said. "Wouldn't want you to get your feelings hurt. It's just we've got more to do here than rescue a fern."

Martin looked at Jordan. "Just for the record, sir. What's good for the Hartford Fern is also what's good for the land and impacts your crops."

"Well, I hope you're not proposing some solution that's going to bankrupt me. I can do cross row cultivation all day, but you said yourself the real culprit is right there." Sam pointed at the horizon where the tire burning plant's smokestack belched out white smoke. "What can you do about that?"

The men looked at each other, then at Jordan. She kicked some gravel with her boot. She had her own feelings about Eugene Martin's superior tone, and she told herself he could handle whatever her father dished out.

Martin said, "Part of the problem is that these tire burning firms are considered waste co-generators because they produce fuel for energy and they're regulated under the Federal Power Act instead of the Clean Air Act, which would be much more stringent. They're considered energy generators."

"Energy generators? For the power company, right?" Martin nodded. "Those tires are trash, not fuel," Sam said. "The power companies have powerful lobbyists. It's just a way for them to escape regulation and here you are nailing me with your elaborate suggestions for better farming practices instead of attacking their pollution. I have a farm to run and a lawsuit to settle. Maybe you heard about it?"

Martin must have heard about the Barbo lawsuit because he didn't seem confused by the reference, but he wasn't about to be dismissed. "Doesn't seem from the water and soil tests that the tire burning plant can be blamed." He scratched the back of his head and waved his papers in the air. They were silent for a moment.

"You're looking at people trying to just keep their heads above water," Sam said.

Martin looked around the farm—at the ramshackle

condition of it all. He regarded Sam with an expression that questioned him, but why? Jordan wondered. "The Connecticut Farmland Trust could help you apply for farmland preservation funds, sir. Give you some extra cash flow while keeping the land open." Martin paid no attention to the scowl darkening Sam's face. He went on. "But you should read this." He waved the paper. "Those soil and water samples—"

"Enough!" Sam yelled. "That's enough from you. I've had about as much as I can stand of you in your sporty car with your arrogance and steady paycheck coming from my taxes—coming out here and telling me how to solve my problems!"

Alice and Dave hastily packed things into their trucks. They'd seen Sam lose his patience with Clay, and it was uncomfortable.

Martin handed Sam the pages. "Well, maybe you want to read this. I'd like to help you if you'll let me."

Sam wouldn't reach for the report.

Martin said, "Sir, there are resources—"

"Resources! Don't tell me about resources."

Martin drew himself up to his full height. "I'll be back next spring to check on the fern, and there might be fines attached—"

Hearing raised voices the geese stirred, squawking and made their way down toward the ruckus. For once, Jordan understood why her father loved them. Still, something made her reach out and grab the pages before Eugene Martin got in his car and drove off.

Chapter 18

Jordan went up to the house and ran a bath with sea salts. She made a mug of green tea, perched it on the edge of the tub, along with Eugene Martin's report, and let herself sink into the warm water and lavender fragrance before she opened it. She thought he needed an education in how to treat people, and she hoped she'd never have to see him again, but as she started reading, she had to admit Martin was a good writer and that his report gave detailed and important information; mainly that the level of ash particulate in the air still didn't account fully for the damage to the Hartford Fern. So, what did? His report recommended more practices to stop erosion and field run-off, but he outlined his doubt about that as the culprit, and then he dove into the water and soil testing. What he had found puzzled him. He'd found trichloroethylene and a host of other chemicals, including benzene in the soil sampling. He noted that benzene was often found where gasoline had been dumped and noted that some old farm practices or trespassing teens might have dumped bad gas or other fuel solvents illegally. But he made a point of saying that even though it was a possibility, he didn't think it was likely that that current farm owners were conducting such a practice. He said the combination of chemicals signaled something more serious in nature and he recommended that there be a follow-up visit made in the spring to check on the fern. "If further or continued distress is detected at that time, a deeper study of soil and water contaminants is recommended." Why hadn't Martin pushed for that now, and why didn't he investigate further? It seemed to her that maybe you just had to live in a place long enough to know its history. As she did. She read back over the report, her gaze stopping on the list of chemicals... words she couldn't pronounce but ones that looked familiar. Where had she seen them? She put the report down, took a sip of tea and closed her eyes. She felt the baby kick, pulling her thoughts away from the Hartford Fern for a moment. Why hadn't Win called her back? Now that he knew she was going to keep the baby, what was he thinking? Would he ever come back to Asheville if he felt his name was clear?

She got out of the tub and dressed in her most comfortable sweats, before going down to the kitchen where she sat at the table and watched her father move around the barnyard. He was a stubborn man, and she knew his anger was really fear over possibly losing the farm, just as clamping down on Clay had been fear, and she wasn't sure what to do about any of it. She opened her computer, with a yellow legal pad beside her. She wasn't sure but something kept pulling her back to Tina calling the mill a ghost looming over her family. Sister Rachael had said the Barbos were at the root of it all and the way to clear Clay's name. The Pascals had said all things were connected—they meant it in a different way, but no one could deny the ways the mill seemed to tie everything together. So, she started with the mill.

Jordan found the facts, easily. The Riverside textile mill covered several acres of the original 15-acre mill site, which from 1809 to 1879 had housed a cotton mill. Dyeing cotton began in 1879 and operated until 1904. Three other textile-finishing companies operated there through the 1900s, using pigment, dyes and solvents to print colors and patterns on fabric. Up until the 1970s drains in the floor flowed directly into the river to dispose of waste. In the late 1970s, when the DEP demanded that waste be stored in drums and shipped away, the mill bosses complied for a while, but when the drum handler folded, the bosses buried barrel after barrel—1500 drums collected on the site. In the late 1980s, a man reported to the DEP seeing an employee dump a barrel of dye into the river. Then in 2006, the mill burned down, the result of a mysterious fire. It had taken years, but finally the DEP investigated and among the chemicals they found? Trichloroethylene and benzene. The Riverside Textile site became a national Superfund site. Jordan closed her eyes and leaned back in her chair. She rubbed her stomach. The mill burning down was beginning to look like a good thing... the only thing that would have stopped the pollution. And the barrels had been removed. Was it possible the pollution had reached upstream? All the way to their parcel of land on Main Street? It was a half mile from the mill site. Jordan didn't know enough about aquifers to know. And what had been the effect on the Barbos of the mill burning, except the most obvious: losing their jobs? Jordan put that question on her yellow pad. They'd lost their jobs, but it was more than ten years ago, and a lot of people had lost their jobs, too, and had since bounced back, at least a bit. But not the Barbos. Did that explain Tony's fascination with the place? Why had Tim thought that exploring the site could clear the accusation against Win? What had Clay gotten himself involved with?

The cursor flashed on the screen.

Jordan knew only one place she could find the information to answer her questions. She tucked into her backpack a yellow legal pad with her questions scrawled across the page, and a sharpened pencil and drove to the Asheville Town Library. The library had been renovated just the year before and moved from the old town hall to its own space, which was light and airy with the familiar smell of dusty books mingled with new carpet and freshly sawed wood. A class of kindergartners flocked around the head librarian Mrs. Grady's desk waiting to check out books. Jordan stepped into the stack, not ready to be seen. She remembered how years ago the grades had walked from the school to the library to get books for the week. It had been that way for decades, but now a bus waited in the parking lot. The town really did need a new school, Jordan thought, just not on their field. She waited for the last of the children to take their books to Mrs. Grady, who stamped them as she greeted each child by name.

Mr. Pascal had said that he and Mrs. Barbo had graduated in 1999. There on the shelf were the yearbooks from the high school. Jordan pulled the 1999 yearbook off the shelf and went quickly to the individual photos. T. Toulousse, Angela. There she was. Mrs. Barbo. Favorite movie: *Coalminer's Daughter.* Favorite Singer: Patsy Cline. Favorite song: "Walkin' After Midnight." Those things seemed like ancient history. Could that really be Mrs. Barbo as a teenage girl? Beautiful. Voluptuous. Movie star quality. Dark blue eyes, almost violet and high curved brows and cheekbones. And there was Mr. Pascal, looking very much the same as he did right now. Jordan flipped quickly through the pages, looking for Mr. Barbo. He wasn't there. She picked up the yearbook from 1998. No, not there either. 1997? There, on the second page, stood Mr. Barbo in a tight T-shirt, Levi's jeans and a hard sexy look. Thick dark hair, feathered away from his face and handsome, yes, but angry handsome. And the editor of that year's yearbook, none other than Mr. Z. She'd forgotten that he'd grown up in Asheville. She picked up the yearbook with Mrs. Barbo's picture and held them side-by-side. Mrs. Barbo as a teenager had the most romantic aura about her. Jordan couldn't imagine how the two of them had gotten together. Except by some mercurial attraction... like her and Win.

The kindergarten teacher saw her in the stack and came over interrupting her. "Jordan? Thank you so much for those adorable pencil cases. The kids really appreciated them."

Jordan jumped and closed the yearbooks. "Oh, no problem," she said, sliding the books back on the shelf. "I had them kicking around my closet."

"About Principal Bennett. I want you to know sometimes we find her difficult to deal with too... she can be a bit rigid about the rules and regulations, but she has a good heart. Mr. Z is working on her, and she's softening her position. I think you'll get approved to come in, so keep your head up."

She bolted out the door to keep up with her class before Jordan could even say thank you. It gave her a little extra confidence to approach Mrs. Grady.

"Hey there, Mrs. Grady, how are you?"

Mrs. Grady looked up and pushed her glasses back in place. She looked at Jordan's stomach as she came around the desk and hugged her.

"You heard?" Jordan asked.

Mrs. Grady nodded. "Small town, as we both know." She looked around to be sure no one was within earshot, and then she said, "I don't tell many people this, Jordan, but I was pregnant before Mr. Grady and I got married."

It was the last thing Jordan expected to hear from Mrs. Grady. Her eyes widened.

Mrs. Grady seemed amused. "Well, no need to look so shocked. Us old folks weren't always old, you know."

Jordan laughed. These people were surprising her. She thought she knew this town and its nature, expected narrowness and judgment, but she was wrong. In the front room, three rows of stacks held adult fiction and nonfiction. Mrs. Grady shared the librarian's desk with her assistant and there were no plush chairs to welcome visitors but rather simple straight-backed wood chairs around tables, but Mrs. Grady was still like a proud mother. The top half of the fresh white walls contrasted with the dark green beadboard around the bottom, put up by a local carpenter who'd volunteered his labor. Jordan felt a flood of gratitude to this woman who had for so many years made so little seem like so much with nothing more than a few stacks, and a vision of what was possible for the children. She was the repository for more than books.

"It doesn't have to throw you," Mrs. Grady was saying.

"I know," Jordan said. "Thank you. The… baby…" It was still hard for her to say these words out loud, "… is due in February."

"You could enroll at a community college," Mrs. Grady offered.

Jordan told her she'd applied.

"I'm so sorry about your brother, honey. It's a tragic loss. He was a good boy."

"I know," Jordan said. She trusted Mrs. Grady. She told her about the boys being at the waste site and also about Win's phone conversation with Tim and lastly about Tony's fascination with the site, according to Tina, because it somehow haunted their parents. She told Mrs. Grady that she wanted to research the Riverside Mill and what chemicals had been found there, but she didn't tell her about Eugene Martin's report.

Mrs. Grady was looking doubtful. "What do you hope to find, Jordan?"

Jordan stopped. What did she hope to find? "I just want to understand what they were looking for."

"Nothing good is going to come from digging up that history. Those were hard times for the town." She pushed up her gold-rimmed glasses and seemed to understand what Jordan wasn't saying about needing to know to be able to move forward with her life. "Honey, if it helps you move on, then of course, I'll help." She grabbed keys out of her desk. A middle-aged woman with a soft face came from the back room.

"Jordan? Nina Fitch. My assistant. You might want to grab a table."

Nina smiled at Jordan and beckoned her to follow to the back room.

Mrs. Grady came back a few minutes later rolling the library cart stacked with binders. "Do you want them all now or do you want to look at them one at a time?"

Jordan shrugged and when Mrs. Grady gave her a binder, Nina said, "I worked at the mill. So did my mother and my first husband. It was a terrible thing when it burned down. I was a tuber. I rolled cloth onto the tube once it had been dyed and when it was ready for a shade, if it needed one, I yelled, 'shade!' and the shader would come over and put that in."

"What was Mrs. Barbo?"

"We had tubers and crimpers and shaders," Nina said. "But

Angela Barbo wasn't any of those." The two women exchanged glances, then Mrs. Grady left the room and came back with a file full of news clippings. She started laying them on the table. As Mrs. Grady spread out the clippings, Nina opened a desk drawer and took out a brown paper towel with thin printing, "To Evelyn. Open." Jordan opened the paper towel, hoping Nina was sharing something more about Mrs. Barbo. But it was a poem Nina's mother had written.

"If Mrs. Barbo wasn't any of those things, what did she do?" Jordan asked, her voice growing impatient.

Nina regarded her with a funny look. "She worked in the office for the big bosses. Always had her nose stuck up in the air. She came in and walked right by like we were invisible. We didn't like her one bit. The rest of us were like family. That's how I met my first husband."

Mrs. Grady had run to the front desk to help a patron. She came back with an album. "I've got some old photos here." One collage included an old black-and-white aerial photo of the mill complex in the 1920s and another of men harvesting refrigerator-sized blocks of ice from the pond into a wooden sleigh drawn by two great Belgians. In the background, children skated, and men hovered.

"Ice never freezes like that anymore," Nina said, seeming to forget Jordan as she entered history, trying to name some of the 'old-timers' as they referred to them, from a picture. Hearing one of the names, an elder woman who'd been sitting in a chair reading a newspaper, came over to the table.

"Jerry Chamberlain was my father."

"He was one of the big bosses," Nina said. "You're—"

The woman seemed pleased to be acknowledged that way. "Evelyn Chamberlain. Yes, we lived on Bonus Row."

"Bonus Row?" Jordan asked.

Nina pointed out another photo from the 1960s of the row of houses lining the river next to the mill. It was the same row of houses where the Barbos now lived, only as one-family homes, well-kept. "They called it Bonus Row because the bosses lived here with their families and every year they got the big bonuses," she said.

Jordan glanced back to the photo of the workers in front of the mill. A tall handsome man stood out in the center of the group. "Who's this?" she asked.

"That's Jimmy Barbo," Mrs. Grady said.

Jordan bent closer to the photo where Mr. Barbo's arm circled his wife's waist. But her attention wasn't on him. Her head tipped away from him, her hair tumbling to one side as she looked toward the far end of the group—the very corner of the photo. Unfortunately, the photo was overexposed and whoever had been standing in the line of her gaze showed only as a white blur. Jordan squinted, analyzing the gaze of Angela Barbo. It was not sly, but rather yearning, though not for her husband.

Nina nodded. "There were rumors about Jimmy Barbo."

"They never proved them," Mrs. Grady said.

"No, they never did," Evelyn Chamberlain agreed.

"What rumors?" Jordan asked.

"That's why they're called rumors, Jordan. Because there's no truth to them. Don't go there," she warned.

"He never could get another job," Nina said.

"Weren't any jobs to get," Mrs. Grady said sharply.

"Took a bad turn after that," Evelyn Chamberlain said. "With the drinking."

Before Jordan could push, Mrs. Grady said, "We should let Jordan get back to work." She'd spread clippings from the front section of *The New York Times* describing how the 150-200 workers had escaped unharmed from the fire. A photo showed people sitting on rooftops to get a better view as a mushroom-shaped cloud of black smoke shot from 300-foot flames. Underneath, the quote said, "This used to be a mill town, you see."

"The mill paid us good money," Nina was saying. "Nowhere else around here could we have jobs like that."

"My father didn't know about the dumping," Evelyn Chamberlain said. "We lived right there on the river."

"That's what I'm trying to find," Jordan said. "Do you have the DEP report on chemicals found at the site?"

"It's that second binder," Mrs. Grady pointed. "But I'm telling you, Jordan, the things that happened back then are better left buried."

Chapter 19

When Jordan pulled into the driveway, she was relieved to see both her father and mother's vehicles gone. She climbed the stairs to her room and plopped down on the bed. Her neck felt stiff, her shoulders ached, the muscles weaving across her abdomen cramped and pulled or were they stretching? God, she had no idea what was happening to her body. She lifted her shirt and unzipped her skirt so she could get a better look. She'd never known her stomach could get so huge! It looked like she'd swallowed a balloon, and this was just the beginning. She got under the covers and pulled the comforter up over her head. She could hear the leaves scraping against the house on their final descent and the calves calling in hunger. She couldn't roll over because her breasts hurt no matter which way she turned. Hot tears streamed down her cheeks. On the bookshelf near her head, an empty space. She'd returned her library books, books four months overdue, books she'd borrowed when she was preparing her summer reading list. Mrs. Grady had waived the fines and taken the books back with a sigh. Jordan looked up at a wooden whale Clay had carved for her and felt a resolve float up from deep within reminding her why she'd started this—for him, though she was beginning to see that she needed to finish it for herself, and maybe, for all of them.

Reading the DEP report of the Riverside fire stirred anger that Jordan didn't really know how to handle. The report described the ruins, visited by the DEP *seven months* after the fire. What had taken so long? Was it that Asheville was a poor town, easy to ignore? *Seven months* before the DEP came to see those 1500 drums of waste leaking into the ground. Thirty different compounds, many known carcinogens, along with heavy metals, running into the ground water that 200 nearby residents drank *every day*. Among those chemicals: *trichloroethylene* and *benzene*. But like the toxic chemicals, her anger flowed from the mill to the residents, who according to the DEP report, vandalized test sites, shot bullet holes through the drums, and largely ignored the DEP call for public comment on the pollution. Jordan read Eugene Martin's report, again. How had these chemicals come to be on their land when the DEP map showed the aquifer flowing into town, and the river—far downstream from their land. And what did any of this have to do with Clay and Tim and Tony?

Jordan picked up her cellphone. Tina answered on the first ring. How much could she share over the phone?

"My mother's home," Tina whispered. "Not now."

"Okay, let's set that study date. I'll text you," Jordan rushed to get the words out before Tina hung up. She heard her father calling her. She was supposed to have completed all the outside chores so that they could begin milking. "Cows are out. Come now," he called from the foot of the stairs. Chasing cows was the last thing she wanted to do. If the fence was down, they were going to have to fix that before they could even catch the cows. "How are we going to manage this farm if you come in for afternoon breaks?" Sam said as she descended the stairs. "Do you think we're running a retirement community here?" She saw his face held affection—he was teasing, just a little like his old self.

She brushed past him and out the door. The cows were nowhere to be seen. "Where are they? How'd they get out? Do we have to fix the fence?"

Sam shook his head. "Floppy opened the gate again. They're down in the lower lot." He smiled. The cows and their personalities amused him, and he particularly liked this smart little heifer. She'd led the heifers to freedom several times before and now Sam declared he'd reinforce the gate with double electric wiring.

"I hate that stupid cow!" Jordan said.

But Sam only laughed. The cows' antics still had the power to lift his spirits. Walking beside her now, he handed her a long stick to wave the cows in the direction they intended. They walked down the road and Chestnut followed. She loved a good cattle round up and it had been a couple months since the last one.

"You went to the library?" Sam asked.

Jordan nodded her head. "I had to return some overdue books." She was sure her father would disapprove her digging into the mill, chasing the illusive past when there was so much to do in the present.

Sam kept his gaze on her. "I'm glad to see it. The library—that's your world."

"Dad, did you ever have any dealings with the people who ran the dye mill?"

Instead of looking at her, Sam squinted at the herd. He was good at keeping a stone face, but underneath that ran a ripple of fear. "We should just let them eat it now. When their bellies are full, we'll take 'em home and start milking." Cows in the fields spelled sacrilege for a farmer, but as if to prove himself, Sam settled on a boulder, and watched the cows rip through the stalks.

"Dad?"

Sam tapped his stick on the tar. Tap. Tap. Like he was tapping out some mystery coded for her.

"Dad?!"

Tap tap. "What makes you ask a question like that?" Just then, a car rounded the bend, interrupting them and illuminating Floppy, who'd stepped onto the pavement to eat a few green leaves hanging there. Sam jumped up, shouting, "Slow down!" The driver stopped and opened his door. He looked at Jordan and Sam standing in the road. Jordan felt the adrenaline pumping. It could have been a terrible accident. She saw the man's mouth moving. She was afraid he might scream and be unpleasant.

But the guy was laughing. "I've never seen anyone walking their cows on the road!" he said. "You do this every day?" His license plate had a dealer sticker from Hartford.

Jordan held her breath, waiting for Sam to yell, but he didn't. "Cows got loose," he said. "We're just about to walk them home. You need to drive slower on these country roads."

"You need a hand?" the guy asked. "I always wanted to be part of a cattle roundup." His wife was saying something from the passenger's side and Jordan noticed she wore a scarf wrapped around her hair.

Sam shook his head in disbelief. "This isn't Hollywood," he muttered, but the man didn't seem to notice.

The guy spoke to his wife. "Come on, honey. Be a sport. Just slide behind the wheel and follow." He closed the door as she slid into the driver's seat, yanking the scarf so that her long, dark hair tumbled around her shoulders. "Thank you," he said, even though they hadn't invited him to help. "Tell me, how does this work?"

Sam handed him a stick. "Don't let them get into those woods." He seemed amused by this man in his Red Sox baseball cap and sweatshirt. "Their bellies are full so they should come right along now. They'll want to be milked. Jordan, you take the lead." Sam climbed between the strands of barbed wire to reach the herd. "Time to get you girls home," he said and then to the man, "You're not local?"

"No," the man said. "This is beautiful country. You own all this land?"

"We do," Sam said, "but we're just caretakers, really."

"That's a nice way of seeing it," the man said, easing into the silence with them. "We just came out to see Gravity Hill. We're making our way around the country documenting these mystery spots for a book we're writing, and we read about this one on someone's blog, talking about three boys who were killed. Tragic thing."

Her father was having trouble holding back his tears. There they were, finally, his tears for Clay, and in front of a complete stranger. "Eh, it is," Sam said, as if taken by surprise by his own emotion. "One was my son. Clay."

"I'm so sorry," the man said. "Forgive me." They walked the cows straight into the barn without incident or further talking and Sam closed the gate. The man shook Sam's hand. "Thanks for letting me help," he said. "Again, I'm very sorry for your loss."

Sam held the man's hand, as if he was taking his measure and whatever it was he wanted to say was stuck in his throat.

Jordan could feel Clay beside her. "Whatever you write," she said, "remember to tell people that it's always the things you can't see that hold the most power."

The man pulled out a little spiral notebook and scribbled in it. "Will do," he said before he slid in beside his wife and they drove away.

Jordan began getting the machines ready for milking, when her phone rang. She recognized Win's number and answered immediately. "Why haven't you called me?" she asked in a brusque tone.

"I'm sorry," Win said. "We had a big storm and I got put on a crew working 24/7 to get the damage cleared and the power going. It took days."

"You didn't have time to even text?" Jordan hated the way she sounded.

"I was out there, no reception whatsoever. I said I was sorry."

"I was worried. A text takes one minute. You know what? I'm busy. I can't talk to you right now." She hung up, regretting herself, because this wasn't the way she wanted to act. Win was the very person she wanted to talk to and what he said was reasonable. Her father worked silently beside her. He hadn't answered her question about the Riverside mill, either, which made her feel even more he was hiding something. And what made it worse, it was her birthday and it was clear that her parents had forgotten. Clay would never have forgotten. She longed to talk to someone she could relate to.

Chapter 20

The only people her age, besides Tina, (who hadn't yet answered her text), were the Dexter twins and Dale Thomas. She hadn't seen them since the shower, but when she called the twins, they immediately agreed to call Dale and meet her at the ice cream shop in Killingly. There was nothing in Asheville and although she didn't want to eat ice cream, the only other choice was the pizza parlor, with few booths and no privacy. Jordan got to the ice cream shop first, selected a booth, and ordered a cup of decaffeinated coffee. A few minutes later, the twins came in with Dale and greeted her cheerfully as they crowded into the booth. Jordan immediately began to feel better.

The waitress, her name tag said Patti, poured them coffee and chirped, "Here they are. The three musketeers."

"We come here every day," Lynne explained to Jordan.

Patti reached into her apron for a few creamers. "And they're the worst tippers," she joked. They all laughed. Jordan saw that they were happy. The twins ordered a sundae to split, Dale ordered a burger and when Jordan ordered chicken soup, Lynne glanced at her stomach.

"I really appreciate you guys coming out on such short notice. I've missed you." Their faces, which had been so open and generous at the Woodstock Fair, were now a bit guarded. Jordan remembered her erratic behavior in the barn and leaving the shower so early after dancing with Win and understood why they might proceed with caution. She'd garnered the support of some adults—Alice and Mr. Z and Mrs. Grady, but those were adults who understood the events of the past few months.

"First, let me say I'm really sorry about how I treated you guys at the fair, when you did so much to help me." She looked down at her hands... her napkin lay in a shredded pile.

After a moment, Laura said, "You were under a lot of stress."

"It's true, but that's no excuse. Everything... everything that's happened is not an excuse to treat you guys badly. I value your friendship." They sat back in their chairs and so did she. "You've probably heard some rumors by now." They averted their eyes when she pointed to her belly. "It's a long story and I don't really want to get into it."

"You don't have to," Laura said. "It's your business."

"Thank you. You probably know that Mrs. Barbo has brought this claim against my parents and our insurance only pays a part of it. So far, she's not backing down. She wants a million dollars."

"A million dollars!" Spoons clinked against bowls as they absorbed this.

"Pretty unreal, huh?" It felt good to talk about it with people her age.

"Was it the guy that showed up at the shower, Jordan?" Lynne asked. "Are you going to marry him?"

"Really, Lynne?" Laura said.

"Yes, it's him and let's just say that marriage would not be a good move right now. I've got to figure some things out for myself." Silence. She thought they probably would like Win. "I... have a proposal for you guys. It's something I think could be good for all of us. Are you guys still working part-time?"

"We've got three days at Hasenbaum greenhouse," Lynne replied. "The Thomson tree farm might give us some work during the holidays making wreaths and stuff—but no commitment."

"It's not enough," Laura said. "We need full-time work. We can barely keep our car insured."

"What about you, Dale?"

"I'm on the waiting list at UConn for spring semester. Radcliff Hicks. It's like a fifteen-percent chance," he said.

"And if that doesn't happen, I'll apply again for next semester, but I have to find something. My parents want me to pay rent. They're afraid I'll never stand on my own two feet." He smiled at Laura and she, in turn, smiled at Jordan. "The wedding is set for next spring."

Jordan pushed her soup away untouched. It hurt, thinking of two people so easily planning a life together, even though she was happy for them. No matter how much work she gave herself, she sometimes wondered if she would ever have someone to love her like that, especially now with a baby in tow. She took another napkin from the dispenser and folded it neatly in her lap. "Well, maybe you will like my idea, then. Without Clay, there's just too much work for me and Dad to do alone, but even if we could handle it, the farm would continue to struggle. We need to do something differently. My mom has gotten involved with these farm stands and this slow—"

"Slow food movement?"

"Yes, and community supported agriculture."

"Right. CSA! Mr. Hasenbaum says that the future of farming is people willing to pay more for produce without chemicals and that it's better for the land."

"Really? So, you're interested? My mom could really use some help and I thought, what if we had our own farm stand? You know—"

"With organic milk," Dale filled in. "And eggs, they're easy and you can make a big margin of profit."

"And beef," Lynne added. "Lots of people in this area are interested in organic beef."

"With the holidays coming up we could start with wreaths and greens," Laura said.

Jordan smiled. "And my dad could use some help with the chores, too, because to be honest with you, I don't plan to work the farm." Jordan felt a weight lift from her as soon as she said it. Before she was even finished, the twins were planning how they could arrange their schedules at the greenhouse and what materials they might find for wreath-making, and how much lumber they would need for building a makeshift roadside stand at the farm. Jordan decided this was the best birthday present, and it was one she had given herself.

Dale was more cautious. "I can commit for the rest of the fall, but beyond that—I need to see if I get into school."

"That's fine," Jordan said. "Whatever you can do."

They spent a few more minutes talking. The waitress came over to clear the table; she dropped the checks in the middle and Jordan snatched them up. Dale and the twins tried to grab them, but Jordan insisted. "I want to—please." They slid from the booth. "You all go ahead—I have to pee, it's a constant thing now." They said good-bye, promising to call within a day or so. Just as Jordan was unlocking her truck, a car pulled up beside her. Mrs. Barbo slid out muttering something to Tina who sat hunched with the GED book open on her lap. Jordan tapped on the window and smiled at Tina. Tina looked up and waved. Mrs. Barbo came around, her eyes on Jordan's stomach.

"If you can resist eating ice cream right now, you'll thank yourself later. It's hard to lose weight after the baby's born."

Jordan wasn't surprised by Mrs. Barbo's direct reference to her pregnancy, but she was surprised that she sounded genuinely concerned. She opened the truck door as far as it would go, another few inches, to shield herself.

Tina opened the window. "Mom, let's go. I don't want to be late for work." Mrs. Barbo hoisted her purse over her shoulder and went inside. "Sorry I couldn't talk earlier. I'm working tonight. We stopped to get sherbet for my dad," Tina said. "It's one of the only things he can digest now."

"When can you meet?" Jordan asked.

Tina twisted the safety gloves in her hands. "It'd have to be when my mother's not around."

Jordan could still feel the way hot bottles coming down the line burned through the thin cotton gloves. "How about tomorrow? Around 11?"

Tina watched her mother inside, scouring the sherbet

selection in the freezer. "That's good. My mother is going to visit her sister." Mrs. Barbo had moved to the cash register and was handing the cashier money.

"Okay," Jordan said, getting into her truck. "See you then."

Chapter 21

When she got home, her parents were sitting at the table. Sam was explaining to Diane the conversation he'd had earlier that day with the insurance company lawyer. The lawyer had assured Sam that the company would do whatever it could to settle the claim with the Barbos but was clear that the $500,000 limit of coverage was what the company would pay. The check was being issued to complete their portion of the claim, but the attorney had continued the dialogue with Mrs. Barbo and her attorney, raising issues he thought might deter the suit. He threw words out at Sam such as contributory negligence, which Sam now explained meant arguing that Tony might be partially to blame for getting into the car drunk himself, but he'd also told Sam the Barbos had a claim with provable damage; pursing the Hawkins for more money was within their legal right.

"Well, I would like to understand why, if the insurance company is going to pay the Barbos $500,000, how Mrs. Barbo thinks she can ask for more?" Jordan interrupted.

Her father took a deep breath. "There's a legal answer, and there's a psychological answer. Let me try to explain what the attorney said." He had a note pad with his neat printing on it and he consulted it. "The fact that Tony survived the accident with burns over sixty percent of his body and died three days later, brings in the issue of pain and suffering. While this is very emotional for all those involved, the court is going to look at this as a practical matter. They are going to try to measure exactly *how much* pain and suffering."

Diane pulled herself up straight and pressed her fingers

to her temples as if squeezing her head to get rid of the painful image.

Sam went on. "Three days is three days. While heart-rending for Tony's parents to watch him die, he didn't linger for months so this reduces the amount any court would award in damages." Jordan had never thought about the Barbos sitting hunched in the hospital watching Tony die. She didn't want to feel any compassion for Mrs. Barbo, but now, being pregnant, thinking about the life growing within her, she couldn't help but feel a little of Mrs. Barbo's grief. "And Tony was a machinist at a little tool-and-die place in the industrial park," Sam continued. "He didn't have any benefits at all. He couldn't even afford health insurance."

"Well, there's not going to be much loss of income then," Diane offered.

"That's what the attorney said. He said that when parents bring these suits, the courts argue that at some point in the deceased's life, he was likely to have moved out and lived independently, perhaps started a family, so the parents would not have benefitted from his future income." Jordan understood that the attorney needed to build this kind of case against the Barbos, and one part of Jordan was relieved to hear it, but hearing her father recount the attorney' assessment was also giving Jordan a chance to absorb the fact of what had been lost: three lives, not just Clay's life, but Tim and Tony's as well. She had been so focused on her own loss, and her family's loss. Did Mrs. Barbo fear if she let the suit go that she would be abandoning justice for Tony? Was it possible to get justice when they had all died in a truly tragic and accidental way?

"Are you all right, dear?" her mother asked.

"This is sad, Mom."

Diane nodded. She pressed her palms into the table and wiped away some invisible dust. "I know, honey. That's why I've been saying not to see Mrs. Barbo as the enemy. They just want someone to compensate them for their tremendous loss."

"Well," Sam said, "The attorney said that how the court values that loss of life can cause more trauma for the family, instead of bringing healing. That's what they're trying to get through to the Barbos now."

It might be they were all in need of healing, Jordan thought. This made her feel not better or worse for knowing it, but simply connected and strangely, not so alone. Her parents had so much to deal with, she decided not to remind them they'd missed her birthday.

She stood up. "I need to go to bed now," she said shifting through the stack of the mail on the table. There were two envelopes addressed to her, one in bold handwriting, no return address. She snatched it from the pile along with the second, more formal envelope, and hurried up the stairs, locking her bedroom door behind her. She plopped down on the bed and ripped open the hand printed envelope. Three one-hundred-dollar bills fluttered to the floor. She scooped them up and read the lines.

> *Dear Jordan,*
>
> *How are you? Sorry I haven't called. But I was on an emergency crew, and we were in the mountains where there was no reception. I made extra money and I'm sending some now and have more for later I'll try to call tonight.*
> *Win.*

Jordan looked at the date and figured Win must have cashed his check and gone straight to the post office to mail the money, even before he had called her. She felt bad about hanging up on him. She was going to have to apologize. The other letter was an acceptance to the community college in Maine. Was it a coincidence that Win should send money and that she should get into the community college in Maine the same day? That made two birthday presents, and they'd both come in unexpected ways.

Chapter 22

The next morning, Jordan stopped into the General Store. She'd been avoiding Maxine, but now she needed her. She waited for people to clear out and once they did, she explained to Maxine that it was Mrs. Barbo pushing the lawsuit and still pursuing her family even after the $500,000 the insurance company was awarding them. Maxine once again expressed outrage about the Barbos' demand for additional money, which was exactly what Jordan wanted. She hoped that by Maxine broadcasting this, Mrs. Barbo could be shamed into dropping the suit.

But Maxine wasn't letting Jordan off the hook so easily. "Please don't tell me this is your whole mission now, Jordan."

Jordan stood at the door, looking out at the bridge as Maxine spoke. Brother Michael and Sister Rachael were just crossing the bridge, heading toward the General Store. Sister Rachael was the last person Jordan wanted to see.

"No, Max," she said as she hurried out the door. "I'm taking positive steps, okay?" It was eleven o'clock. Would Mrs. Barbo be gone, as Tina had said? And what about Mr. Barbo? But Jordan didn't let fear stop her. She rapped on the door. Tina opened it. She wore her hair up in a ponytail. She was pretty with her angled cheekbones and deep-set eyes, the chiseled chin and her creamy complexion, things generally hidden by her baseball cap.

Tina cocked her head and looked at Jordan for a moment, then pulled her oversized sweatshirt up over a curve of delicate shoulder and opened the door wide.

Jordan stepped inside and Tina shut the door behind her.

The hallway was dark and musty, with a carpet worn thin in places. Tina shifted her weight from one foot to the other.

"Is this still good?" Jordan whispered.

"Yeah. Come in." Tina reached up, tore the elastic from her ponytail and swept it tighter, winding the elastic around the thin little tail of hair. "I'm just about ready to give up."

"Don't," Jordan encouraged. "We can do this." She scolded herself—helping Tina came before her own interests.

"I hope so," Tina said. "You always were the smartest kid in the school."

"Well, for a smart kid, I haven't been very smart." At that Tina laughed.

"Mama!" There was a little call from inside.

"Mama's right here, Tori." Tina turned and walked into the adjoining living room, where her baby was standing in the playpen, rattling the side, her face pink with sleep, and one side creased with the lines of the blanket upon which she'd been resting. Tina picked her up and kissed her.

"God! These reading passages are so boring," Tina pointed to the GED book.

Jordan went to the table and scanned the passage. She pulled the book toward her and another chair beside her for Tina. She had a million questions she wanted to ask Tina about her mother and anything that might help stop the lawsuit, but she waited while Tina read the first passage. The place was neat, but a film of dust hung over everything. Jordan stared at Tony's graduation photo on the wall, and when Tina finished reading, she said, "He looks just like your mom did in high school."

Tina looked up abruptly. "How do you know that?"

"You can see the resemblance," Jordan explained.

Tina narrowed her focus. "No, you said how my mother looked in high school? How would you know that?"

Jordan squirmed. Tina kept her stare. "At the library, I was flipping through old yearbooks while I was waiting for Mrs. Grady to finish helping kids and I saw her picture. She was beautiful." On top of the TV in the corner sat another 8x10 glossy photo of Tony, kneeling in his football uniform. There were no other photos in the room. In fact, the room was almost devoid of mementos, almost as if the Barbos themselves had no comfort in their lives. "I never got the chance to say this to you. I'm sorry. We're all sorry." Jordan decided to take the plunge. "Sister Rachael snuck up to my car window after you left the parking lot the other day and she said everything goes back to the mill and your parents."

"Is that the only reason you're here?" Tina stood up, hugging her daughter.

"No, I want to help you *and* I want to get to the truth."

Tina took a few toys from a basket, tossed them in the playpen and set her daughter down. "But why go back all those years, to the mill and—my parents?"

"Sister Rachael—"

"There's something you should know." Tina interrupted her. "Rachael is my mother's sister."

"What!? Sister Rachael is your aunt?"

"I don't think of her that way. They haven't talked to each other in twenty years."

"Well, what—?" Jordan tilted her head away from Tina, as if trying to see her more clearly as related to Sister Rachael. She didn't see any physical resemblance between Tina and Sister Rachael, but the photo of the young Mrs. Barbo bore a striking resemblance to the wide set and expressive eyes of Sister Rachael.

"My grandparents were hardasses. When Rachael hooked up with Brother Michael, she was just 16. They couldn't deal with it, and they cut her out of the family."

Jordan murmured and Tina went on. "Rachael and my mom never talked after that, even though my grandparents did the same when she married my dad. Just erased us and boom, gave their farm, everything, to my uncles."

"That sucks." Jordan felt bad, even though she didn't want to, for Mrs. Barbo. She didn't think Tina knew the other part of the story the one Mr. Pascal had told her of Mrs. Barbo wanting to leave Mr. Barbo.

"So, I think Rachael might be just a little obsessed with my family."

Jordan picked up the GED book and flipped to the scoring page. Even though she didn't think Tina meant to imply it, she felt maybe she and Sister Rachael had that in common. An obsession about Mrs. Barbo. She didn't like to think of herself that way. She turned her attention to the scoring and explained the answers to the ones Tina got wrong. The girls put their heads together and worked on another reading comprehension passage. Tina took a second test and scored better.

"See?" Jordan said. "Already you're doing better."

"Yeah, I feel like someone finally explained it in a way I can understand," Tina said. "Thank you." Tina went to the refrigerator and pulled out a bottle and a syringe. She dumped tealeaves in a pot. Essiac tea. Cindy Pascal drank Essiac tea when she was sick.

"They didn't get all those barrels when they cleaned up the mill site," Jordan said. Without giving too many specifics she explained about the carcinogens. "Maybe we should report that barrel our brothers found. Those chemicals could be the cause of your dad's cancer."

Tina handed Jordan a little cup of Cheerios. "Jordan, it was one barrel. My family's been drinking that water for decades. Would you like to feed these to Tori while I take my dad his tea?" She picked up the tray and went down the hall. Jordan went over to the playpen and picked up Tori, who gave her a big smile.

Jordan had never babysat. She didn't have much experience with kids.

"Hi!" she said. Tori smiled. The child was heavier than she'd imagined. She sat at the table and settled the baby on her lap and put a Cheerio on her finger. The little girl leaned forward and took it with her mouth, leaving glistening saliva on Jordan's finger. She chewed and swallowed, and they repeated the process. Tina came back to the living room just as footsteps sounded on the stairs and the door opened to Mrs. Barbo.

"Hi Mom. You're home early." Tina took her daughter from Jordan and stood up, moving toward her mother.

"What's she doing here?" Mrs. Barbo addressed Tina as if Jordan was invisible. She came into the room and her look went to the books spread on the table.

"What are you doing here?" Mrs. Barbo plucked the child from Tina as she spoke.

"She's helping me study." Tina yanked hard on her ponytail. "We were just finishing up."

"Gamma!" The toddler put her chubby little hands up to her grandmother's face and Mrs. Barbo's face lit up. "Hello, pretty girl. Let's go to the playground, shall we?" The Mrs. Barbo talking to her granddaughter was not the woman Jordan thought she knew and certainly not the woman talking to Tina. Mrs. Barbo put the baby's coat on, kissing her on the head as she did so and then went to the door and held it open, gesturing to Jordan.

Tina stood in the corner looking small. "Thanks for your help," she said, weakly.

"Goodbye, Jordan." Mrs. Barbo gave her a penetrating gaze and closed the door firmly behind her.

That night her mother made her favorite dish for dinner, chicken and biscuits. "Thanks mom. I love this," Jordan said, pulling her chair into the table eagerly.

"I know you do," Diane smiled. "Comfort food. Hardly any vegetables in it."

"It's still my favorite."

Sam teased that she had enough for three people on her plate. "But that's okay. We're celebrating."

"Celebrating what?" Jordan asked.

"Why didn't you tell us about your acceptance letter? I

didn't mean to snoop—I saw it when I was picking up laundry upstairs. This is great news, honey," she said.

Jordan decided to just appreciate her mother's positive response to her college acceptance this time around. "Mr. Z encouraged me," she said. "When Mrs. Bennett kicked me out, he said I needed to take a positive step. Our community college accepted me too—they sent the letter electronically. Either way, it's still not practical to think of school for next semester."

Diane and Sam exchanged looks. "Sure it is." Diane asked, "Have you been talking to Win? Does he know you're keeping the baby?"

"I told him," Jordan said.

"And?"

"He sent some money and told me to call him."

Her parents looked at each other and said nothing for a moment and then her mother spoke again. "This is a very good step—to begin school next semester."

Chestnut barked as headlights swung into the darkness. Jordan went to the window and peered out. "It's Tina Barbo."

Diane pushed herself back from the table and went to the door. "I'll go."

They heard Tina talking and then Diane saying, "Who's this little sweetie pie?" as she drew Tina into the living room.

"This is my daughter, Tori." Tina's face beamed with pride, then she glanced over to Jordan in the doorway and gave an almost imperceptible nod. "She has a rash and Jordan told me you might look at it?" Sam retreated out the back door, and Jordan wondered if he was offended by a visit from anyone in the Barbo family or if he was fed up with pregnant teenagers. Of course, they hadn't talked about a rash earlier. Tina's daughter had seemed fine. Why was she really there? Showing up on their doorstep was a bold move, and Jordan hoped it meant something more as Tina showed Diane the faintest of rashes.

"Oh, I have some cream you could use on this." Diane went out of the room.

Tina pulled Tori's shirt back down and hurried over to Jordan. "Maybe you're right about those chemicals, Jordan. I came to tell you... after you left, my parents had a big fight. My father told my mother to drop the lawsuit. My mom said no. She forbids me to see you and she took my phone so don't try to call me or text. But I need your help to get this GED, Jordan."

"I'll help you," Jordan said, caressing Tori's hand while she spoke. It was tiny and soft.

"Can we study at the coffee shop in Moosup before I go to work tomorrow? One o'clock? They have Wi-Fi."

Diane came back with a tube of cream, holding it out to Tina along with a slip of paper. "If the rash continues, call Dr. Beltone. Tell her I told you to call. She'll see you right away."

Tina hugged the little girl tight, and Diane put her arms around both of them. "You poor girls, worrying about these things. It's just a little irritation. I wouldn't worry much about it."

Tina said, "I better get her home and in bed before I have to get to work. See you tomorrow, Jordan?"

"Sure, see you then."

As soon as Tina was gone, Diane asked, "Since when did you become friends with Tina Barbo? And why did she say she'd see you tomorrow?"

"I'm trying to help her get ready for her GED test." Jordan explained seeing Tina at the glass factory trying to study on one of her breaks. She waited for her mother's criticism, but instead Diane left the room without a word and a moment later came back with a little velvet box. She placed the box in front of Jordan. "What's this?" Jordan asked.

"I'm proud of you, honey. What you're doing to help Tina when you have so much on your own plate." Inside the box lay a tiny gold cross and a baby ring. "My mother gave this to me when you were born," Diane said. "You may think your life has gotten off track, but I see a beautiful young woman developing. I was wrong to call you selfish. Pursuing your dreams and helping Tina pursue hers—I'm proud of you."

Jordan fingered the tiny cross and placed the box in front of the sonogram picture on her desk. "I can't wait to put it on him. Thanks, Mom." She didn't say it, but her mother's apology meant more to her than the gift itself. She decided it wasn't the right time to say anything about Mrs. Barbo and Sister Rachael being sisters, or to ask her mother about her father avoiding her question regarding the mill. Instead, when her mother left the room, she picked up her phone and texted Win. "Sorry I hung up on U. Thk U for note and $. Call me soon."

Chapter 23

The next day before meeting Tina, Jordan went to the local community college and picked up a catalogue. Dale and the twins were cleaning the calf pens and putting clean sand in the barn stalls. The pears, a mix of rotten and ripe, needed to be picked up from under the pear trees and separated into baskets. Each day, more customers flowed into the farm for raw milk and organic eggs. The teens' plan was meeting with more success than they'd imagined. They were already buying greens, too, even though the holiday was more than a month away. She had not yet heard from Mr. Z or Mrs. Bennett about going back to volunteer at the school, and Win hadn't yet responded to her text of apology for hanging up on him.

Tina waited inside the coffee shop, sitting at one of the booths, books spread before her and two cups of coffee on the table. She waved to Jordan. "Hey."

"Wow. Look at you."

"Yeah. Look at me," Tina said. "I just took a practice test, and my math score is in the eighty-fifth percentile. Not bad for a dummy."

"You're not dumb," Jordan said, sliding into the booth. "You're going to get your GED and get a really good job as a bookkeeper."

Tina opened the GED book to the reading comprehension. "Maybe so, if I can pass this." She seemed eager to get started so they got right to the passages and strategies for analyzing an author's rhetoric. "But why do they have to use words like that?" Tina asked. "Can't they use plain language and just say the message?"

"Sometimes it's not just delivering a plain message," Jordan explained. "They intentionally use language to persuade an audience."

Tina groaned. "Okay, go on."

And so, they did. Tina's score took another leap with the next practice test. She sat back, eyes bright, and said, "I'm going to pass this test. I feel it. Thank you, Jordan."

"You're the one doing the work," Jordan said. "Thank yourself." They slid out of the booth and Jordan noticed they were the same height. "Last night my mom apologized for the way she treated me. She said us becoming friends made her see me different. When I saw the way your mom loves Tori, and how she looked in those pictures Mrs. Grady showed me at the library—I started to see her different too. Do you think Tony was trying to get to the bottom of this whole mill mystery to help her?"

"Maybe." Tina hefted her backpack over her shoulder and headed for the exit.

"You could ask your dad. You're close to him, right?"

They got to their cars and Tina shoved her backpack into the back seat before answering. "He's not doing well, Jordan. I don't know how much time he has left."

"I'm so sorry," Jordan said, but she couldn't let it go. "All the more reason. He may be the only one who can help."

Tina said nothing as she slid behind the wheel and closed the door between them. Jordan couldn't imagine the stress she was under, but she hoped Tina heard her because they needed each other, and time was running out.

Chapter 24

Jordan had two more tutoring sessions with Tina over the next week and both times Tina told her she hadn't had an opportunity to talk alone with her dad. Jordan was losing patience. At home, they were finishing chopping corn into silage. They pushed it into an enormous pile in the barnyard, which they then covered over with long sheets of black plastic, like a thick sausage wrapped in Saran Wrap. During those long stretches of chores, Jordan thought about Win. She wondered when they would ever see each other again. They'd talked a couple of times now, but it seemed the more pregnant she got the more she thought about things she wanted to say, and she wrote them down until she had them all collected. She'd started to think about how much this baby was going to have to forgive her. Forgive her for getting pregnant so young, for being conceived not out of love but some crazy mix of grief and desire and most importantly, for not even trying to make a family with Win. One early morning as she was thinking that way, she called Win even though it wasn't yet six a.m. He answered. "Jordan. Is everything okay?"

"I had a dream I was having the baby and I called for help, but no one came. It was a just silly dream. Those kinds of dreams are pretty common, I hear." Jordan realized she was trying to reassure herself.

There was silence and then Win said, "Do you want me to come down?"

She did want Win to come down, but not if she had to suggest it. "No. No. I'm good... but thank you for offering. I have to get back to chores."

"You can call me anytime, and you can ask for help when you need it," she heard him say before she hung up.

She felt sad. Win was far away and when they talked on the phone, she felt she was getting to know and like him even more, but he wasn't there to share silly little things, like a bad dream and those things sounded stupid to her on the phone.

That morning the Pascals stopped by. It was late October and Jordan was five months pregnant. She'd put on her first maternity top, purchased on a shopping trip with her mother. The Pascals fussed over her for a few minutes, before saying they'd come to buy some of Diane's organic produce. They bought a fifty pound bag of potatoes and a twenty-five pound bag of onions, but Jordan felt glad they had come by to check on her. When they seemed satisfied that she looked healthy and happy, they turned their attention to her parents. Mrs. Pascal hugged Diane. She whispered something into her ear and Jordan saw tears and a softening in her mother's face. Mr. Pascal shook Sam's hand and drew him into an embrace. The suffering of parents losing children was a silent and solid bond between them, but Jordan felt she was also part of the living bond they now shared. Jordan felt her own spirits lift seeing the connection between them.

Jordan and Sam had finished milking early so Sam could go meet with the attorney regarding the lawsuit. Diane was off bringing vegetables to market. Dale and Laura rolled in after eleven o'clock with their thermoses of coffee and lunches in brown paper bags. They stuck their food in the refrigerator down in the barn and reported to her for work. They were laughing and carefree. Each day they treated her exactly the same as they had before she got pregnant, maybe even with a little more respect as they saw how hard she was working, but she didn't join in with their jokes—and today, she couldn't help but resent the fact that they seemed truly happy and content. When she waved the list of the day's chores at them, snapping because they were an hour late, they looked at each other and took the list. But instead of moving away, they huddled together and faced her.

"You know, Jordan," Laura said. "You don't seem happy."

"What do you mean?" Jordan asked. "I'm happy enough." The two looked at each other.

"It just doesn't seem like you are. Do you want to talk about it?"

"No," she said, moving away. "I do not." Her friends watched her walk away. Only Chestnut followed. "Shit," she muttered to him. "I wouldn't want to be around me, either." She went up to the house and took a nap even though it was still morning.

She was feeling better than she had been earlier when she returned to the barn, but still in no mood for what she stumbled upon. She was feeling groggy and leaden. The baby just seemed to weigh her down like an anchor and the hormones made her feel weepy and vulnerable. Yes, it was likely she was going to college in January and yes, Dale and Laura and Lynne were making vast improvements to the farm, but sometimes a person could have a million positive thoughts and not feel positive. She felt lonely. Which is why she was in absolutely no mood for the grunting sighs of passion she heard from the hayloft. At first, she thought perhaps it was a cow in heat and she peeked out to the aisle to see just who it might be so she could make a call to Dave, but the cows were lined up peacefully at the feed bunk, eating silage, their long tongues curling over the steaming feed. Then there it was again, a grunt, a groan—a giggle! Who was up there? Who the hell had the nerve to trespass on the farm and climb into their hayloft? She climbed the steps carefully, testing each rung first to make sure it would hold her pregnant weight. When she reached the top, she peeked over and saw two sets of legs, pants down around ankles and before she could stop herself—she knew those work boots with the red laces—she shouted:

"Laura!"

There was a scurry and flurry of activity and "Oh, shit!" uttered in a voice she also knew and the boots with the red laces disappeared behind a stack of hay bales and the larger, male boots which had been pinned in place by those on top, were next to disappear. The giggles became more easily identifiable. "What the hell, you two?" She hated the way she sounded. She hated that edge in her voice, the miserable jealousy.

"Jordan, be careful climbing down that ladder," Laura called. "If you fall…" Her voice caught and that made Jordan even unhappier that her friend whom she'd yelled at was more worried about her well-being than angry at her discourteous treatment. When she reached the solid cement floor, she went into the storage room and closed the door behind her. She slumped on an overturned five-gallon bucket. She could see her reflection distorted in the galvanized medicine chest on the shelf, the pulled down mouth, and the puffy eyelids. "Well, shit," she muttered. "Get over yourself. Don't you want them to be happy? Huh? Then let them be happy. Go out there and apologize and tell them you're sorry." But before she had the chance, a timid knock sounded on the thick wooden door.

"Jordan?" It was Laura. "Are you okay?"

Jordan opened the door just a sliver. She was going to apologize, but she didn't want Laura to see she'd been crying. "I'm sorry," Jordan said. "I had no right… I didn't mean…"

But Laura was laughing. "Oh, Jordan," she said, sticking her hand through the barest cracked opening in the door. "Look at my ring! Because of you and working here, Dale finally had enough money to get it."

And despite her earlier blues, Jordan threw open the door and grabbed Laura's hand to inspect the tiny diamond on Laura's finger. "Oh my God," she squealed. "That's great." And she meant it. It *was* great. Before Jordan could find Dale to both apologize and congratulate him, the loud motor of a motorcycle pulling into the barnyard interrupted them.

"Who's that?" Laura asked.

"Shit," Jordan uttered. "That's Win."

"The baby's father?" Laura said.

Jordan nodded. She and Laura peered out the window as Win dismounted his motorcycle and removed his helmet. His hair fell around his shoulders.

"Wow. He's gorgeous," Laura said. "How old is he?"

"Older," Jordan snapped. She poked her head in front of the tiny mirror hanging on the wall in the milk room to see her own hair poking out like snake coils from her head. "I look like a mess. Look at me."

"No, you don't," Laura said. "You look pregnant. Are you going out to greet him?"

Jordan zipped up her barn jacket and jammed a ski cap on her head. "I guess so."

"Lose the hat," Laura advised.

Jordan yanked it off and handed it to her.

"You go, girl!" Laura pushed her out the door.

Win stood in the barnyard, gripping his motorcycle as if he was afraid to go too far from it, but when he saw her, he did let go, and gave her a big smile. "Girl of the fairground, here I am."

She stepped up close to him. "This is a surprise."

"A good one?" Win asked.

"Yes."

"It's my day off," he said. "I know you said you were fine, but I thought I would take a ride to see you." He smiled again looking her over from head to toe. "New look."

"Well, I wasn't expecting company."

He considered her. "Prickly, that's what you are," he said. "I meant you finally look pregnant. A very nice look. Can I help you with chores?"

"We just finished giving the cows hay. Not quite time for afternoon chores yet. Would you like to come in and have some coffee or lunch?"

"Lunch sounds good," he said. He looked around the barnyard. "Your parents?"

"Not home at the moment," Jordan said. "You afraid to meet them?"

"If I was afraid to meet them, I wouldn't be here."

Jordan could see her rudeness wearing thin. Why was she being rude to him when all she really wanted was for him to wrap her in his arms?

Laura came out of the barn with Dale behind her. Jordan introduced them and Win stepped right up and shook Dale's hand. "I remember you guys were the couple who got engaged and had the party at the Legion Hall."

"Yes," Laura said, "but we didn't get to meet you. You're the mystery man. It's a pleasure to meet you now, Win."

"Dale just gave Laura her ring," Jordan said.

"Congratulations," Win gave them a broad smile.

He really had a great smile, Jordan thought as she took his hand. "I'm going to make some lunch. You guys want lunch?"

"No," Laura answered a little too quickly. "And take your time. We've got the chores covered."

Jordan ignored her friend's lack of subtlety and led Win to the house. When they got inside, Jordan took off her jacket, aware of Win's stare.

His face got very serious. "A lot has been happening. Can I feel it?"

They took a step toward each other, and Jordan took Win's hand and cupped it over the top of her stomach.

"He's asleep now, but sometimes this wakes him up." And sure enough the baby began to stir. Not a kick, but a hard knob poked across the top of her belly. "His elbow," she said. She went over to the refrigerator and got the most recent sonogram and handed it to him. Win turned it one way and then the other. Jordan put the sonogram up right and pointed. "There's his nose and his mouth and his hands. He always has them up in that funny position, like he's praying."

"And this?"

"That's his heart," she said. Win's eyes were full. "You can have it," Jordan said, turning away. She both wanted and didn't want to see his emotion. "I should have sent you one before now. It probably doesn't look the same on a text."

"It's okay. Thank you," he said, and he placed it carefully in his wallet and put his wallet back in his pocket. Jordan opened the refrigerator, pulled out a container, and ladled some of her mother's minestrone soup into a pot and set it on the stove.

Before she could turn the burner on, Win stepped up behind her and slipped his arms around her. "You're doing a great job," he said. "I know this isn't easy." Why was he here giving her so much affection? What did it mean? "Hey, did you hear me?" He pressed himself closer and his lips were caressing the back of her neck.

"I heard you. And I heard you in Maine when you said you didn't want to be a father."

He put his hands on her shoulders and turned her toward him and tipped her chin up so she would look him in the eyes. "I needed time to think about it. That's what I said then. And I thought about it. Now I'm saying you don't have to do this alone. I want to help. I want to be a parent." He kissed her and his lips found hers in the same way they first did on Gravity Hill with no apology and a tender longing that she found her own body answering. "And I'm hungry," he said, "but not for soup. How about you?"

She responded by putting her arms around him. He kissed her again with real tenderness. Jordan took his hand and led him up the stairs to her room, which looked entirely too small with him in it. Win locked the bedroom door, and then began to undress her. Jordan watched his face as he uncovered her stomach. He bent down and kissed her stomach and then he stopped. "It's okay," she said. "The pregnancy book says it's safe." That was all the permission he needed. They woke sometime later to the door of the house opening and Sam calling from the bottom of the stairs.

"Jordan?"

"Shit!" Jordan said. "My father's home."

Win started to laugh and then Jordan laughed too. "This is a little crazy," she said.

"Girl of the fairgrounds, you have a knack for stating the obvious. Let's go meet this head on."

"Wait, Win, what does that mean?"

"What do you want it to mean?" he asked.

She pulled her jeans on and stood, looking into his face. "Well, what are your thoughts about Asheville?"

"Non-negotiable," Win said. "I can't live in Asheville."

"But—."

"Jordan—" Sam's voice again, a bit more insistent.

"Coming, Dad."

"But if we cleared your—"

He shook his head. "My life's in Maine. I have a house and a job."

"Well, I'm not ready to get married."

"You could move in."

It was tempting, but if it didn't work, she'd be left with no solid ground beneath her feet. She said so.

"Well, then we'd know we tried. And we'd know each other better, which would be good for both of us—and the baby. And you would be getting solid ground under your feet because you'd be in school and getting help from me." And so, they opened the door and went downstairs to find Sam and Diane at the kitchen table with a pot of coffee brewing and four bowls of minestrone soup steaming hot on the table. Win had met Sam before, on the night of the Jack and Jill shower, but not Diane. He stepped over to her now, shook her hand, and smiled straight into her eyes.

Her mother was disarmed by him, Jordan could tell because Diane blushed and then looked at Jordan as if to say, "Okay I see how this happened." Jordan gave a little shrug and laughed nervously, and Diane said, "Let's have some soup, shall we?" Their attention went to the soup and Win said it was delicious and Diane sliced a loaf of whole grain bread that she gave Jordan credit for making and when Win tried it, he said it was the most delicious bread he'd ever had, and he ate most of the loaf.

When they were through eating, Win cleared his throat. He looked at Sam and Diane and he said, "I know you weren't expecting this—Jordan being pregnant—and you probably have a lot of questions about a lot of things, which I understand." He brought his water glass to his lips and took a quick sip and went on. "But I want you to know I respect your daughter, and I'm not going to leave her alone in this. I am going to be a parent and that's why I am here." He squeezed Jordan's hand.

Then, Sam cleared his throat, but before he could speak, Win said, "Jordan and I still have a lot to talk about, but we are talking about it and we're figuring it out."

"It's a little late for talking," Sam said, pushing his bowl away. "She's a nineteen-year-old girl, getting ready to become a mother when she should be thinking about four carefree years of college."

Win wiped his hands on his pants, looking down as if trying to find the words to speak. He looked up at Sam and said, "Yes, sir. I understand your point."

"And I don't think you should 'sir' me—how old are you?"

"Thirty, sir—I mean Sam—if I may. No disrespect here, but how old were you two when you got married?"

"Marriage? Don't tell me you two are thinking marriage right now? You hardly know each other."

"We were eighteen, Win. Straight out of high school, and we started dating our junior year." Diane spoke in an even voice as she got up from the table to clear the soup bowls.

"Jordan's mature beyond her years," Win said, getting up to help her. "There's still a lot for me to know, but I know that. And it's more than the two of us meeting up that changed her path, sir." Win paused for emphasis. "Life does that. It put the two of us together and we're taking this one step at a time. I appreciate you want to protect your daughter. And I hope you'll believe me—so do I. Her and our baby."

Diane took the dirty bowls from Win. "That's a very mature attitude and it's much appreciated. Would you like some coffee, or dessert?"

Win put his hands on the back of Jordan's chair. Just the feel of them there steadied her. "I better get going now," he said. "I have to work tomorrow and it's a long ride back."

"You got any other wheels?" Sam asked.

Win smiled, evenly. "Yes sir, I have a truck. And, I have a house and I have a decent job."

"Well," Sam answered. "Good. That's good."

"Dad, this isn't some horse trade," Jordan snapped. "I'm not doing anything crazy. And I'm asking you, please treat Win with respect." It grew quiet. Sam got up from the table, and he hesitated, but then he looked at Jordan, and shook Win's hand.

Win winked at her and said, "Sometimes crazy works." Despite herself, she laughed, and so did her mother, which then forced a begrudging smile from her father—that broke the tension and left her feeling that maybe she could fall in love with Win, but she couldn't leave Asheville, and follow him to Maine, not yet.

Chapter 25

The following Monday, Sam gave Jordan a list of errands to run after milking: buy supplies at Agway, parts at NAPA, pay bills at the post office and deposit checks at the bank. These were things he never asked her to do, so she was glad to do them.

"You'll probably be gone most of the day," he said. "Take yourself out to Friendly's for lunch." He handed her a twenty-dollar bill.

But she was tired after the errands and decided to go directly home and take a nap before starting afternoon chores. She could see lights on in the kitchen, glowing behind the steamed-up windows. Jordan wondered at first if perhaps someone from her mother's group of friends was over for a cooking spree, but those people drove smaller cars and pick-ups with stickers plastered all over with messages like "Be the Change You Want to See in the World." This Buick was new and shiny. Jordan hurried up to the house. When she opened the door, the sweet smell of her mother's beef stew enveloped her. There at the table with her parents sat a burly man who looked like a lumberjack stuffed into a dress shirt and tie with his sleeves rolled up.

Her father leaned toward the man and the open document; he was saying "But you guarantee the government has no other rights besides those we got here." He tapped the paper between them. "You rent that strip of land and we promise not to grow anything on it—just a cover crop and some conservation tillage, right?"

"That's correct," the man said. "For ten years."

"What's this?" Jordan said. The man frowned at the interruption and looked back at Sam, sliding the document closer to him. Sam sat back in his chair and folded his arms. "This is Mr. DeWitt from the Land and Water Conservation Fund. Bob, this is our daughter, Jordan."

Jordan's gaze went to the stack of papers on the table. "And what's going on here?"

Her mother and father exchanged glances. Her mother got up from the table and ladled Jordan a bowl of stew. "Come sit with us, honey," she said. Mr. DeWitt offered her his hand, but then his attention went back to Sam and Jordan immediately disliked him, thinking maybe Eugene Martin had alerted senior officials to the chemicals found in testing the Hartford Fern. Was this guy here in a legal capacity? To accuse her father of some crime? She'd asked him one more time about involvement with the Riverside Textile Mill, to which he'd replied flatly, "stop asking." Maybe Eugene Martin had understood more than he'd let on when he left his report and had referred it higher up the DEP chain of command.

Sam pulled his chair up to the table. "The federal government's got a program."

He looked at DeWitt for help.

"We're interested in conserving land and water for the future," DeWitt said. "This is a partnership where the government rents land—pays farmers like your dad not to plant their regular crops to help prevent runoff and get the waterways clean again."

"What piece of land are we talking about?" Jordan held her father's gaze.

It was Mr. DeWitt who answered. "That big field on Main Street. It slopes back to the river and that endangered fern, the Hartford Fern."

Jordan set her spoon back into the stew without taking a bite. "Isn't that the one you called the heart of the farm, Dad?" Sam squirmed as if he were sitting on a hot stone, trying not to look at Jordan. "The one Eugene Martin wrote his report on?" Diane poured more coffee for the two men and sat next to Sam, sliding her chair close to him. The steam wisped up from his cup casting a haze over his face; Jordan didn't think her mother knew whatever it was her father was hiding—but *she* knew he was hiding something—not planting that field could mean only one thing. She swallowed and her breath quickened. "Why?" was all she could say.

Her mother put her hand out across the table. "We've done a lot of thinking and talking this over, Jordan. The state is in the last hour of accepting applications. We're going to do this."

"But Dad, you always…"

"I know what I always said." He looked past Mr. DeWitt, out the window. "But we have a lawsuit to settle, and this is something we can do so this place doesn't turn into Hawkins Estates someday."

"Is there anything you *wouldn't* do, Dad? To keep the land?"

"Oh Jordan!" her mother said, "What makes you ask such a thing?"

But her father dug his fingernails into the table so hard his fingertips turned white. Through clenched teeth he said, "It's a legacy—taking care of this land. This gives us cash to do things we need to do around here to survive. And you can go to school."

"But you couldn't do it earlier, for Clay?"

"Jordan!" her mother snapped, causing Mr. DeWitt to jump in his seat.

"If you're not ready—" he said.

Sam pulled the paper toward him. "We're ready. Jordan, this is *renting* the land for ten years. Not *selling* it or the development rights, like the town wanted."

"What about Dale and the Dexter twins?"

"This doesn't change them working with us," Sam said. "In fact, we're going to invest in some of their ideas."

"Jordan—" Her mother saying her name was begging her to let it go. Jordan saw between her parents an intimate connection she hadn't seen for so long. Her mother had forgiven him, and she was pleading for Jordan to do the same. "We can grow the organic produce and build a real farm stand, diversify the farm. Don't make this harder than it already is. It's our choice. And we get to do what we feel is best for us and the farm."

Jordan looked at Mr. DeWitt. He was staring at the set of encyclopedias gathering dust on the bookshelf in the hallway.

Her father cleared his throat. "You can stay if you want, but now you can go to the kind of college you wanted. There will be enough money for that."

Jordan wondered if he was hoping she'd make a different choice about her future, but this wasn't about her future. It was about Clay. She could barely get out his name, "Clay..."

Sam's hand shook as he took a sip of coffee and sloshed it over the side. "What about Clay?"

She knew what she could say. If only. That perhaps Clay could still be alive *if* her father hadn't pushed him to live a life he didn't want. *If. If. If. If he was going to do this, why couldn't he have done it earlier? But the man seated before her wasn't the same man he had been. Not one of them was the same.*

When Jordan didn't say more, Sam put his coffee cup down. "All right, Bob. We're ready to do this. Jordan, I left those calves for you to feed."

Jordan left the house before he signed, without saying goodbye to Mr. DeWitt. The unfairness of it to Clay made her tremble with anger. It wasn't right! She wanted to talk to someone who loved Clay too, someone who would understand her feelings about this.

The last bus was pulling out of the school driveway as Jordan pulled in. Mr. Z often worked late and his beat-up Volvo sitting in the corner of the lot told her he was, in fact, still there. She approached his classroom from the parking lot and saw him hunched over his desk correcting papers. She tapped on the window. Mr. Z looked up and waved. He came over and opened the window.

"Come around," he said. "Are the doors locked?" Then after he got a better look at her face he said, "Wait a minute. I'll come around." Less than a minute later he rounded the corner of the building braced against the wind, his jacket collar flipped up and his hands in his pockets. "I'm sorry we haven't been able to get the clearance to have you back yet."

"No, I—" Jordan didn't know how to preface what she wanted to say so she just dove in. She told him about the meeting and her parents' decision. Mr. Z listened intently; it was one of the qualities she loved about him.

"Which field?" he asked.

Jordan told him and as she was explaining about the stressed Hartford Fern and Eugene Martin's report, and the chemicals—some of which were the same as chemicals at the Riverside site, Mr. Z shifted nervously away from her, pulled out a pack of cigarettes and lit one. "And it's all because Mrs. Barbo won't back down on the amount of the lawsuit. I'm going to start telling people she had an affair with that mill boss."

"What mill boss?" Mr. Z asked, the cigarette hovering in front of his mouth.

"Some mysterious guy who disappeared after the mill burned down. I saw a picture at the library—"

"Enough of this!" Mr. Z snapped. "You are going to do no such thing." His hands trembled as he pulled a second cigarette from the pack, held it to the nearly spent one to light it, and then stubbed the first beneath the toe of his shoe and took a long deep drag, regarding Jordan as he did.

Jordan wrapped her arms around herself prepared for one more scolding under Mr. Z's squinting glare.

"You are going to do no such thing, because the person Angela had an affair with is me, Jordan."

"What?!" Mr. Z's words knocked her off balance. She reached out and leaned against the rough brick. "You and Mrs. Barbo?" Jordan tried to imagine it. She couldn't, even though Mr. Z had never talked about a wife or kids, he'd always just been everyone's favorite teacher. "How?" she couldn't get any other words out.

"We starred in the high school's musical of *Coalminer's*

Daughter. If you ever heard her sing, you'd understand." He looked away. "I don't imagine she sings much, now."

"But that was high school. When did you… you know?"

"Not then. It was years later. I went to work as a manager at the mill while I was getting my master's. I worked the night shift at that time and so did she. I could have made her life different. When she got pregnant, she wouldn't say if Tony was mine or Jimmy's and she wouldn't leave him. For all his bad qualities, his anger, the drinking, she was still afraid of what people would say, what they'd think."

"Oh, Mr. Z, I'm sorry. Is that why you never married or had any kids—any other kids?"

"I had kids. Decades of kids coming through my classes," Mr. Z said. "You kids all were my family, and I told myself by staying here, I'd get to watch Tony grow up, too—that if he were mine, I'd see myself in him."

Jordan felt him crumple into himself. She knew better than to say anything. She knew how sometimes just being there mattered more.

"And Mrs. Barbo, do you ever see her?"

Mr. Z shook his head. "Funny how it fizzled out." He shrugged and pressed his lips together, thinking. "Once she said it could never work, it just closed a door in my heart, you know? But people talked about her, regardless and they still do. We were naïve to think this small town would ever just let her be. That's one thing I regret—I couldn't protect her from all that rancor against her, but she put herself in prison, too, by caring about it so much."

"How long did you work at the mill?" Jordan asked.

"Nine months, which turned out to be nine months too long."

"Did my father have anything to do with the mill when you were there?"

Mr. Z ground the second cigarette under his foot and pressed his back against the school wall. "Jordan, I tried to tell you to leave it alone, didn't I?"

"Did he?" she asked. "Because those chemicals didn't get down by the river by themselves."

"You should ask him, then."

"I did. He won't tell me. And I know he's hiding something. I'm tired of the secrets in this town."

"I hear that," Mr. Z said. He looked at her, gazing deeply into her eyes, as if gauging her readiness. She held his gaze. "Maybe this is what we needed after all, someone to push us to clean out all this shit."

Jordan didn't know this side of Mr. Z. She waited.

"Your father accepted some barrels, just one load to my knowledge, before the pollution got cracked open—before any of us understood the full extent of it."

Jordan tilted her head back. The sky had darkened enough that bats had come out. They flitted over the parking lot. "I got into a community college in Maine," she said.

"Near Win?" Mr. Z asked.

Jordan nodded.

"And?" He asked softly, almost imperceptibly.

"I think I want to go. I think I need to go." The truth surprised her as it unraveled on the air, but after hearing Mr. Z's story, it was clear.

"I'm glad," Mr. Z said. "I think Clay would want you to go, don't you?" When Jordan didn't answer he said, "Maybe you can give yourself and all of us a little forgiveness, Jordan. What do you say?"

"Yeah. I'll think about it." Jordan pushed herself off the wall. "Your secret's safe with me by the way."

"You don't need to keep secrets for us—I think that's also something Clay would say."

She felt Clay beside her as she drove home. His energy felt peaceful, not angry, and his presence softened her heart. She sensed him, full of something she wanted, compassion. Was he asking her to have compassion in this moment? Was this one of those gifts the Pascals had referred to? She pulled into the driveway—Mr. DeWitt's car was still there—blinked in the cold autumn air and went to the edge of the drive where the winter pears nestled like eggs around the trees. Jordan knelt under a tree, plucked a pear, rubbed it against her sleeve and bit into it. It was juicy and sweet. Perfectly ripe. She gathered a few more and set them on the passenger's seat of Mr. DeWitt's car. It was the best she could do for an apology.

That night, Sam stayed in the barn past chore time and Jordan went out and found him in the milking parlor with Bucky. He'd brought her in and given her a scoop of grain and when Jordan slipped into the room, she caught him just standing there, petting the heifer while she ate. Jordan thought she might be able to get to the place of forgiveness if she understood more.

"How many barrels did you let them bury, Dad?"

Her father turned to her; his face winced in pain. "Not now, Jordan."

"Not now? What do you think Mom would say if she knew Clay and others were digging up barrels *you* let the mill bury?"

Fear blanched his face. "We don't know that. And that was a time people didn't think twice about dumping stuff in the ground. The whole country did it." Jordan squeezed her eyes shut. She didn't want to let him off that easy, but she also knew what he was saying was true. Her father continued. "It was just once. We'd had a bad year for crops, and milk prices dropped at the same time. I had to buy feed for the cows."

"You only did this rental thing because of Eugene Martin's report. You were afraid he'd report you if you didn't."

Sam shook his head. "No. It was just one load—." He wrapped Bucky's lead tighter around his hand. "And when the mill got exposed—I dug 'em up and snuck everything back there to be cleaned up."

"But that's what Tony was showing Clay and Tim that night," Jordan insisted. "Benzene's highly flammable. They must have put some of those chemicals in the truck. That's what made the truck explode."

Sam waved his hand in the air as if waving the words and their truth away. "You don't know what they were doin', and we're never gonna know. Hell, I might have missed a barrel, sure. But those kids! Not a damn lick of sense. I wish to God your brother never got tangled up there." Sam swiped at his face, leaving a streak of wet. He averted his eyes from Jordan and nudged Bucky, who'd finished the grain and moved with him down the aisle away from her and by his slumped shoulders despite his words she knew his suffering and that he'd continue to suffer, maybe for the rest of his life. Her forgiveness or lack of it wouldn't change that, but could perhaps soften it.

"I'm not going to tell Mom. If she knew just how far you were willing to go to hold on to your *legacy...*"

Her father slipped the halter off Bucky and before he stepped out into the barn's dark interior, turned toward her and braced himself against the doorway. "It'd kill everything." But he meant it'd kill him. That was the only thing that stopped her from asking if he knew how much it was going to cost her—after trying so hard to get the truth—not to speak it.

Chapter 26

The next morning, it was easy to find Sister Rachael at the intersection of the gas station and Main Street in Moosup. Jordan pumped gas slowly to give Sister Rachael time to separate herself from Brother Michael, leaning on his staff more like a crutch, and cross the street.

"I see you're not afraid of me anymore," Sister Rachael's teeth gleamed white and straight. Her face, though unlined, bore a resemblance to the fine boned proportions of Mrs. Barbo.

"I just wanted to clear Clay's name. You said it all went back to—*your sister*—but did you see them, Clay and the others, in the back field that night? Or just up on the ridge like you said?"

Sister Rachael wrapped her robe tight around her. "We heard kids partying back there that night. But we didn't see. I told you only what I saw."

"You wanted me to figure it out—that it wasn't Clay's fault because it wasn't the drinking. It was the chemicals. You knew that. How?"

Sister Rachael nodded and pulled her long hair back from her face, as if revealing the part of her hidden from people for so many years. "Michael gets treatments at the hospital every week. We were there the day after they brought Tony in and it was all the staff talked about—chemical burns, not crash burns."

"I can't clear Clay's name. I can't tell anyone because the chemicals might've come from a barrel left down that back field from years ago, when my dad..." Jordan couldn't say it. "All I wanted was the truth and now it's me keeping it secret."

Sister Rachael put her hand out to stop her. "You needed to know that for you." Her voice barely a whisper on the air. "But don't stop now."

"I'm more confused than ever. That night of the accident, you could have just reported the barrel on the ridge? Why didn't you?"

Sister Rachael straightened her robe around her shoulders. She looked back at Brother Michael, who was waving for her to return to him across the street, but before she did, she said, "Toxic secrets started this whole thing and no one's going to listen to me. It's bigger than a missed barrel down behind your field."

Jordan drove slowly toward home. As she crossed the bridge on Main Street, she remembered the photos of the river, a lollipop red one day, lemon yellow another, a deep indigo the next. She tried to imagine just how much dye would have been dumped in the river to make such vibrant colors.

The next morning, Jordan and Sam were just finishing milking when Mr. DeWitt showed up in the barn looking subdued. Sam called out hello, but his enthusiasm dipped when Mr. DeWitt asked if he could have a few minutes.

"Sure." Sam looked at Jordan.

"I got this, Dad." She'd milked out half the switch when Sam returned to the milking parlor, his expression grim. "What's the matter?" she asked.

Sam didn't answer right away. He finished getting the machines off the cows and releasing them from the stations, then descended into the pit and turned the radio down.

"It seems the program folks want this lawsuit settled with the Barbos." Sam stared over Jordan's head, out the window, as he talked. "I should have thought about it beforehand," he said. "Up until now, I didn't really think she could take us down. I don't even know how to tell your mother." Her mother was off at a regional meeting of CSA farmers with

Dale and the twins, already excited to begin collaborating on new ventures.

They finished the chores in silence, which was okay because in that silence, it became clear what to do.

Chapter 27

"Tina's off taking the test," Mr. Barbo said when he answered the door. "We appreciate what you done to help her." Tori clung to his leg, and he patted her head as he spoke.

"You're welcome, Sir." Jordan wasn't sure why she said sir except maybe his impending death lent him authority. She'd brought a bunch of flowers to congratulate Tina on passing her GED, for she was sure her friend would pass. Mr. Barbo let her in and slumped into a dining room chair, watching her cut and arrange the flowers into a vase she set on the table before she sat too. She was there with a purpose.

Tori scooted up to her grandfather's chair, throwing herself into his lap. Mr. Barbo's face lit up, pain and tension slipping away as his hand cupped the silky head. The toddler leaned forward, and Mr. Barbo fed her an apple slice. The silence deepened. The plate of apple slices was almost gone before he spoke. "You saved her that day."

"I need your help," Jordan said. When Mr. Barbo looked up, she went on. "Our town has been through so much."

"Humph!" Mr. Barbo said. "You think I don't know that?"

Jordan cocked her head. "Maybe we can let something good come from it all."

"You sayin' I owe you?"

"My parents can't go on if this lawsuit doesn't get dropped. Paying more than the insurance company agreed to would destroy them. I know Mrs. Barbo had an affair." Mr. Barbo squeezed his eyes closed, as if he were being tortured. "And I know how much she still cares what people think. Tim and Clay and Tony dug up a barrel of chemicals that night and that's why the truck exploded. If I told that, the insurance company might fight paying even one penny."

"You know this—how?"

"Your *sister-in-law* saw them and she told me. I found a barrel on the ridge and covered it back up. I can just as easily show it to the police. And Win told me that Tim had said they were going to find something that would clear suspicion about him burning down the mill."

"What do you *really* want?" Mr. Barbo asked.

Jordan swallowed hard; she needed him to think she understood more than she did. She didn't want him to see she was still trying to figure out how the two things connected. "Look at what this secret has done to you, Mr. Barbo—it's been eating you up, hasn't it?"

"It's cancer eating me up," he said.

"Secrets are a cancer," Jordan said. Mr. Barbo glared as if she was someone else now, his body tense. Sensing the change, his granddaughter began to whimper. He got up from the table, put her in her playpen and slumped back in the chair, one arm braced against the table. He was a big man, and his presence filled the room, but he was running out of time. He looked at the photo of Tony smiling at him from the top of the TV.

"Tina doesn't know you're not Tony's dad, but Tony knew, didn't he?" It was a stab in the dark, but when Mr. Barbo pushed the empty plate away so the space between them was clear, she could see she'd hit a nerve.

"He was always running up there, spyin'."

Before Jordan could ask another question, footsteps sounded on the porch and the door opened to Tina and Mrs. Barbo. Tina looked surprised, but Mrs. Barbo understood right away what was going on. "Get out," she hissed. Mr. Barbo's face grew pale. Jordan slid her chair out slowly. "Out!" Mrs. Barbo shouted.

Tina looked angry now too, as she swooped up Tori from the playpen. "I know you've helped me, Jordan, but right now,

I swear, I hate you." Despite the GED certificate in her hand and the celebratory flowers on the table, she gave Jordan a look that severed their connection. Before Jordan even looked back, she closed the door.

She drove to the playground, parked her truck, and went to the swings. She could see the back of the Barbos' house from the swing. The air was empty, except for the gentle sound of the river babbling over rocks. It hadn't rained for a while and the water was low, the current slow. Within a few minutes, Mr. Barbo backed out of their driveway and headed past her. He tipped his head curiously toward her, but he didn't stop, continuing on toward Moosup. She almost got in her truck to follow him, but a heaviness swept over her, and she couldn't move. She felt all the anger, all the recrimination draining out of her—she could almost see the mist from the river reaching up like hands to receive it and carry it away. She didn't know how much time passed before she felt able to get in her truck and drive home.

Hours later, she received a text from Tina's phone though it was clearly from Mrs. Barbo. "Come to Day Kimball ER soon as you get this. Jimmy wants to see you. Hurry."

She texted back. She was on her way.

Mrs. Barbo scowled at her when she entered the hospital room. "Why couldn't you leave things alone? You have absolutely no idea about anything!"

"Angela! Stop." Mr. Barbo squeezed her hand. "Please."

"You made him upset."

"No," Mr. Barbo said. "Tony wanted this, Angela. You know that. He begged us. You should be thanking her—she saved Tori from getting hit by one of them dump trucks. She saved her life. We owe her this." That stopped Mrs. Barbo. Mr. Barbo forced out the words in a gasping whisper. "Angela, you gotta stop—now. Promise." He reached for her hand and held it. "Promise." When Mrs. Barbo shook her head, he squeezed her hand tight. "Look at me. You don't want this, please, promise."

Jordan looked around the room.

"She took Tori to the cafeteria," Mrs. Barbo said. "You'll see soon what mothers will do for their kids." Jordan wrapped her coat tighter around her stomach, protecting herself and her baby from Mrs. Barbo's gaze. Mr. Barbo seemed to be having more trouble breathing, but he wouldn't let Mrs. Barbo call the nurse. He gestured Jordan to sit in the chair by the bed. "Tony snuck up to the mill." He caressed Mrs. Barbo's hand as he spoke. "I went up to fetch him home and when I called his name, it scared him. He was smokin' a cigarette; he was just eight, and he panicked and tossed it. There was a chemical pit—he didn't know it, but I knew. I grabbed him and jumped out the window just in time. All these years we swore the whole thing to secrecy."

"No one got hurt, except Tony himself," Mrs. Barbo cried.

"That's not true, Angela," Mr. Barbo said. "No one got hurt in the fire, but a whole lot of people got hurt by what that mill did and losing their jobs to boot."

"You're right," Mrs. Barbo looked at his hand and caressed the wrinkles away with her finger. "I'm sorry, Jimmy. I am." Mrs. Barbo covered her face with her hands and wept. Mr. Barbo waited for her to stop crying. He looked at Jordan but spoke for his wife to hear. "My anger and my drinkin'— that's what pushed her straight to another man. I was out of control. You want the truth. There it is. From a dyin' man." Mrs. Barbo looked up and locked eyes with Jordan. Jordan felt death enter the room. Mr. Barbo didn't say another word. He closed his eyes. She got up from the chair, leaving them alone. She escaped down the back stairs, taking them two at a time, not wanting to see Tina. Her body shook and though she didn't have far to drive, she turned the heat on. Her teeth rattled. *Oh Clay. Clay.*

Her mother was in the yard and when Jordan opened the door of her truck, her mother saw the emotion on her face and rushed over and hugged her. Jordan told her about Tony and the mill, and they cried together, crying for all the boys, their tears finally helping them feel lighter.

That night, she and her mother got on the Internet, and she made notes of courses and talked about how she could balance her spring semester's courses at a community college with the baby.

"Do you think here or are you thinking Maine, honey?" her mother asked.

"I can't stay here, Mom. Even if it weren't for Win and this baby. It's time for me to go. But Maine's not that far, Mom. We'll come home and you can visit."

Her mother patted her shoulder. "This is what kids are supposed to do, honey. They're supposed to fly."

How could she tell her mother that knowing the truth she'd insisted on finding had forced her to understand human vulnerability, including her own. She'd never see home in quite the same way as she had before Clay died, and she didn't think she'd ever be able to come home and be known or accepted in quite the same way ever again, either. Someday she'd have to tell her mother the rest of the truth about the chemicals the boys had in the truck, for she thought this couldn't really be finished until she did. But, for now, she'd move forward feeling the presence of Clay helping her to have some compassion for everyone, including herself.

Jordan heard the bed squeaking in her parents' room later that night. It had been such a long time since she'd heard those sounds. The house felt peaceful afterwards and when she heard their rhythmic, sleeping breath, she got up and snuck downstairs to the kitchen. The light on the stove lit the room and Chestnut came over, wagging his tail. Jordan made herself a cup of tea and drank it in the dark. The moon turned the trees and corn stubble to liquid silver and Jordan opened the window, just a crack to feel the presence she'd once identified as the invisible giant, but a bigger divine presence now, stretching everywhere—in the dark and the light.

Chapter 28

On the night Jimmy Barbo went to the police and confessed that he'd burned down the mill, the punctured barrel was delivered in the middle of the night to the police station. Jordan felt sure it was Sister Rachael's contribution to healing both the human and environmental toxicity. Another twenty barrels were found on the ridge; it was all anyone could talk about for a week. So, in a sense, her goal had been achieved, but Jordan felt terrible that Tina wouldn't return her calls or texts. Jordan worried how Tina would live in the midst of the turmoil about her father's confession.

When she called Win, his reaction surprised her. "If only I hadn't told Tim that story," he said. "They'd all be here."

"Win, please, don't blame yourself. Every single one of us could take a little blame, but what good does that do?" She understood now why Mr. Z kept urging her to take positive steps for her own life and not to attack Mrs. Barbo. Jordan called the Pascals and when she told them how people were turning against the Barbos and she felt responsible for that, Mrs. Pascal said the mill was like an infected wound and the truth had to come out so it could be healed. "Remember our conversation about what led you to us? I think the town is ready now and so are you."

Jordan wasn't sure exactly how to set things on the right path, but she wanted to ask people to forgive the Barbos, for Tina's sake. Her parents were busy with the farm stand and making changes to the farm, so she asked Maxine if she could call a gathering at the General Store, and Maxine said yes. Jimmy Barbo had died two days after his confession. A week had passed since then. For many, life moved on. Only twenty people had gathered at the store when Jordan arrived. They looked at her, their faces revealing their feelings because, she thought, they didn't understand how anyone, least of all the Hawkins family would call for forgiveness of the Barbos, or they just plain didn't agree with what was being asked but were too polite to say so directly to Jordan. This was the old way things were done in Asheville, and she felt some impatience because her family had been on the receiving end of it too, and she wanted them all, herself included, to learn something more.

"Well, that was some detective work," Maxine quipped. "A person can't pee in the woods without someone knowing it in this town, and look at this secret that was right under our noses all this time. Girl, how did you do that?" The sun was a vague ball behind a cloud sending light down over the bridge. A group of kids was still hanging out there, but Tina was not among them.

Emmet Owen, owner of the hardware store, was eating from a plate of cookies Jordan had brought and he offered a joke. "Here's one for you," he said. "There was this guy on his death bed."

"Oh God," Bette Sullivan, the town clerk groaned, thrusting her sensible brown shoes out in front of her like brakes. "A death joke now? Really?"

"No, it's funny," Emmet went on. "Just wait." Bette rolled her eyes. She and Emmet had "made time" as she referred to it and although no one knew who had broken it off, Jordan suspected it wasn't Emmet, since he seemed to be looking for her approval as he told his joke. "He was on his death bed, and he smelled chocolate chip cookies and he said to himself, 'that's my dying wish—I want a chocolate chip cookie straight out of the oven with the gooey chocolate melting as I take a bite.' So, he crawled downstairs into the kitchen, barely strong enough," here Emmet gestured with his long lean arms, and he reached his hand up to the counter and—*thwack!*—Emit slapped the air with his hand. "Don't touch those," his wife said. "I'm saving them for the funeral."

Laughter erupted from the room, even from Bette, which Jordan could see pleased Emmet immensely. Jordan put her hand on her stomach. The baby was kicking. Emmet's joke had softened the mood, so Jordan summoned her courage. Mr. Z was standing in the back corner talking to the Pascals, and Jordan overheard them talking about community programming. When he saw her getting ready to speak, Mr. Z gave a thumbs up.

"Well, I don't have a lot to say," Jordan said, "except to ask that we try not to be so quick to judge and maybe be a little more forgiving?" She looked around the room and she couldn't tell from people's expressions how they were receiving her words. "It turns out things are never quite the way they look, as we've seen. I'm learning this myself, because I had some good teachers," she gestured to Mr. Z and the Pascals, "and they kept telling me forgiveness is the only way forward. I kept wanting to blame someone, but if the boys were here, they'd want us to do better. They *died* trying to dig up the truth about the mill. They wanted the truth to heal us and the environment." She could feel them there, Tim and Tony and Clay. She knew they were helping her. She looked out the window, just as Brother Michael and Sister Rachael crossed over the bridge, their white robes glowing in the dusk as they disappeared into the woods for the night.

"So, I think they're trying to help us clean up our act. The way I see it, this is what we can do to honor them."

Chapter 29

Everything looked gray in the cold November afternoon. It was Thanksgiving weekend and the farm buzzed with holiday activity, visitors buying fresh cut Christmas trees brought in from Maine, wreaths and roping made by Dale and the Dexter twins, and hot cider and cider donuts served by Diane. Sam oversaw a small petting pen of calves and a recently acquired goat and Chestnut wagged his tail, greeting each and every person.

Jordan guided her truck from its spot near the barn and slipped away from the farm without being seen. She approached the hill slowly, shifting into neutral at just the right moment and let herself feel the delicious sensation of being released from gravity. The three crosses glowed in the overcast light, caught by her headlights, which she always kept on now for safety. Someone had placed three miniature fir trees with red bows behind the crosses. She rolled down the window and inhaled the dank river, rolling the truck off the road.

Jordan had not been to the accident site since that night with Win. Now, she pulled off the road and parked. She put the Garth Brooks CD in and hit play, letting his voice fill the air as she headed for the river. The river roared, the current white-capped with its dark stream rushing underneath. She and Clay had loved the river most when it was like this. They hardly attempted to talk when the river was so swollen because the water rushing, rushing over rocks, past them, drowned their voices out. They had no need to talk then. In those moments by the river, they listened to the water play its music against the rocks and watched the rainbows form in the mist.

Jordan found the oak, still fire charred. The rain soaked the area with the smell of fire, but the canopy of the tree was so vast that there was a dry spot beneath it. Jordan swept away twigs and acorn caps and then she propped herself against the trunk. She found herself praying. *Forgive me, Clay. Forgive me for not hearing you. Forgive me that when you needed me to hear you, I turned you away.*

She closed her eyes. She wished to see him one more time; she wished she'd hugged him one last time that day. Oh, if she'd only known how short his life would be, there were so many things she would have done. She couldn't remember the last time she'd hugged him. The silence expanded around her, and as she sat watching the river, she felt a warm sensation around her heart. A presence.

"Clay?" She opened her eyes. What must Clay think of her? She wanted to know, in a deep and passionate way, how eternity worked. She believed in it, even if she didn't believe in fate, and she wasn't sure anymore whether she could say she believed in destiny or choices. Maybe life was a mix of the two. But there was always going to be some regret, knowing she could have done more to help him to be free too, free on earth. Just by letting him speak his truth, she could've done that. She would have liked for them to be part of each other's lives, for him to hold her baby and teach it to throw a ball, instead of leaving it to her. But then there would have been no baby and the town would never have come together and all the secrets and lies would have remained buried, just like the chemicals, destroying people. *At least we did something there, Clay.* She was just nineteen, with life ahead of her and a lot more appreciation for it. All because of Clay.

"If you're here Clay, just a little sign?" The next second a trout broke the surface of the water, jumping to show its glistening scales in the moon's light. "Thank you, Clay. You're here. I know you are." She knew because she felt his love for her. She felt in that moment that Clay had never blamed her, not really. He'd loved her and contrary to staying stuck, he would have wanted her to be free. After all that had happened, she had a responsibility to live the best life she could. She heard the ancient cassette player in the truck and Garth singing, "We shall be free." She knew no one but Clay would hear her, and so she let her voice join with the crash and rush of water coming around the bend.

When the song finished playing, Jordan walked back to the truck. She felt the baby kick as she adjusted the rearview mirror to see the moon and the dark woods and her own face, shining. She looked back one last time before she shifted into gear, and headed away from Gravity Hill, vowing to hold it always in her heart.

About the Author

SUSANNE DAVIS is the daughter of a sixth-generation dairy farmer and lives near her dad's farm where the real Gravity Hill exists. Her dad works every day to keep his farm from developers, just like Jordan's father. She has an MFA from the Iowa Writers' Workshop and a short story collection, *The Appointed Hour* (Cornerstone Press). Individual stories have been published in *American Short Fiction*, *Notre Dame Review*, *Clackamas Literary Review*, and other literary journals. Her work has won awards and recognition, including 2nd place in Madville's Blue Moon Novel Competition and mention as distinguished story in the *Best American Short Stories* series. She teaches creative writing at the college level and beyond. For more, see her website, susannedavis.com.